Praise for *My Be...*

'A stunning, thoughtful debut which explores the nature of friendship, addiction and how events of the past stay with us. Utterly compelling'

Catherine Cooper

'Gut-wrenching and powerful . . . This is a thoughtful, nuanced and authentic portrayal of female friendship and addiction'

Charlotte Duckworth

'A powerful novel . . . Emily Freud brilliantly captures the destructive inner voice of a woman struggling to stay on course'

Jane Lythell

'A raw depiction of addiction and examines the complexities of female friendship. Filled with beautiful writing and devastating twists, this debut is not to be missed'

Miranda Smith

'A pacey, heartfelt story about the perils of addiction and adolescence, from a writer who clearly understands the world she creates. Moving and compelling, I read it in one sitting'

Charlotte Philby

'An absolute page-turner of a book'

Samantha Hayes

MY BEST
FRIEND'S
SECRET

Emily Freud has spent her career working in television production and development. Credits include Emmy and BAFTA award-winning television series, including *Educating Yorkshire* and *First Dates*. Her debut novel, *My Best Friend's Secret*, publishes in 2021. Emily lives in north London, with her husband and two small children. She is currently working on her next novel.

MY BEST FRIEND'S SECRET

EMILY FREUD

Quercus

First published as *Closure* in eBook in Great Britain in 2020 by Quercus
This paperback edition published as *My Best Friend's Secret* in 2021 by

Quercus Editions Ltd
Carmelite House
50 Victoria Embankment
London EC4Y 0DZ

An Hachette UK company

A CIP catalogue record for this book is available
from the British Library

PB ISBN 978 1 52940 7 532
EB ISBN 978 1 52940 7 518

This book is a work of fiction. Names, characters,
businesses, organizations, places and events are
either the product of the author's imagination
or used fictitiously. Any resemblance to
actual persons, living or dead, events or
locales is entirely coincidental.

10 9 8 7 6 5 4 3 2 1

Typeset by CC Book Production
Printed and bound in Great Britain by Clays Ltd, Elcograf S.p.A.

Papers used by Quercus are from well-managed forests and other responsible sources.

For Dan

A thin piercing noise is all she can hear as her eyes flutter over the message. She shuts her lids tightly. The noise turns into crashing rain – she can still feel it seeping into her hair and dripping into the creases of her skin. It makes her teeth chatter. The memory of a tap on her shoulder, his lips moving as he said hello.

This is what she thinks of when she finds out he isn't coming: the first moment she saw him, when she'd been caught in the rain on Waterloo Bridge. His eyes on her had felt invasive, as though they were already three layers deep.

She walks downstairs. Her dad smiles up at her. She smiles back momentarily, caught off guard.

'He isn't coming,' she says, still not quite believing it's true. She drops her pretty bunch of simple spring flowers onto the floor and hands him the phone. Her dad's wearing a suit. He had his hair cut especially for the occasion.

She is wearing a white silk tea dress with lace detail. Neither of them wanted a big wedding. She has a smattering of daisies in her loosely plaited brown hair. She balances herself on the

1

armchair and, catching herself in the mirror, she feels sorry for the girl standing there. Abandoned on her wedding day. This will hurt once the numbness passes.

Her father holds her in an embrace, and she turns her cheek onto the shoulder of his cold jacket. She stands still, just breathing. That is all she can manage. A binary in and out, hoping that if she just does that enough times it will be over.

1

Several weeks earlier

'Why didn't I bring a coat? I'm freezing!' Kate jumps up and down on the spot. Ben puts his arm around her and squeezes. It has been one of those spring days where you are fooled into thinking summer has started, but by 7 p.m. your bare arms have goosebumps, and your exposed ankles are chalky and white.

'Come on, let's get inside,' he says, pulling her up onto the dip of the worn stone step.

Ben rings the bell and they wait. In front of them is a large panelled wooden door, which dwarfs them both. An irritated buzz summons Ben to push. Kate holds his hand, her other clasped around the top of his arm so she can observe the reception area safely from behind his shoulder. She watches as the haughty woman at the desk develops a smile and a warm inclusive tone as she takes his name and registers his reservation. It is as if, suddenly, she has met him many times before. Kate can't help but notice the perfect wisps of hair which have escaped expertly from her loose bun and the neat pearls which sit exquisitely on her dainty lobes. Kate tucks a strand of hair behind her ear as Ben laughs along with something the woman has said.

She has been to his club before, but it always makes her feel on edge, as if everyone is watching her, wondering who she is and how she got in. They are whisked through, past the busy bar area, to a table by an imposing sash window which commands the attention of the whole room. Ben is well versed in getting the best. They sit down, she smooths her skirt over her legs as she takes it all in. Light ripples of laughter entwine with quiet rumbles of conversation. Everyone is wearing dark hues of block colour; the waiters wear long navy butchers' aprons and crisp white shirts folded up to their elbows. Candles twinkle against large bulbous glasses on sparse tables. It feels edgy, in a conformed sort of way.

Ben is looking over the wine list, one finger poised over his bottom lip as he thinks. She gets a feeling of deep pleasure when she watches him just being. He readjusts his glasses and strokes her hand absent-mindedly as he turns the page. As he softly touches her that warm feeling spreads within, reminding her she's here, now, in this lovely place with her wonderful fiancé. Everything really is OK in the end. *This too shall pass*, they said. And it did.

He looks over at her and touches her cheek. 'Happy anniversary, darling. You look beautiful tonight,' he says. Her stomach tingles. Ben is classically handsome; he's got thick dark-brown hair and a roman nose. He wears tortoiseshell glasses that

4

make him look smart, and he is, very. A friend once told her that nice guys don't dress well, but Ben does. Tonight, he's wearing a light-blue shirt that goes with his eyes. He has a dimple in the middle of his chin, which is so perfect that sometimes Kate runs her finger across it, just to check it's real.

'Thank you,' she says smiling, blushing. She still finds it hard to accept a compliment; she spent half her life convinced she was worthless, and even now she can't quite quit all those old feelings towards herself. The remnants hang in the air like particles of dust floating around her face, impossible to catch. She often has to remind herself that she never has to go back. She is safe now; she doesn't need to hurt herself any more. She takes a deep breath and leans forward, kissing his cheek. He kisses her back, tenderly.

'Soon we'll have a new anniversary to celebrate,' she murmurs into his ear.

He looks at her intently. 'Then I can call you my wife.'

The wedding. Six years ago, she would never have thought a man like this would want to marry her. But, one day at a time, so much has changed. Like a flower in bloom, her petals have gently spread open, and now she feels as if her transformation is almost complete. A gentle smile of contentment dances on her lips as she looks out of the window, onto the street and the steady flow of people: couples walk arm in arm, groups of friends laugh jovially in clusters, holding up the solitary figures trying to dash ahead. Everyone is participating in life, and so is she. She is no longer cowering away, afraid of everyone and everything.

'I'm just going to go to the bathroom,' she says as she stands up. She wants to check her make-up. She had decided to wear red lipstick, but fears it may have smudged during the journey into town, or that an unsightly smear may have made its way onto her top teeth. She is sure the woman at the desk gave her a sympathetic look. Ben looks up and nods, and then goes back to studying the wine list.

Her shoes make obtrusively loud clicking noises as she walks towards the back of the building where the toilets are. Glamorous faces peer up, and then quickly down when they realize there is nothing there to see. She pushes the door into the quiet sanctuary of the bathroom.

On the far side of the dark room are five oval mirrors with brass light fittings hanging over the top of each. She walks through and moves her face under one, allowing the light to slowly cascade over her features. It is as if she is on a blacked-out stage, with only a spotlight hovering above her. She raises her hand to her lips and leans in. She stops before she touches them; there is nothing to amend. She crushes her top lip up to her nose to check her teeth, but pearly white is all that reflects back. She looks exactly how she did when she left the house. She gives herself a reassuring smile.

Then she hears the quiet thud of the door open and close. Footsteps walk up behind her. Quickly, her eyes fall towards the basin and she turns the tap on, washing her hands with expensive-smelling soap. The other person props their bag on the surface of the sink, and rummages around, removing a pouch. Kate concentrates on her hands, and the job of ensuring all the soapsuds make their way down the plughole.

'Kate!'

She looks up and over at the head suspended in the next mirror along.

It takes her a moment to place who the person is. She definitely knows them somehow. She cocks her head to one side, pausing in the hope it will come to her quickly, to avoid any embarrassment.

'It's Becky,' the woman says.

Kate almost gasps at the transformation. Becky's fuzzy curls are sleek and tamed. She used to wear an overeager dab of blue eyeshadow, but in its place is a sexy slash of liner. Her brows were overplucked; now they are just the right amount of bushy and dark. She is wearing tailored trousers and a tight black halter vest that accentuates her slim figure and full breasts. Her handbag is designer and she has a Burberry trench coat over her forearm.

'Becky,' Kate chokes, coughing. 'Becky,' she says again, more confidently. She goes to hug her, but Becky kisses her impersonally on each cheek. A waft of perfume drifts away as they part. 'How . . . how nice to see you,' Kate breathes.

'It must have been over ten years,' Becky replies. The statement hangs in the air, like washing on the line on a windless day.

'I thought you lived in America?' Kate fiddles with her necklace, trying to smile politely.

'I moved back a few weeks ago. Are you a member here?'

'No, but my fiancé is.' Kate smiles.

'Fiancé?' Becky's eyebrows rise. 'Congratulations,' she says flatly. Kate isn't sure that Becky sounds happy for her.

'What are you doing here?' Kate asks, wondering why her tone sounds accusatory.

'I was just meeting an old colleague for a drink, bending his ear about a job. I'm on the hunt for something new.' Becky turns back towards the mirror and sighs. 'Oh, for God's sake, was that there the whole time?' she mutters before curtly wiping the side of her lip, where her make-up has smudged ever so slightly. She takes out a tube from the pouch and reapplies her lipstick.

'Beck, I can't believe . . .' Kate starts.

Becky turns to face her. 'How much I've changed? Well, living in New York will do that to someone. It slowly chips away at you and before you know it you've conformed.'

'Ben, my fiancé, he's from New York.' Kate nods her head towards the door, towards where Ben is sitting at their table.

'Really?' Becky zips up her make-up bag and puts it back.

'Yes.' There is a pause Kate wants to fill. 'Do you want to meet him?' she finds herself asking.

Becky watches her as she thinks; she blots her lips together once more before she answers. 'Yes. I'd like that.' Kate wishes she could take it back; she should have just said it was nice to bump into each other and walked away. Now she has invited something into her evening she hasn't prepared for.

Her heart quickens as they walk back into the busy atmosphere, thudding louder and louder the closer they get. She sees his face smile from across the room as he registers her return, and then a slightly confused look unfurls across it as he sees the woman following her.

They stop in front of him. 'This is Ben,' Kate says. He jumps up straight away and shakes Becky's hand. He is looking at Becky, intrigued.

'This is Becky . . . we . . . she . . .'

Becky interjects, 'We used to be best friends.'

Kate's lips part in surprise at the admission. She watches Becky, still shaking his hand, as if she has forgotten to let go.

Ben smiles, welcoming her. 'You must join us for a drink.' He breaks his hand away and ushers over a waiter.

Becky nods and accepts the extra chair produced for her. Kate still remembers the last time she saw Becky. They were about eighteen. Kate was hungover, as usual. She was trying to piece together the night before. Her hair was muddled, her mascara was halfway down her face, as if someone had wiped soot under each eye. She was shaking, too afraid of what she might have done to ask an angry Becky what happened. They hadn't spoken since.

'Kate said you're from New York. Whereabouts did you grow up?' Becky asks Ben.

'I was born in Manhattan; my family have a brownstone on the Upper West Side.'

'Slightly more glamorous than Camden Town,' Becky says with a knowing smile.

Kate watches her old friend so confidently converse with a practical stranger. It used to take Becky some time to warm up around people she didn't know; she'd always let Kate take the lead. The waiter approaches again, a pad and pen in hand.

'Would you like to start with a drink?' the waiter asks.

Ever the gentleman, Ben hands the wine list to Becky. 'The Shiraz looks nice,' he says. 'I've had the Pinot before and found it a bit heavy.' Kate watches Becky study the options. They used to like Blossom Hill or anything two-for-five-pounds. They would never have come to a place like this – *why eat when you could drink?*

Ben turns to Kate. 'Kate, what would you like? They have a few mocktails here in the back,' he says. Kate can't help feeling excluded, like a patronized child allowed on the grown-up table as a treat.

'I'm fine with sparkling water,' she says. She can feel Becky watching her, confused.

A few minutes later the waiter returns and pours Ben an inch to try. Kate can imagine the taste in her mouth, the initial sting and the caustic tang, like poison. She takes a sip of her water.

'I love your ring,' Becky says, catching Kate's hand between her fingers and staring at the large set diamond. 'Congratulations,' she says to them both.

Kate watches Becky study Ben's face and wonders what she is thinking. Is she impressed? He is more than Kate ever wanted, more than anything they could have dreamt up back when we wrote lists of their perfect man and burnt them over the sink.

'When is the wedding?' Becky asks.

'It's next month. We're just having a registry office do,' says Kate, her cheeks tinged red. 'We didn't want a fuss, and Ben didn't want everyone feeling like they had to travel from the States . . . It's going to be intimate.'

Becky nods thoughtfully. Kate always wanted a big show-stopper of a wedding; they used to discuss it for hours. She used to love the idea of the drama of an event like that. But now she just wants something simple. She wants it to be about them, not about fuss or stress or other people. She loves Ben. She wants the marriage, not the wedding.

'Then over the summer we'll go stay with my folks on Long Island. My mom's threatening to throw us a party while we're out there,' Ben says.

'You'll never come back,' Becky says with a knowing smile.

'I can't see that happening!' he laughs.

Kate shrugs. 'Ben is a complete anglophile, and besides, I'd never leave the kids.' Becky looks at her quizzically. 'I'm a teacher,' she explains.

'It's like she doesn't think every inner-city school is begging for talented teachers,' Ben says.

'What do you do?' asks Kate.

'I was working for a big pharmaceutical company. I'm looking for something new now I'm back,' Becky says. 'Staying at my parents is beyond demoralizing.'

'Oh God! How are you coping?' asks Kate. Memories of Becky's parental home swim at her like hungry ducklings: dancing drunk in the living room, tidying up after another house party that got out of hand, lying half naked in Becky's

11

bed talking about boys they fancied who didn't fancy them back. It feels like Kate's adolescence is stored inside that house.

'Fine, you know. I'm just too old for their bullshit.'

Becky's father is what you would call eccentric. Kate was there almost every day after school and every weekend, and she barely saw him. Becky's mother, Susanna, is another story. Part of Kate aches still when she thinks of her. The way she would put Kate's hair behind her ear for her and smile, the way they would smoke around the kitchen table together, talking long after Becky had gone to bed.

'How come you came back?' Kate asks.

Becky pauses, and straightens her cutlery as she talks. 'My mother . . . she isn't very well, and Alexa thought it was time I helped out. Older sisters, do they ever stop bossing you around?' she asks with an irritated shake of the head. Kate wonders what is wrong with Susanna. Becky changes the subject before she can ask.

'So . . . how did you guys meet?'

Ben coughs. 'I was on a business trip, a meeting about a job in Glasgow . . .'

'He's an engineer,' Kate says, holding her hands a metre apart. 'Big ships.'

Ben pushes her jovially for interrupting. 'Anyway, I was flying through Heathrow and had one night in London. It was a chance meeting, really. I was lost . . .' He smiles at Kate.

'How romantic,' says Becky, taking them in. Kate watches her give Ben another side glance, and she almost thinks Becky blushes.

'I took the job once we met; I just knew.' He looks over at Kate and smiles again, before kissing her cheek.

'You're so soppy.' Kate shakes her head and pushes him away as if she is embarrassed. But really, she's more than happy with the public display of affection in front of her old friend.

'A toast,' says Ben. They raise their glasses, 'to old friends and new'. The glasses chink. They make a show of looking each other in the eye very seriously before they take a sip. It is painful to look Becky in the eye. It is as if Kate is looking directly into the sun. She quickly looks away and watches their red wine slosh and takes in a drink of her water.

'God, this wine is heaven.' Becky looks at Kate expectantly, and takes another sip.

'I don't drink any more,' Kate says, feeling the moment requires an explanation.

'Oh.'

'I've been sober six years.' She wants Becky to know that, after all the broken promises, she finally did it.

'That's amazing, Kate.' Becky sets her glass down. 'That really is amazing.'

Later, in the cab home, Kate puts her head on Ben's shoulder and sighs. Seeing Becky again has exhausted her. Kate has tried hard not to think of her old friend much over the last few years. She has been focusing on the present and the future. It was one of the things she used to mull over, while she was drinking herself into oblivion: what really happened

13

that night, why their relationship broke off like it did. Kate was incapable of being a good friend when she drank, she knows that now. Becky was completely justified in giving up on her.

She thinks about how different Becky is now. Not just the way she looks. She used to have an exuberant energy, a self-unaware buoyancy, like the way she would smile naively at someone giving her a dirty look. She is measured now, sophisticated. Kate found her intimidating, but maybe that is because of all that is unsaid.

'I've never heard you talk about her,' Ben muses.

'We lost touch; I haven't seen her for years.'

'Well, I thought she was nice.'

'She used to be very different,' Kate says. 'Not like that.'

'Oh yeah, how so?'

'You'll think I'm being a bitch.'

'Come on, dish the dirt.' He tickles her. He has a glint in his eye, and she knows he's tipsy. It doesn't take much. He left his glass half full at the restaurant. She's always amazed when he does that. She never left a drop.

'She's had some sort of body and personality airbrush. I swear her teeth were never that straight or white,' Kate says.

'Ha, Yanks don't stand for your snaggly British teeth.' He tickles her again.

'Hey! Stop it. And I don't have snaggly teeth.' She sits up.

'No, you have lovely teeth.' He cups the side of her face and brings it towards him.

Their lips tease each other, gently pressing against each

other before going in deep. Their tongues touch and she feels a familiar surge.

The car comes to a stop and they pull apart. She grins, her eyes shine, and her cheeks are mottled pink. Feeling happy when she hasn't had a drop to drink is better than any high she had experienced drinking or using drugs. Because she knows it's real. He is here, loving her, wanting to marry her. With Ben, it's not the sort of one-sided toxic relationship of before.

He climbs out of the car and turns, holding his hand out to help. 'Mademoiselle,' he says in a fake French accent.

She takes his hand and allows him to pull her onto the kerb. 'Why, thank you,' she giggles. Arm in arm, the couple walk up the steps to their apartment. Kate turns as she hears a sort of bedraggled howl, like a fox in pain, or a cat. Her eyes look up and down the road, which is bathed in orderly pools of soft yellow light. A car goes past, and the noise stops.

She turns back just as Ben opens their door, guides her through and kisses her on the mouth, pushing her against the interior wall. He uses his foot to nudge the door shut and, giggling, they go upstairs.

2

Kate is enjoying watching him get ready for work. She is lying in bed, on her side, face plumped against her pillow, half a leg out of the duvet. She doesn't move; her eyes travel with Ben as he ferrets around trying to find everything he needs. He is looking for his only clean shirt. It's hanging on the back of the door.

'Have you seen my shirt?' he asks finally.

'It's on the back of the door,' she says.

He looks up from tying his shoe and leaps forward, holding the hanger as he undoes the top button. He leaves the room as he pulls his arm through a sleeve. She rolls onto her back and looks up at the ceiling. There is a water stain she hasn't seen before. She can't work out where it's come from. It bothers her that she spends a lot of time worrying about bad things happening, and they are never the things she should actually worry about.

She hears him shout, 'Bye!' and a moment later the front door bangs. She closes her eyes and repeats the words she has said every morning for the last six years: *Just for today, I will try and live through this day only . . .*

There is a sudden whirring noise from outside. Her eyes spark open. She gets out of bed and looks out of the window. There are two men with hi-vis jackets dangling precariously from the branches of the large tree across the road. It has always felt too big for their residential London street. Kate loves how much green it dashes across the view, how it reaches like children's arms stretching as far as they can go, fingers splayed up to their very tips trying to reach the sky. She watches as a branch tumbles to the ground and sighs.

Since last night she's felt uncomfortable, as though her skin isn't on right. She feels lopsided. It is the unnameable feeling she dreads, as if everything is right and she is just wrong. It has taken her by surprise. Nowadays she's contented the majority of the time, so when something like this pops up out of nowhere, it reminds her of what used to be a constant state. Her go-to impulse is to quickly change the way she feels. Before, the monkey on her shoulder used to scramble around looking for a way to blot out the unpleasant feeling. And then she would drink. Now, she has been given the tools to deal with this sort of unease. She decides to make a call, one she hasn't felt the need for in a while because everything has been going so well. It rings three times.

'Kate!' Clare sounds relieved to hear from her. 'I was hoping you'd call.'

'Hi, Clare,' Kate says. 'Is this a good time?'

'Let me just give the baby to Greg.'

Kate hears a commotion and a few murmurs before Clare

17

comes back to the phone. 'What's been going on? It's been months.' She sounds breathless.

'Sorry . . . I should have checked in. I've just been so busy with school and the wedding.' Kate knows she's making excuses.

'Right,' says Clare. 'Have you been going to meetings?'

'A few,' Kate murmurs noncommittally.

'Well, that's the main thing,' Clare says kindly. Instantly, Kate feels terrible that she lied. 'How are you?'

'I'm fine, I mean, there is loads going on with work and stuff. And the wedding is soon and . . . I bumped into Becky last night.'

'Becky . . . your old friend?'

As her sponsor, Clare knows everything about Kate, her darkest secrets, her deepest worries, the thick gangrenous rot that swirls inside her brain at night and stops her from sleeping. That is because of Steps Four and Five, the two most feared and most transformative steps of Alcoholics Anonymous. It was only after she'd completed these that Kate really began to feel free from the chains of addiction.

The purpose of Step Four – *Made a searching and fearless moral inventory of ourselves* – is to uncover all one's secrets, everything she was feverishly hoarding away. All the things she'd ever done to anyone else, because of her ego, or vanity, or self-pity. All the things she used to use to keep herself drunk, 'because that happened to me', or 'because I'm like this'. All transferred from inside to outside.

She had dreaded Step Five, which is where she had to read

the list she had created to her sponsor. But oddly, after she did it, Kate felt better. She felt as if she could let it all go, as if she'd removed the central point of a blockage and could watch the debris rush down a fast-flowing river. Not forgotten, but no longer clogging up her mind with useless worries and regrets.

This is why Clare knows everything about her relationship with Becky.

'I thought she moved away?' Clare asks.

'She's back.'

'OK . . . and how did it go?'

'Ben was with me, which kept it light.'

'Kate, do you think she's back in your life for a reason?' Clare asks, leading her to the point. 'You always said you didn't want to do it over Skype.'

Kate stares at the tree across the road as it is cropped further and further back. The feeling of trepidation grows, like an old chest being opened, the dust blown off and a key rattling inside a sticky lock.

'Maybe it's better just to leave it,' Kate says.

'Right . . . and why do you think it's a good idea to leave this unresolved?' The kindness in Clare's voice has been replaced with a no-nonsense tone. 'Out of everyone you felt you had hurt during your drinking, Becky was near the top of your list. You've put it off, Kate, but she's stepped back into your path for a reason. Don't you think?'

Kate nods, but doesn't say anything. She thinks of Becky and her shiny hair and glamorous outfit. 'She's so different now, she won't care. She'll think . . .'

'What? That you're weak?' Clare says, knowing Kate's pride will be desperate not to do this.

'Yes . . . maybe . . . I don't know.' Kate walks backwards and slumps onto the edge of her bed, wiping her forehead.

'You shouldn't care what Becky thinks of you. The purpose of doing your Step Nine with her is to deal with any situations from your past that could come back to bite you and possibly trigger a relapse,' Clare says forcefully.

'What if she doesn't want to hear it?'

'She sat down and had a drink with you last night, right? I'm sure she'll want to hear what you have to say,' Clare says.

'You're right.' Kate knows she is. Clare always is.

'I think this will be an important part of your recovery, Kate,' Clare presses. 'All we can do is keep our side of the street clean.'

'OK, I'll arrange to meet her,' Kate says, trying not to grit her teeth.

'Great! I've got to go. Let me know how you get on.' Clare hangs up.

Kate puts her hand on her chest, trying to calm the swirling anxiety. Part of her had hoped Becky would never return, so she could put this off forever. Seeing her has brought up so many memories of who Kate used to be. She can't just live in her lovely new bubble if she meets with Becky and opens up the past again. She moves her hand off her chest and glances over at the mirror. She looks herself in the eye and swallows. She has worried about it all these years, what awful thing she did that caused Becky to break off their friendship with no explanation. Becky's dark wounded eyes have haunted her since she saw them, that last time, over a decade ago.

Finally, Kate leaves the flat. Her bike is in the hallway downstairs. Their landlord who lives below lets her keep it there. She lifts it down the steps and onto the pavement, pulling her other arm through the strap of her backpack. She loves cycling in the city. Ben often jokes that it is her final vice – the buzz she gets from weaving through London traffic, deep house music blaring in one ear. The adrenalin is euphoric.

Kate is covered in sweat by the time she arrives at school. She feels as if she has ridden out the anxiety a little. She takes off her helmet, gasping for air. Looking down, she checks the time on her phone: a new record, which makes her happy. She squints as she looks up at the modern red-brick building in front of her. Felix Road Academy is among the largest and toughest schools in Hackney, one of London's most deprived areas. She completed her teacher training here. It was one of the hardest years of her life, almost breaking her. Three years in, and finally Kate feels on top of her lesson plans and more confident in her abilities. The kids don't mess with her like they used to when she was shiny and new. They could smell her inexperience back then. Kate hasn't cried in the toilets all term, which she feels is massive progress.

'Nice wheels, Miss.' Kai saunters past, a fourteen-year-old with a Nike man-bag around his neck, clutching an elaborate metallic vape cigarette. He blows out a plume of smoke as he walks towards the main entrance.

'Er . . . not in school, Kai!' she calls after him.

'Technically, I'm not inside yet,' he says, mischievously taking another drag and blowing the smoke behind him before making his way inside.

Kate shakes her head, smiling at his audacity as she locks up her bike. Every morning she feels proud that she has made it here. When she got sober, she made a promise to herself that she was finally going to finish something and get a proper career. She'd always wanted to teach, and for those first few years of sobriety Kate barely had a life. All she did was focus on getting her degree and attending AA meetings. But it has paid off, laying the foundations for everything she has now.

She is grateful that she scraped through her GCSEs and A levels back when she was a teenager, before her disease really took hold. It meant that once she got sober, there wasn't so far to climb to get to where she wanted to be. If she hadn't passed her exams back then, would it have been too daunting to start again? Where would her addiction have taken her? To heavy drugs? To prostitution? Over six years she has sat in hundreds of AA meetings listening to thousands of people's stories, and she is well aware of how dark that road can get. She feels blessed to have got her life back in her twenties, before her illness had the chance to take too much away, and when she still had so much of her life to live.

She follows Kai through the main door. Inside is a porch area that the receptionist has to buzz her through. Maureen, who mans the front desk, can be incredibly fierce if necessary.

'Kate!' Maureen calls from inside her glass case. Kate turns, suddenly worried she's done something wrong. 'Not long to go now,' Maureen smiles.

Kate's shoulders relax and she nods. 'Thank God!' she replies. There are only a few weeks until the GCSE exams start and then it will nearly be the summer holidays. The countdown is on. The door is electronically released, and Kate pushes through to the main corridor. She takes off her backpack and cranks her neck to the side. It clicks. She showers in the staff changing rooms, feeling refreshed and energized when she steps out of the hot mist and onto the cold tiles. She applies her simple daytime make-up, and dresses. Six years ago the thought that she would ever start her day with exercise would have been laughable. But, back then, brushing her teeth without gagging would have been an accomplishment.

First period she has her favourite, but most challenging, class: her bottom set, Year 11. The class has been incredibly important to her this year. Kate has to work hard to build energy and excitement for their work. There is one girl in particular, Lily, who is far too talented to be there. She joined the school two years ago, having been expelled from the more desirable state school up the road. Kate has made it her mission to get her through with a good grade. She has become too emotionally involved, but she's seeing results and that's all Kate cares about. She desperately wants them all to do well, but it's a tough gig. Most of them have been predicted Fails; it will be an achievement for any of them to get a GCSE pass grade. Malcolm, the head teacher, wasn't sure she was ready for such an undertaking, but Kate pushed for the class and he decided to give her a chance. She wants to prove herself to him, and she wants Lily to get the grade she deserves. She also wants to be there to give Lily the extra support that she so desperately needs; the girl could easily slip under the radar with a less committed and more jaded teacher. Kate unlocks the classroom and switches the lights on. She moves the desks so they are facing each other in a circle and places a worksheet on each surface. Best friends Lizzie and Emma are the first to arrive; their ties are bunched at the top with a fat knot and their skirts are pulled up high. Their hair is matching in style, tight buns that pull up their ears. They are talking at each other briskly as they look down at their phones.

'Yeah, and then she said that she hadn't slept with him, but she definitely did, fucking slut,' says Lizzie to Emma.

'Morning, girls,' Kate says. 'Take a seat, please.'

'Hi, Miss,' they say sweetly, in unison.

Over the next five minutes the rest of the class file in and take their seats. Kate allows them to chat for a while. She finds that if she lets them get it out of their system, they are not bursting to distract each other throughout the class. The chatter comes to an abrupt halt when Lily walks in. She has striking pale, clear eyes, plump lips, and a thousand tiny freckles dashed across the top of her nose. She wears her long dark hair down. It reaches the small of her back. Kate wonders if she has ever had it cut. She is petite and doll-like but has a huge presence. Everyone stares as she pulls out a chair, sits down and takes out a pen which she places between her teeth.

'Hi, Miss.' She props up her chin with her elbow on the

desk. She looks tired and wary and completely unaware of the effect she's had on the room. That is the thing with Lily, she can be loud and mouthy, or quiet and timid, depending on what she got up to the night before. 'Hi, Lily,' Kate says, smiling. 'Right, I think that's everyone.' She opens her book to the poem they are studying for the English exam: 'Human Interest' by Carol Ann Duffy. 'Can you all look at the sheet of paper on your desks. We're going to look again at the poem we discussed last time. Who can remember what a *volta* is, and which part of the poem is an example of one?'

She looks out at their blank faces encouragingly. Finally, Emma slowly raises her arm.

'Is it the last bit, Miss?' she says quietly, as if it's painful to try.

'Yes! Very good, Emma, do you know why?' Emma's cheeks run red. Kate doesn't want to embarrass her. She turns to the rest of the class. 'Anyone else?'

'It's the sudden change in the emotion, Miss.' It is Lily. 'He goes from being nasty about his girlfriend to being sad that he killed her.' She's looking out of the window as she talks, not wanting to fully commit to the answer, in case it's wrong. Then she can pretend she didn't really care anyway.

'Yes! Spot on, well done, Lily,' Kate says, proud.

Lily doesn't acknowledge the praise, but the corners of her mouth turn upwards ever so slightly.

'So, I've set you a few questions to do during the class, they are on the printout in front of you . . .'

Audible moans.

25

'You should be able to complete these by the end of the lesson. I'm here to help.' They spend the rest of the class getting on with the work. Kate is so focused on them she doesn't think of herself the whole time – another reason she loves teaching; helping others quietens her busy mind.

At the end of the session Lizzie raises her arm. 'Can we see a picture, Miss?'

'Of what?' Kate asks, confused.

'The dress! You said you had to go and get measured on the weekend.'

'Oh, the fitting!' She smiles, pleased that Lizzie remembered. 'I think it might be bad luck to show it to anyone.'

'But we won't even be there, Miss! Come on . . .' All the girls have a pleading look in their eye.

'Yeah, go on, Miss,' says Lily, who rarely pushes for anything.

'OK, it's really simple, though.' Kate gets out her phone. The girls gather round and look at her screen. 'Aw, Miss, it's lovely,' says Lizzie. 'Very classy.'

'I'm going to have a full-on princess dress when I get married,' says Emma. 'It is pretty, though, Miss.'

'Yeah, it's nice, but I want a few more sparkles in mine,' says Lizzie, twirling around as she imagines a wedding dress of her own.

'You'll look beautiful, Miss,' says Lily sorrowfully, as if she has something else on her mind entirely.

'Thanks, Lily.' Kate wants to reach over and hug her, to tell her everything is going to be OK. But she can't promise that.

The bell rings and the class starts to disperse. 'We don't

have many classes left before the exam so make sure you do the work I've set,' she calls over their chatter. 'Lily, can I have a quick word?' The teenager nods and walks over. She stops before she gets too close. Kate takes another step forward. She can smell it instantly. Lily's tried to cover it up with cheap perfume, but it doesn't mask last night's booze. Kate wonders if anyone else would notice. It takes one to know one, as they say. Kate hands Lily her workbook open at the last page. In big, scrawling capital letters Lily has written, *THIS IS A FUCKING WASTE OF TIME*. Kate can see she has attempted the first few questions; her handwriting started calmly and relatively neatly, but as she goes on it becomes ratty. Lily looks shamefaced for only a moment, then she backs away a few steps, her shoulders rise and her eyes narrow, a cat backed into a corner.

'It *is* a fucking waste of time, Miss,' she starts. 'There is no point . . .'

'Lily, you are one of the most talented students in this class,' Kate says firmly. The girl stops; her large eyes look up, unsure how to take the compliment. 'You're on course to pass, or do even better if you really focus these last few weeks.'

The girl looks down at her shoes. 'I should sack it off,' she mumbles miserably.

Kate pauses, and then with a soft, encouraging voice says, 'It's just a few more weeks, Lily. Once you've got that grade it's forever.' She perches on the desk and puts her hand on Lily's shoulder, trying to encourage eye contact. 'Come on, you've worked so hard for this. You're nearly there.'

The girl looks up at her. Dark circles under her eyes shine. 'OK, Miss, I'll try.' Her chin is wobbling.

For a moment Kate thinks Lily is going to cry. 'If there is anything you want to talk about, Lily, you can talk to me,' Kate says softly.

Lily sniffs and takes her book. 'I'm fine.' She hurries out of the room.

Kate wishes she could do more. She always wishes she could do more. She can almost taste the raw emotions. She can see in Lily so much of herself when she was that age, always hungover or stoned. Always chewing gum furiously, spritzing herself with that cheap body spray they used to steal from Boots, and squirting eye drops before lessons. Kate knows all the tricks.

The school is aware that Lily is having issues and has laid on counsellors and extra support, but Kate doubts that the girl turns up for any of it. She desperately wants to wade in, but it isn't her place to get overly involved with a student's emotional well-being. Supporting Lily through these last few weeks of school is something productive she can do to help. On days like today Kate isn't sure she's getting through to the girl at all. But then, teenage Kate would have ignored advice too. If she alone could feel her pain, how could anyone else know how to fix it? Kate slouches in the wheelie chair, manoeuvring in circles with the tips of her toes. As she pushes against the floor, she looks up at the ceiling, revolving above her head. Lily is so close, just a few more weeks.

She halts the movement with a sudden toe on the floor and bends down to undo the side zip on her bag. Inside is a cold metal coin; on one side a triangle with the words *To Thine Own Self Be True* along the edge, and the number six in Roman numerals, dead centre. She turns it in her fingers. On the other side is the Alcoholics Anonymous serenity prayer. She looks over the words . . . *accept the things I cannot change* . . .

She holds the coin between her hot palms. It is the sobriety chip she got the day of her sixth sober birthday. She takes it everywhere with her. She closes her eyes and allows the chair to spin her further around. About six years of living in reality. About 2,190 days of waking up and thinking, *just for today I won't drink*, and miraculously getting into bed that night without having taken a sip. She should feel proud. She sighs and thinks back to her conversation with Clare that morning. One of the AA steps, Step Nine, involves making amends by apologizing to anyone you may have hurt during your drinking. She picks up her phone and looks at Becky's name in her address book.

Maybe she could just leave it, lie to Clare and say it went well. But what would be the point? The only person she would hurt is herself. She has always known she'd have to do Step Nine with Becky. The weight of guilt about their relationship is heavy. It's not as if their friendship was in a good state before that last night in the pub. As Kate's disease became more ingrained, their friendship became more and more fractured. Back then, she never once thought how Becky felt, holding Kate's hair while she puked in a toilet, or leaving a party early to help her get home, or when Kate kissed the boy that Becky

29

fancied, just so she could feel some sort of personal validation. During those teenage years, it was Becky that bore the brunt of Kate's selfishness.

She shudders; no wonder Becky couldn't wait to dash off to university to start a new life, away from her. Kate took Becky for granted; she had no idea how much she relied on her friend until after Becky left, and Kate went to pieces. Sometimes she placates herself by thinking that nothing specific happened that last night, and Becky had just outgrown their chaotic friendship. But deep down, Kate just knows she must have done something truly awful. She presses on Becky's number and listens to the phone ring. It rings and rings until Becky's voice chimes in with a recorded voicemail message. Kate hangs up, relieved. Just as she puts the phone down, it starts buzzing on the spot like an amputated bee. Becky's name flashes.

'Kate?' Becky says, sounding thrown.

'Hi . . . I wasn't sure if this was still your number.' Kate pauses. 'It was lovely to see you last night.'

'Yes . . . you too.'

'I was wondering, would you like to meet up this evening? There is something I'd like to talk to you about.' She coughs nervously.

'Tonight? Is it important?'

'Yes, I suppose it is,' Kate says.

A pause. 'OK. Let's meet at the Vulture.'

Kate makes an inaudible gasp and starts to protest. The Vulture is the last place they saw each other. She blinks. Could she really do her Step Nine with Becky in the very place they fell out? She knows what Clare will say: why put yourself in unnecessary danger? And: why not create new memories in new places that aren't riddled with ones you'd rather forget? But she wants to go along with the suggestion – maybe there is a reason they are meant to end up back there.

She also wants to prove to Becky that she isn't weak. She doesn't have limitations. Enough time has passed. It won't trigger anything.

'Sure,' Kate says. 'I can be there for seven.'

She looks down at her outfit and feels frumpy in her old cream blouse and black work slacks. Before, Kate had always been the pretty one, the one who gained the most attention, mainly because everything about her begged for it. As a teen-ager she'd saunter around with her navel out, her pert breasts always on show. She'd be the one making the most noise, laughing the loudest, wearing the most make-up. She was screaming out to be noticed, as if that would be proof that she really did exist. A teacher once called her gregarious. It stuck with Kate because she had to look it up. When she saw the meaning, a person fond of company, sociable, it just reinforced her view that no one understood her at all.

Kate looks up at the ticking clock; she will just have time to cycle home and change before meeting Becky later. It feels strange that she needs to impress her old friend at all. Becky is the last person she ever cared about impressing before. She calls Ben to let him know her plans but can tell he's in a rush.

'Just going into a meeting,' he says.

'I'm going to meet Becky for a drink tonight, is that OK? I know you said you were going to cook,' she says.

'Oh, you want to talk about me, don't you?' he jokes.

She can picture the mischievous look on his face; his pupils will be shining, the deep creases either side of his mouth will have appeared. 'Yes, and everything else we couldn't talk about with you there.'

'Of course it's OK, have fun,' he says. 'I'll order in and watch that Vietnam documentary you keep saying you'll watch with me.'

'Sounds wonderful.' She puts the phone down and bites her thumbnail. She reminds herself what she has learnt since getting sober: the things that frighten her the most often offer the biggest reward. Someone in a meeting once said that you can't die from a feeling. That was a revelation. Courage swims ahead, beating the fear she feels to the fifty-metre line. She's going to do it, then. She's going to make amends to Becky. Kate has spent over ten years worrying about what happened that night in the pub, and by tonight she'll know the truth. She must trust that everything will be OK, whatever happens, whatever she has to say.

Kate used to run away from pain, terrified, thinking she might get trapped inside it forever. Until she allowed herself to stop, to feel feelings, to sit with them; sometimes it lasts a few hours, or days, or weeks. But it always ends, and she always feels stronger and more able to deal with that feeling the next time. It is such a basic life skill that simply passed her by. She's heard people share in AA meetings that they feel as if they missed a vital lesson at school, or that there is a rule book that got handed out while they were in the loo or something. She can relate to that, there have been so many light-bulb moments over the last six years.

Maybe, once it is over, the lingering feeling that follows her around whispering in her ear that something isn't right, will go away. Maybe she'll get the closure she craves. Maybe, just maybe, Becky doesn't hate her after all.

3

Kate looks in the mirror, sighs, and starts to undo her dress. It is short and made of navy-blue chiffon, one of the more expensive items in her wardrobe. She throws it on the bed. To wear it would look like she is making too much effort. She walks back over to the wardrobe, her fingers sliding her pendant on its chain as she thinks. She is nervous, on edge, her mind revolving, rehearsing what she will say tonight. Her lips move silently as she practises lines, before discarding them with disdain. She is so engrossed in her projections of the evening ahead that she almost jumps when she hears the flat door slam.

'Hey!' she calls down so Ben knows there isn't an intruder. She listens to him pause, and then climb the steps up to the second floor of their flat.

'I thought you were going out.' He walks into the room. 'Oh, heeeey!' he says, seeing her for the first time. He walks over and takes her in his arms, putting his cold hands on her bare butt cheeks.

'Oi!' she giggles.

'I thought you were going out?' he says again, nuzzling her neck.

'I am!' She moves backwards, laughing. 'I can't decide what to wear.' She pushes him back on the bed. 'Help me?'

'I'll do whatever you want. Just please don't put any clothes on.'

She hits him playfully. Lifting up the discarded dress on the bed he asks, 'Where are you going, anyway?'

'Just to the Vulture.'

'The pub? Didn't you use to work there?'

'I'd hardly call it work.'

'Are you sure you want to go there?' His voice has changed from playful to concerned.

'Yes! I'm looking forward to it.' And then, 'It will be interesting to see how it's changed. It was sold to a gastro-pub chain a few years ago, apparently.'

He lies back on the bed and rubs his face, feet still on the floor. 'Well, if you think it's a good idea.'

'We go to pubs all the time,' she says, annoyed that he is delving into her plans, telling her things she already knows.

'I know . . . you just said you never wanted to go back, that's all.'

'It's not a big deal,' she says softly.

He sits up. 'OK, why are you thinking of wearing your most expensive dress, then?' He nods towards the discarded crumple of fabric.

'I wasn't. It just fell off the hanger,' she lies, picking out a simple black boat-neck top and some jeans. 'This is just right.'

35

He goes downstairs to order some food and she applies her make-up. She does all the extras: a hint of eyeshadow, a dab of plum lipstick, highlighter on the side of her cheekbones. She wants to look better than she did the night before.

Ben looks up from the sofa before she goes out of the front door. 'You look lovely.'

'Thanks.' She never believes him. He always thinks she looks wonderful. Men are completely blind to detail. Not like the way girls scan you when you walk into the room, taking in every nuance. She goes over and kisses his forehead.

'Bye, then.' She looks up at the black-and-white archive footage playing out on the television. 'Enjoy your programme.'

'Don't leave me here all on my own for too long,' he jokes. 'Have fun.'

Kate checks the contents of her bag and moves a strand of hair behind her ear. Before she leaves, she turns one last time. He smiles at her as she slips out of the door. That smile. When she first saw it, she thought she was going to die.

They live in Newington Green, a tiny pocket of north-east London that straddles the sophisticated affluence of Islington and the trendy deprivation of Hackney. In its centre is a pretty square of green with small independent shops huddled around. It has a leafy, village feel, even though it is just minutes from the city. It feels like the perfect setting for this phase of Kate's life. There are more coffee shops than pubs. It is full of young professionals just like her, on the trail to marriage and starting families. Women in their thirties push buggies around the square wearing big black sunglasses and clutching flat whites. She likes to watch them, thinking it will be her turn soon. Everything is orderly and clean, and it is just far enough from the dirty streets of Camden, where she grew up and did most of her drinking.

She steps into an Uber and looks out of the window. The evenings have become longer, the sky bright and hazy with a low-hanging sun. The white moon is already visible. It hangs there dormant, like an uncomfortably early guest. She watches the familiar streets canter past. This area of London is a film set from years gone by: a street corner where she had an argument with an ex, a shop she threw up outside, a bus stop where she begged for money to get home having lost her purse.

Camden Town goes in and out of fashion every decade. Currently, it is very much out of vogue. During her teenage years it was the height of cool. The dirty post-punk ambience lent itself well to the indie rock and roll scene. All the boys from bands hung out there, with their pointy shoes, impossibly tight jeans and trilby hats. The nightlife was alive with gigs and club nights.

Kate felt like she'd won the lottery getting a job at one of the local pubs when she turned eighteen. She felt ingrained in the place, her own personal playground. There was always something going on, always someone to drink with, always someone to score drugs off. Looking back, it should have been fun. But it wasn't. She was constantly chasing those rare moments she used to have when she drank, where everything was happy, fun, and sparkling – like a music video or one of those adverts for beer or rum where the clinking of a drink with another person's somehow magicked a connection, and suddenly you were dancing through a sunroof in a limo, or holding hands running through the streets, laughing.

But really, the more she drank the more depressed she got, and the more she couldn't stop, and the further she felt from everyone around her. If it weren't for Becky, those years would have been the loneliest of her life. Ever since Becky left, Kate missed the connection they had, and no matter how many times she tried to replicate it, it just didn't work. She was on her own.

She remembers a big fire, which took out a big chunk of Camden Market and one of the most popular drinking holes in the area. As they watched it burn from a friend's council flat high above the skyline, someone joked that it was God getting rid of the rot. She stood there watching, half wishing she was burning with it.

The lights turn from red, to amber, to green, but the transient crowd ignores the traffic-light system and crosses the road at will. The taxi beeps and people scurry, allowing them entry. Camden is busy day and night, crammed full of tourists walking slowly; tramps sitting under cash machines with dogs; home county kids buying drugs off dealers by the canal bridge. To have been a resident of Camden Town is to see past the dirt, the wasters, the leather-clad heavy metallers.

They turn into a quiet back street and pull up to the corner.

'Thanks.' She opens the door and jumps out. The car zooms

off behind her and she looks up at the place where she used to spend the majority of her time: the Vulture.

It is far enough away from the high street that only locals know of its existence. The pub board has the same old painting of a half-spread vulture. She looks up at him and smiles warily; he peers down at her mildly amused that she's returned. She feels nervous as she walks towards the entrance. It used to be the place she came for refuge, to feel safe from the scary outside world. The irony is not lost on her.

She gets a rush of nostalgia as she pushes the door; it has the same weight and creak she's heard a thousand times. It's the stuff that stands still and stays constant as she has grown and changed. It's funny, she almost feels like she's come home, but looking around, she realizes it has completely transformed. Everything dishevelled and debauched has reformed. *Just like me*, she thinks. Maybe there is something poetic about doing her Step Nine with Becky in this place. She will have come full circle.

She lets the door close behind her as she surveys the scene. Kate started working here over ten years ago when she was in her late teens; sacked before she turned twenty. Back then, it was owned by a rich party boy who basically wanted somewhere to host his own private lock-ins. The manager was careless, the staff were high most of the time, and the customers were a heady mix of old-timers and fashionable scenesters. Local drug dealers would congregate before a busy Saturday night, getting a pint in before beginning their rounds. It was a community, albeit a very dysfunctional one, but Kate remembers it being the first place she finally understood the rules. Mainly because there weren't any.

It is quiet. Music plays but the volume is so low she can barely make out the track. There is a clatter of cutlery and the homely smell of roasted food. She had heard on the grapevine that the venue was sold two years ago. Everything has been smartened up: the paintwork glistens; the tables twinkle with varnish; the wallpaper is new. The booth where she used to sit with off-duty bar staff has gone. She looks at the bar and thinks of the time she fell off it, drunkenly dancing to impress a boy, and broke her wrist. She touches the area and looks down at a small scar. Chris, the manager, took her to hospital and had joked to her that she 'wasn't in *Coyote* fucking *Ugly*'. She thought she would die of shame when she sobered up.

There are a few tables scattered around the bar which aren't set for dinner and she sits down. It is oddly familiar but so implausibly different at the same time. She picks up the menu balancing between the salt and pepper shaker, and touches the flowers sitting in a tiny vase. It is all so grown-up. She shifts in her seat and takes a deep breath. She can't quite believe she is here or what she's about to do.

Becky walks into the room and Kate can't help but stare. The man behind the bar drying glasses is looking too. Kate has never seen Becky looked at like that. Men would look through her when they were younger. Kate waves at Becky, who acknowledges her and walks over.

'Wow, this place . . .' Becky plonks her bag on a chair and

looks around. 'I mean, are we even in the same pub?' Becky did the odd shift in the pub the summer before university, but she never dropped out of her education and she got a proper job after she graduated.

'I know. Crazy, isn't it? Barely recognizable.' She scans Becky's outfit. It is perfect, like an Instagram post. Black biker boots, washed jeans torn at the knee and a simple sleeveless blouse. Sunglasses dangle over the neckline; just a touch of peach lip gloss. It looks effortless. Kate's fingers curls around her pendant and swing it on the chain.

'Ah well, it's kind of a relief.' Becky takes her seat, scraping the chair back with one hand.

'I know what you mean,' says Kate.

There is a bang; the barman has opened the door to the cellar. A sudden memory makes her feel sick: racking up lines of coke down there with one of the local dealers. He was much older than her and had a constant green, sweaty sheen. He put his hand on her bum as she snorted the line, and she let him – anything to get out of her head. She twisted herself away from him with a sexy smile once she'd got the drugs she was after. She shakes her head, wanting to shift the memories. They come in short, sharp flashes of shame and cling on like a cat's claws digging into skin.

'Are you OK? Shit, sorry. Do you mind being here?' asks Becky, suddenly worried.

'Oh God yeah, I come to pubs all the time.'

Becky watches her. 'But here . . .'

'Yes, my misspent youth!' Kate chuckles. 'Seriously, it was

41

a long time ago; I've put a lot of space between that Kate and this one.'

Becky looks relieved. 'God, do you remember what we'd get up to here?' She shakes her head. 'All the lock-ins, the parties.'

Kate smiles weakly. 'Yes. Crazy. Becky . . .' She wants to get on with it. Kate leans forward, lets the words escape from her mouth before she has a chance to decide against it. 'There is actually a reason I asked you to meet me.' She coughs nervously.

'Yes . . . you said there was something.' Becky looks up, waiting.

'I got sober using the Twelve Steps . . . Alcoholics Anonymous.' She turns the little vase in front of her in half circles as she speaks. 'One of the steps, number nine, is making amends to those you feel that you hurt during your drinking.' She lets herself look up to gauge Becky's reaction. Her forehead is creased in thought. She has caught the corner of her bottom lip between her teeth. Kate feels her cheeks heat up.

'I think about you a lot; how close we were, and how much I hurt you. About how I took advantage of our friendship. You were always there looking out for me, looking after me. And I behaved really badly. The way our friendship ended; it has always bothered me.'

Her eyes dart up to Becky's face again. It is unreadable, her hands are settled on the edge of the table, waiting. Her mouth hangs open ever so slightly.

Kate quickly looks down again and continues. 'I know you must have been sick of hanging out with me. I was a nightmare. I don't blame you for going off to university and leaving all this behind.'

Kate remembers going home that next day and sitting in her room composing text message after text message to apologize. But the problem was, she didn't know what she'd done wrong. And she knew Becky was bored of her hollow apologies, rendered meaningless from overuse. She had the feeling she'd done something awful: shouted at her or embarrassed her in front of everyone, or worse. When the other Kate came out, the drunk version, she just never knew what she was capable of.

'I know that I used to say sorry to you all the time for my behaviour. But I hope you can see from the life I have built for myself that this is not just a flash in the pan, this is who I am, this is who I was always meant to be. That other Kate was my disease trying to push everyone away . . . even you.' Kate stops and looks over at Becky, still unable to decipher what she is thinking. She ploughs on.

'One day at a time, I got it back. A career, a boyfriend. If it weren't for Ben, I don't know what I would do. I mean . . . I'd probably go on a massive bender,' she laughs, joking. Becky doesn't join in. Kate stops and takes a deep breath. 'I am trying to say I'm sorry, and this time I really mean it.'

There is a long pause. Kate blinks: there, she's done it. She has no control over what happens now.

Finally, Becky speaks. 'I came to see you, that first Christmas I was home from university. Your dad said you were in Margate with your grandmother . . .'

43

'I didn't know . . . he never told me . . .' Kate closes her eyes and remembers that lonely time she spent by the seaside, walking along the promenade, white-knuckling her fists. She didn't drink for seven whole months. They were some of the darkest days she'd had in her life. She didn't want to ask for help, she thought she could do it all on her own if she just got out of London, got away from her friends at the pub.

'I nearly got on a train to see you,' Becky says. 'But then I thought maybe it was best to leave you to it, to work everything out . . .'

'You probably did the right thing,' Kate says. 'I wasn't ready then; you would have only been disappointed with who you found. It was another four years before I got sober.' The problem was inside her. It wasn't where she was living.

'I'm so pleased you got there in the end,' Becky says with a soft smile. The comment creates a warm well of hope within Kate. 'How is your dad?'

'He's OK. He's moved to Margate. Grandma died last year.'

'Oh, I'm sorry.'

'She was an old battleaxe, but I miss her. Dad sold the house and bought an old fifteen-room bedsit that he's renovating.' The usual pang of guilt; she hasn't seen him for months.

'I bet he's so excited about the wedding,' Becky says.

'Yes, he's excited for me.' She has barely spoken to him about it, really.

'I bet his eyes well up every time he talks about walking you down the aisle.'

Kate hasn't even invited him. She and Ben were thinking it would be romantic to grab some witnesses off the street.

Becky continues, 'It must be such a big deal for him. I bet there was a time he thought he might not get the chance.'

Kate looks down; the comment is almost too personal for someone else to articulate. 'Yes,' is all she can manage.

Becky's eyes run over Kate's features, as if she is checking for something. 'I'm really proud of you, you know?'

Hearing Becky say that, after all this time, means so much to Kate. 'Thanks, Becky. I'm happier than I've ever been.'

'You deserve to be happy,' Becky whispers, almost to herself.

Kate knows this could be her only chance. There is no other moment where they'll be this close, this intimate, this honest. If she wants to find out, she needs to do it now. 'Becky, do you mind me asking, what happened that night?' Kate leans in. 'What did I do? Did we have a fight?'

Becky's fingers drum on the table, she opens her mouth to say something and then she shifts in her seat. Finally, she says, 'Oh Kate, it was nothing really. You were a mess. You were all over those guys, it was embarrassing to watch. I was just tired of looking after you.'

Kate nods, understanding. 'It was just the last straw.' She is relieved.

Becky nods and then stands abruptly. 'Do you want a drink? I mean . . . a lime soda or something?'

Kate sits back in surprise at the sudden movement. 'Yes, thanks.'

She watches Becky walk confidently over to the man

behind the bar, whipping her hair back over her shoulder and laughing gently at something he says. It is so interesting to just watch her, to see how her mannerisms have changed. The way she raises the back of her hand to her face to check her nails as she waits, the way she carefully slides her finger on her bottom lip to smooth her gloss. Kate is sort of transfixed, and she has to tell herself to stop staring when Becky returns.

Becky sits down and takes a sip of her wine, a large measure, so clear it is barely tinged yellow. It must be dry, Kate thinks as she takes a sip of her water with fresh lime. She inhales a wet ice cube and crunches it between her teeth.

'So, are you still going to AA meetings?' Becky asks.

'Yes, it's an ongoing process. It hasn't been easy. I've had some pretty low points. But it's all been worth it. My sponsor used to say to me that if I just didn't pick up a drink, one day at a time, I'd get all the stuff I used to dream about when I was drinking. I never believed her.'

Becky nods slowly. 'Like meeting Ben.'

An image of his face drifts into Kate's mind. He was drenched and gleaming. She couldn't hear what he was saying at first, the noise of the wheels against sodden tarmac deafening.

'On Waterloo Bridge, in the rain.'

'And he's an engineer?' Becky asks.

'Yes, he works up in Scotland three days a week. To be honest, in term time I'm so busy I barely notice he's gone.'

'Is he nice to you? Treats you like you deserve and all that?'

Kate smiles. 'Yes, to be honest, Becky, I never thought I'd have a relationship like this. So easy, you know? Nothing toxic.

Nothing dark. He's just kind, and funny. At the end of the day, what more do you need?'

'And now you get your happy ending,' Becky smiles. It is something they used to say to each other when they were younger. That none of these stupid scrapes they got into would matter one day . . . because they would get their happy ending.

'Are you seeing anyone?' Kate asks.

Becky shakes her head sadly. 'I dated a few guys in New York; never anything serious. But I think subconsciously I always knew I wanted to come home, you know? I just didn't plan on coming back so soon,' she shrugs.

Kate nods. 'Your mother, is she OK?'

Becky takes another long sip of wine. 'She's not herself, and Alexa is nine months pregnant. She needed me home.' Becky looks down at her drink. Kate opens her mouth to find out more, but suddenly Becky looks at her, smiling. 'Six years, Kate! Could you ever have imagined you wouldn't drink for so long?'

Kate laughs. 'No! I couldn't even stay off it for a few days by the end.' She shifts in her seat, and a waft of cool air breezes in from an open window.

'You know, you don't really have anything to apologize for,' Becky puts her hand on Kate's. 'I missed you.' Becky's voice catches. 'I just couldn't watch you do it to yourself any more.'

Kate nods. 'I understand.'

Their eyes meet. All the teenage angst, all the anecdotes that bound them together, now dance between them. All the old resentments . . . for a moment they are gone.

*

47

Later, Kate rests her forehead against the window of the car that takes her home. She is exhausted; the evening has been emotionally laborious. She is trying to work out how she feels. She had played that scene out in her head many times over the last few years, and few times had it gone as well as that. Kate is forgiven. She doesn't have to worry about Becky hating her any more, and there is nothing darker lurking that she wasn't aware of. *Poof*, she thinks, the well of darkness she created in her head didn't even exist in the first place. She has closure. She looks out onto the dimly lit street and wonders why she doesn't feel the sense of relief she was expecting.

Kate thinks of Becky, that awkward almost-teenager she first met. Her frazzled hair that she could never tame, and the dodgy make-up that Kate never thought to correct. Kate used to like the fact Becky always got it just a bit wrong. She knows that now. It was so that Kate always felt as though she was better than someone else. She thinks about that as she looks out of the window at the streets they would roam together, and lets the shame roll over her. She will make up for it now, if there is any way she can. She'll prove to Becky she isn't that person any more.

4

Kate loves listening to his voice when he reads to her in bed. She closes her eyes and lets the story take her away. She'd always thought the New York accent was brash and twangy. Ben's is soft and methodically timed, as though he's never rushing to get a point across because he has so much confidence in its validity.

Just a few words from his mouth can calm her. Anxiety can dissipate in a moment – a tiny look, or a hand on the small of her back, and it just floats away. No one has ever been able to make her feel like that, like everything is OK. His ability to conjure serenity has baffled her from the first moment she laid eyes on him. But she'd never really been in love before she met Ben.

She can't help but feel that Ben is her prize for not drinking, for getting sober and doing all this work on herself. They say that you can only really love someone once you've learnt how to love yourself. Her previous relationships were fraught with anxiety, with blurry nights out involving passionate arguments and rabid make-up sex.

She was a magnet for that kind of chaos. The highs and lows offered an adrenalin fix, and she often confused that energy for love. The men she chose usually had the same issues as her and were unable to look after themselves, let alone cherish someone else. She would never have been able to hold down a healthy relationship six years ago, and a 'Ben' wouldn't have looked at her twice.

Kate readjusts her chin on his shoulder and places a folded leg across him. He moves some of her hair away from his mouth as he speaks. There is something about this closeness that makes her want to pinch herself; it is more intimate than sex. It is the connection to another person she always used to crave. The simplicity of sitting with someone else and feeling comfortable, not on edge or like she's putting on an act, being able to be the most authentic version of herself and being accepted. That is one of the best feelings in the world.

He closes the book with a dull snap and shuffles down the headboard to where she is lying.

'Goodnight.' He kisses her mouth and goes to turn off his bedside light.

'I'm really happy,' she whispers. He turns over and kisses her again.

'So am I,' he smiles.

'School's nearly over, and the big day . . .' She pauses to sigh. 'I wish we could just fast-forward to the good bit.'

'Ah, you see, that's where you're going wrong.' He kisses her again. 'This is the good bit. All of it is the good bit.' He kisses her more intensely this time and places his fingers around the elastic of her knickers, slowly taking them off. He chucks the duvet over his head and gives her a look before diving under. She lies back.

The next morning, Ben places a coffee on her bedside table and sits on the side of the bed fixing the knot of his tie as she lies behind him. His small wheelie bag is by the door. He's flying to Scotland straight from work that evening.

'Will it be a stressful week?' she asks, curling her body around his back.

He shrugs. 'It'll be fine.'

'I'll miss you.'

'Bullshit, you'll be too busy with all your kids.' He laughs.

Kate watches him disappear out of sight and then, with a groan, flings off the duvet. Today is her busiest day, she has five lessons back to back. A day without any free periods always makes her feel chaotic and disorganized. She didn't do any prep the previous evening, wanting to enjoy her only night in with Ben before he went away for the rest of the week. She doesn't have much to do, just a bit of marking and some lesson plans to run over. She can easily get it done before the bell for first period.

Kate enjoys the warm sun on her face as she races through Hackney on her bike. She heard on the radio that a heatwave was due to start, and this has cheered her up immensely. The beginning of the year seemed to drag on, with weeks of endless rain, and the sudden sun has opened a new chapter for everyone.

Kate feels renewed; a large part of the reason is what happened with Becky the other night. It's funny; when you have been so set on a certain truth about something, and you later find you were wrong, it makes you feel as if you have shed an old, flaky sheath of skin.

Clare was right, doing her Step Nine with Becky has been an important part of putting the past behind her. She shouldn't have put it off so long. But there is still that lingering feeling that something has been left unsaid. *Stop it*, she tells herself firmly. *It's just because you are so used to that feeling surrounding it, maybe it will take some time to go away.* She needs to look at the facts, that is something she has been taught. Instead of listening to her rambling mind and jumping to conclusions, look at what has actually happened, what has actually been said. She sighs; it is exhausting being herself sometimes.

Cutting past a bus, she waits at some traffic lights, her foot balancing against the kerb to keep her from falling. Music is pumping into her right ear, and she tries not to bop her head in time – the surrounding drivers would smirk and snigger.

Suddenly, a familiar figure walks down the pavement about ten metres away. Kate cups her palm over the top of her eyes to shield them from the sun. Squinting, she sees Lily. The girl is walking back towards her house, the wrong direction for school. Also, she isn't wearing her uniform; instead she has black high-waisted jeans and a sports bra on. Her long hair sways from side to side as she walks. She chews on her lip, occasionally taking a fevered drag of her cigarette, flicking the ash obsessively with her thumbnail.

She doesn't notice Kate; she is too engrossed in whatever she is thinking about. Kate watches her take the next left, and decides to follow her slowly, letting the pedals turn without any force. Before she gets to her house, the girl sits on a bench and flicks through her phone, a worried expression on her face. Finally, she stands, as if she has accepted her fate, and walks up to the Victorian terrace across the road. Kate looks up; she can see Lily's mother standing with crossed arms at the window, a thunderous look upon her face.

Hanging back, Kate watches with keen interest as the front door is opened and harsh words are shared. Then, the anger turns into relief and her mother encloses her in a hug. Lily just stands there; her arms hang uselessly by her body.

Kate has followed Lily home before; she was interested to see the kind of place she lived in. The house is a large terrace with beautiful sash windows. It is well maintained; the brickwork is newly repointed and a fashionable dark-grey colour is painted on the windows and front door. She can see the kitchen through the window on the ground floor, and the decor is contemporary and stylish with muted colours.

Kate studies Lily's mother's worried face. If she hadn't witnessed this, it would be easy to assume the girl had parents who weren't concerned with her well-being. But that is clearly not the case. She is obviously loved and cared for. It annoys Kate that everyone at school keeps saying Lily is just going through a rebellious phase. It makes what Lily is going through sound trivial. Kate remembers what that feels like, having others think she was being disruptive because she was just another silly attention-seeking girl. And after some time, it became easier to live up to that label, because that was what everyone expected of her.

Out of the corner of her eye, she notices a man with a dog staring at her oddly as she gawks through the kitchen window of the house across the road. She gives him a tight smile and quickly turns her bike around, returning her attention to the daily commute. Hunching her back above the handlebars, she shoots forward. Ten minutes later she arrives at school. After locking up her bike she fans her top against her chest and blows some cooler air down between her breasts. Wiping the sweat from under her chin with the back of her hand she pushes her shoulder through the main door.

'Morning,' she says to Maureen, barely looking up as she riffles through her bag for the folder of class plans. 'Lovely weather, isn't it?'

'Good morning Miss Sullivan,' Maureen replies. 'Don't forget the staff meeting this morning,' she chants as though she has been telling everyone. 'It's starting in ten minutes.'

'What?' Kate asks, looking up with a start.

'There is a pre-assembly staff meeting scheduled, Kate, didn't you get the message?' the receptionist replies haughtily.

'Oh yes, thank you.' Kate feels a familiar tightening of her chest. Looking down at her sweaty cycle outfit she rushes down the main corridor; she needs to quickly change before heading up there. She would be mortified to attend a meeting in these clothes. Hastily she turns on the shower in the staff changing room. She dips herself underneath the weak pressure of the piping hot water, careful not to wet her hair as she rinses off the suds. Stepping out, she pulls at the simple black cotton dress folded in her bag. She haphazardly applies some make-up and pulls her hair into a teacherly bun. Taking some deep breaths, she attempts to calm the stressy swirling of adrenalin. Then she unlocks the door and scampers up another flight of steps to the staffroom.

Tired chatter permeates the air as she enters, and she looks around for a friendly face. She notices Gus, who started training at the same time as her. He is sitting in the front row, laughing along with something Malcolm, the head teacher, is saying. She slides into a chair in the back row and puts her bag on the floor in front of her. She slips out the folder of lesson plans and places it on her knees.

Malcolm claps his hands and shouts for quiet. The chatter slowly dwindles, and everyone turns to face him. Kate carefully slips out the first page from her folder so she can cast her eyes over it as the session progresses.

'As we know, there has been a sharp rise in stabbings in the capital, and our school sits in an area high in violent crime,' the head teacher starts. 'PC Alcott is here to give a talk about signs of gang activity and details of things to look out for like street language et cetera.'

Kate looks up as the officer takes his hat off and places it on a nearby table, before launching into his lecture.

Biting her lip, she turns her head downwards to track her

eyes over the sheet on her lap. Kate wouldn't usually do this, but she has 10B next and they are her most disruptive class. She must be prepared. There is one boy in particular that makes her feel uncomfortable, Nathan Kelly. He is the last in a line of five brothers to attend the school. They each had a reputation and Nathan is no different.

At first, she'd assumed that it was a predetermined label that the poor boy had been stuck with. She's tried on many occasions to get through to him, and she knows that if she stumbles over the class hesitantly and seems unprepared, he will be the first to pick up on it and take advantage.

'If you hear or witness anything you feel is out of the ordinary please come and speak to me, my door is always open,' says Malcolm, bringing the session to a close. 'Thank you, PC Alcott, for taking the time to speak to us.'

There is the usual sound of rustling and the hum of conversations starting back up. Kate slips the paper back into her folder and stands, ready to rush off to her classroom and set up.

'Kate!' She turns towards the voice. It's Gus, walking towards her from the front of the room. She is itching to leave; she doesn't have much time.

'Hi,' she says, trying to be friendly.

'How are you?' he asks.

'Yeah good, thanks, in a bit of a rush. I've got 10B now.' She nods towards the door.

'Right . . . I was just wondering if you'd like to come out after school tonight? A few of us are going for a pint in De Beauvoir – it's meant to be a lovely evening,' he says.

She thinks for a moment: a beer garden, freezing cold cider with ice. A dribble of condensation.

'Oh right . . .' she says, whilst thinking of an excuse. 'I can't tonight, I'm so behind on my marking. Have a lovely time, though,' she says, turning to walk out of the door.

'Are you sure it can't wait?' he calls after her.

She stops and turns her head; he looks disappointed.

'Sorry, Gus, maybe another time.'

It's not that she isn't capable of sitting in pubs and having a good time these days, she just hasn't done it with the other teachers yet. She's not sure how she feels about them making assumptions or questioning why she isn't drinking. Inside this building she is a teacher, not an alcoholic, not someone with a troubled past. Just a hard-working teacher. And she doesn't want to do anything that will jeopardize that.

Kate readjusts the strap of her bag on her shoulder and checks the time; the kids will be in assembly for ten more minutes. She hastily unlocks the door to her classroom and logs onto her computer. Shaking, she gets the work out of her bag and quickly organizes the sheets into order. She checks the projector is working and tests the markers on the lip of the whiteboard. She is ready.

The bell rings and she sees the children beginning to gather outside. Kate nods and beckons them in. They troop through, finding desks, kicking chairs out from under tables, sighing and moaning. She gives them all stern smiles, a look she has perfected over the last three years. It took her a while to get the balance right. At the beginning of her career she thought if she smiled, if she was nice, the kids would like her and therefore work hard for her. She quickly learned how naive that was. She has to be more manipulative than that; she has to play a game, one they don't even realize they are playing.

'Morning, everyone,' she says.

Nathan Kelly is the last to arrive. He humps in, his bag hoisted over his shoulder like it's a dead deer he's just shot. He slumps in his chair and tilts the front of his cap over his eyes.

Everyone in the class looks at him and he smirks.

'Nathan, cap off, please,' Kate says sternly.

He crosses his arms defiantly.

'Nathan, you can take your cap off or see the Head, it's up to you.'

He sits there motionless, unwavering.

'OK, Aliyah, can you read the part of Juliet?' Kate asks the pretty dark-haired girl in the first row.

'Nathan, you can be Romeo.' She looks at him confidently.

He smirks. 'Piss off, Miss, I ain't reading that.' He pushes the book away from him as if it smells.

'Nathan, take your hat off and read for me,' Kate says, standing at the head of his desk. 'Come on, you'd make a dashing Romeo, wouldn't he, Aliyah?' She turns to the girl. Kate has seen Nathan blushing in her direction before.

'Come on, Nath,' Aliyah says.

'All right, but I'm not taking my cap off, Miss,' he says roughly.

Kate smiles. 'Deal.'

*

Kate is exhausted by the end of the day; it has been a whirl-wind of questions and quick thinking. She knows she must look bedraggled, her make-up has probably all worn off. She swallows and licks her dry lips; she didn't get lunch and she hasn't even had a chance to drink any water. But she has that feeling of satisfaction she gets when she's left her comfort zone and succeeded. As if the growth has pulled her phys-ically taller. Before she was stunted, restricted, and curbed. She hadn't tried anything that tested her boundaries for years, stuck in a state of perpetual similitude, like a wasp trapped under a glass. Banging against the same wall, able to view the outside world but incapable of finding a route out to join it.

She has one final lesson and it's with her favourite class. Mustering a final push of energy, she claps her hands together and welcomes them into the room. They plod in looking put-upon as usual, chatting candidly and scrolling their thumbs against the lit-up screens of their phones.

Kate wipes down the board. 'Not long to go!' she shouts over the chatter.

'Miss!' Lizzie's hand goes straight to her mouth. 'Don't say that, you're making me nervous, I think I'm going to puke.'

'Please, not on the desk, Lizzie,' Kate jokes. 'Don't worry, we're going to cram everything again before the exam.'

Kate looks at the door. Lily is missing. Maybe she needed to sleep off whatever she did last night.

'Has anyone seen Lily today?' she asks the class.

They all shrug and shake their heads.

Kate nods. 'OK, let's look at the Shakespeare. Did everyone

watch the Baz Luhrmann film over the weekend like I asked?' The girls all start cooing over the Hollywood actor who plays the main part.

Kate cycles home just as the sun loses its bite. She's thinking about Lily, about the sad look upon her face that morning. She'd seemed as though she wasn't paying attention to anything around her, like she was replaying something all-consuming over and over in her mind. Kate knows that feeling: of being so jammed up within a problem that you can't make sense of anything any more. She clicks her tongue in her mouth as she considers ways of getting Lily to focus for these last few weeks. To ignore everything else, just for this short period. If she passes these exams it will be a real boost to her confidence, it may help to pull her out of the spiral of self-hatred she is in. Kate cycles faster, enjoying the burning sensation, gritting her teeth as she rolls her legs around, pressing down on the pedals harder and harder until the pain is all-consuming, and she can't think about anything else at all.

She opens the front door and places her bike against the wall of the communal hallway. Ben is away; she already knows it will be dark and silent inside, the only noise the odd car or motorbike speeding past. Kate doesn't mind, she likes quiet. She spent so many years pretending to be an extrovert, but since she's been sober she's realized the simple truth is that she likes solitude, and quiet, and Radio 4, and cups of tea, and long baths and intimate conversations with only a handful of people she trusts.

She uses the wire of her earphones to fish out the phone from her pocket. It rang a few times while she was cycling. She sees a missed call from Becky. Kate is surprised; she wasn't expecting to hear from her anytime soon. Unbuckling her helmet, she calls her back.

'Kate,' Becky answers. 'Sorry to bother you.' She sounds nervous and a bit put out.

'That's OK!' Kate says, trying to sound cheerful and not too intrigued.

Then Kate hears someone else muttering in the background. 'I'm asking her!' Becky says with force. 'Sorry. My mum . . . she wants you to come for dinner tonight. I know you're probably busy but it's her birthday and I let it slip we met up and . . . she wants you here. Can you come?'

'Oh,' says Kate. She isn't sure what to say, Becky doesn't sound that keen.

'It's just us, Alexa and William. It's not a big deal. But she says she misses you.' Becky coughs. 'See, I've asked her,' she whispers to Susanna who must be standing with her by the phone.

Kate thinks about Becky's mother, her sparkling jewellery and extrovert wardrobe. Her evil punctuated laugh, which she couldn't help but mimic. The funny stories, the voiced characters she'd conjure up while telling an anecdote. The way she made Kate feel so included and present, like she was the most important person in the room. Part of Kate wants to feel like that again.

She should pretend she's busy, that's what Becky probably

61

wants her to do. But Susanna was like a surrogate mother to Kate when she was a teenager. Something pulls Kate towards the offer.

'Are you sure?' she asks, knowing she isn't.

There is a pause. 'Yes, it will be nice,' Becky says in a stunted voice.

'OK then, if you're sure,' Kate says.

'Lovely, see you at seven,' Becky says quickly before hanging up the phone.

Kate stands there staring at her screen, wondering if she's done the right thing. Should she really be getting involved in Becky's life so soon after she's put it all behind her?

5

Kate showers and changes, blow-drying her long hair and brushing it upside down to give extra volume. Susanna used to own one of the most successful model agencies in London and her personality matches that achievement: fierce and charming. She latched onto Kate as soon as Becky brought her home that first time. Susanna always used to say Kate had natural style and presence. She would make Kate feel special, in the way a mother should, in a way no one ever had before. Becky and Susanna were badly suited to one another. Becky was ungainly and awkward, whereas Kate was funny and daring. Kate used to daydream that Susanna was her real mother, that they'd been swapped at birth and a twist of fate had bought them together again. Susanna would never have left her like her own mother did, she would think.

Kate applies some lipstick and blots her mouth on a tissue, the way she imagines someone sophisticated would. She puts on some pearl earrings and pouts at her reflection. She wants Susanna to see her as an accomplished young woman, not the damaged teenager that used to flit in and out of her home.

She walks up the quiet Belsize Park street. The affluent area is full of smart houses with white pillars either side of the doors. When she first went there – she must have been about thirteen – it was like being Alice down the rabbit hole. She'd never been anywhere like Becky's bohemian home. Kate's father, Jonny, scraped together the money to buy his council flat; there was nothing elegant or aesthetically pleasing about their two-bedroom apartment. The only reason the two girls' paths crossed was because Kate had gained an assisted place at their expensive private school in Marylebone. She did so well on the eleven-plus exam the whole fee was waived. Kate was nervous and intimidated by the girls at the posh school, and to combat this she tethered an unapproachable demeanour to herself. When the girls naturally huddled into friendship groups, Kate found herself alone. She spent the first term wondering where on earth she was, feeling isolated. She fantasized about getting expelled and moving to the local state school where she had friends and knew all the rules.

Then Becky turned up halfway through the year with no idea of the social politics. Kate watched her keenly during their first English lesson together; she was smiley and sweet. Kate remembers that when she turned to her and saw her looking, she gave her a big friendly grin, completely unaware of Kate's reputation as the scary girl from the council estate. In that moment Kate decided this was her chance to make a friend. Becky was so unassuming that she welcomed the new friendship unconditionally. Kate was led into this whole new world at Becky's house and, suddenly, she didn't want to change schools or spend time in the flat in Camden, eating macaroni and cheese on her own in front of the telly while Jonny worked. Susanna made her feel wanted and needed and exciting and interesting.

Kate holds a box of chocolates under her arm and looks at the bell she needs to ring, feeling apprehensive in the way that she does when she hasn't seen people this side of sober. She feels as if they are checking her out, to see how she has changed, whether she is still 'fun'. She spent the first few years sober putting on a big show, trying to prove she was still the life and soul, thinking that if she stayed up past 2 a.m. then everyone would still think she was cool or something. It has taken her a long time to come to terms with the fact that she is enough, and she doesn't have to prove anything to anyone. But it's still something she struggles with.

Finally, she presses the bell. It whips up aggressive barking from inside and the door is opened to a tiny dog jumping and shouting. 'Hello, Poppy.' Kate kneels down and caresses the dog's ears; she can't believe she's still alive. The dog nuzzles Kate's hand, suggesting she remembers her too.

'That's actually Poppy number two.' Kate looks up to see Alexa, Becky's older sister, above her. 'I didn't know you were coming.' Ten years have not been kind to Alexa; she must be in her mid-thirties now, but she could be five years older. Her skin looks vacuum-packed across her face. Her cheekbones were once shiny and pinched, they now look bony and worn. Her long dark hair is straight against her face, and there is a

65

startling white line of a parting running across her head. Kate looks down to where her hand is positioned on her stomach.

'Hi, Alexa, how are you? Congratulations,' Kate says, gesturing to her bump.

'Oh God, thanks,' says Alexa. 'I'm on number three so devastatingly tired, as you can imagine,' her posh plummy voice taps. Alexa beckons her through the grand hallway, and Kate follows the back of her dress, which whispers behind her as she glides over the black and white tiles.

Becky comes down the staircase just as they pass it, 'Kate, you're here.' Her eyes are red, and her cheeks are slightly swollen. Kate wonders if she's been crying.

Alexa walks away from them in disdain, as though they are still the fifteen-year-olds they once were, causing trouble and getting away with it. Kate stands awkwardly as Becky reaches the ground floor, unsure whether to kiss or hug her.

'Are you OK?' asks Kate.

Becky sniffs. 'Yes, Mummy's just been dreadful since she got home, she's been drinking all afternoon.' She pats her cheek with the palm of her fingers, trying to calm herself. She looks at Kate and sniffs again. 'I think you'll find nothing has really changed around here.' She beckons her towards the living room.

Inside, there is a man in his early fifties sitting in the large leather armchair wearing dark-blue jeans and brown brogues crossed towards the veiny green marble fireplace. A colourful cravat sits under his bowed chin. His face is a few inches from his phone screen; it is hard to make out his features.

'Oh, William, do get off your phone,' Alexa nags.

He quickly looks up and stands, his hand out ready to shake. 'This is my husband, William,' Alexa says for him. He smiles at Kate. A plastered-on look that says: *hurry up and get this over with so I can get back to my phone.* His nose is slightly adrift, he isn't ugly, but attractive in an interesting-looking way. Kate knows he must be ridiculously wealthy and connected if he managed to pique Alexa's interest.

'Nice to meet you,' Kate says politely.

'Kate is an old friend of Becky's,' Alexa says, as though she is utterly bored of the evening already.

'Nice to meet you too,' says William, shaking her hand. He turns back to his wife. 'I will, dear, I've just got some important emails to get through before dinner.' He leaves the room clutching his phone.

Alexa collapses on the sofa, huffing. She lies back on the orange velvet cushions, her arm resting on her forehead in front of the midnight-blue wall. Kate admires her; in this grand room she looks like an oil painting. Alexa used to be a model; she is willowy and svelte even now, heavily pregnant. Her career was launched in the era of Nineties heroin chic, and by the time the girls were teenagers Alexa was continually away in Paris, Milan or New York. Susanna spearheaded Alexa's career, and it sometimes seemed as though Susanna was so focused on that daughter, she just didn't know what to do with her other, slightly awkward one that she couldn't package and sell.

'I give up, I can't walk another step today,' Alexa moans.

Kate takes a seat on the opposite sofa; Becky sits next to her and crosses her arms.

'Alexa, you have a full-time nanny, it can't be that hard,' Becky says.

'You have no idea what you're talking about,' her sister replies with a tight smile.

'Is Kate here?' Susanna, Becky's mum, walks into the room. Poppy number two is happily yapping at her feet.

Kate looks up at the woman she used to idolize, whom she hasn't seen for over ten years. She stops herself from gasping at the change in her. Susanna's hand shakes as she brings a cigarette to her mouth. She's swaying softly as she sucks in the smoke. Her top is multicoloured and sequinned; a pillbox hat with a tiny flume of a veil perches on her head. Her lipstick is thick and smudged. She doesn't look glamorous at all, if anything she looks foolish.

'Oh, Kate, darling.' Susanna rushes to her.

The pungent smell of alcohol fermenting inside skin hits Kate as her chin knocks against Susanna's shoulder. Her fingers touch Kate's back and press tightly, and she feels taken hostage. Susanna slowly lets go and holds the tops of Kate's arms and looks at her directly, in the same way she always used to. This time Kate sees a crazed look in her eye, something so tangibly familiar, like looking at a view you have seen a million times from a window with a different vantage point. Kate can't believe what has happened to that wonderful, outrageous woman she used to clamour for attention from. It shocks her right to the core. Kate looks over to Becky, questioning. Becky looks back at her sternly, her chin slightly raised. As if to say, *this is the reason you shouldn't have come.*

'You are just gorgeous, darling,' Susanna says. 'You haven't aged a bit, that skin!' She lets go and holds her hands, rubbing affectionately and bringing them up to her mouth and kissing them. 'Oh, lovely, spirited Kate.' Kate can see Becky's jaw clench behind her.

'Mother has been at the Wolseley all afternoon with some of her terrible friends,' Alexa says with disdain.

'How else is one meant to turn seventy other than in style?' Susanna says. A nub of ash falls onto the floor. 'Some of us aren't boring like you two.'

Alexa fans the smoke away. 'Mummy, really, I'm pregnant.'

'It never did us any harm.' Susanna's cackle turns into a hacking cough.

Kate looks over at Becky again; she is silently watching, chewing her lip. She looks very young and vulnerable all of a sudden. As if she is on guard, waiting for something to happen that she will need to react to quickly.

'Maria has been working on dinner all afternoon!' Susanna turns and leaves the room with a flourish. The little dog goes trotting off after her.

'She's getting worse,' Becky snaps at Alexa.

Alexa nods, considering. 'It's her birthday, she wasn't that bad the other day.' She pulls herself out of the deep sofa. 'I swear this one is heavier than the other two put together,' she says, rubbing her stomach and moaning.

'Come on, everyone! Dining room, please,' Susanna calls.

Kate looks around again. It is as if a veil has been lifted and she can now see what is really there. Everything is exactly how it was; nothing has been updated at all in the last decade. There is now clutter and dust, and a bedded-in smell, like a damp mausoleum. Shell-shocked, she walks into the dining room, which too is exactly same as when she last stood there, although the opulence is now tired and worn. The same large print hangs on the back wall. It used to be vibrant, but the sun has bleached the colours on one side. The laid table doesn't look welcoming: the cutlery is blemished and the glassware smoky. Susanna sits at the head of the table. She shakes out a napkin extravagantly and puts it on her lap. There are two types of wine glass by each setting.

Susanna pats the seat next to her and beckons to Kate. 'Come and sit next to me, I see everyone else all the time.' She coughs into her hand.

'Happy birthday.' Kate pulls out the carved Georgian chair she was motioned to, and tentatively takes her seat.

'Pass me your glass,' Susanna says, holding a bottle of red wine out to her.

Kate places a palm over the top of the glass. 'Sorry, Susanna, I'm actually not drinking.'

'Oh right!' she says excitedly. 'Well, you can have one, can't you? Alexa does, and her last two have the right number of arms and legs.' She laughs.

'Mummy, I told you,' Becky chips in, 'Kate doesn't drink any more.'

Kate smiles at her. 'Sorry,' she shrugs, wondering why she feels the need to apologize.

'Why on earth not?' Susanna demands.

Everyone is watching them. William places his phone by his place setting, Alexa's lips part at the exchange. Kate spreads her napkin over her lap, feeling exposed. She has had this moment many times in the last six years, and it is always more of a battle with people like Susanna. People like Susanna find people who don't drink uncomfortable. They don't like the idea that they've stopped; it shines a light on their own problem. It whispers to them: you shouldn't drink either. Kate knows, because Kate used to feel like that too. She used to say she didn't trust people who didn't drink, but really she was terrified of them. It was as if that person could see past the facade, and that was the scariest thing in the whole world.

'It didn't suit me, I suppose. I got myself into a bit of trouble with it,' she says, quietly.

'Mummy, leave Kate alone. If she doesn't want a drink leave it at that, it's rude to go on about it,' says Alexa.

Susanna takes a sip of her own drink and puts it on the table, disappointed probably. She turns away from Kate, who feels shunned. It is strange not to play a part for someone any more. She used to be such a chameleon, chopping and changing her behaviour and principles for anyone she deemed important to impress.

'How's work, William?' Susanna asks.

'Oh, you know, all this uncertainty.'

71

'Yes, awful,' Susanna replies. 'Alexa, how are those naughty grandsons of mine?'

'Oh, you know, Mummy, bloody terrors,' she says, stroking her belly.

Susanna turns to Becky, stops, and then decides to ignore her and goes straight back to Kate. 'I hear you're getting married. Who is the lucky chap?'

Kate clears her throat. 'He's American, an engineer.'

'Oh, a Yank, how exciting,' Susanna says devilishly.

'Really?' says Alexa. 'Whereabouts in the States is he from?'

'Manhattan, but his family has a place in the Hamptons where they spend the majority of their time now.'

Alexa looks impressed, her eyes flick over to her own husband with annoyance. 'I love the Hamptons; William knows people out there. What's his father called?'

Kate has never seen Alexa as interested in anything she has had to say before. 'Erm . . . Hamilton, Bill Hamilton.' Her cheeks redden; she feels as though she is being tested.

William looks up from his phone. 'You are marrying into the Hamilton family?' he asks in surprise. 'The ones who own the department stores?'

Everyone looks very impressed.

'Bloody hell, Kate,' says Becky. 'You didn't tell me that! I had no idea . . . he didn't seem . . .'

'He's not really into all that, he's actually quite an unassuming geek really,' she says by way of an explanation.

She doesn't mention that Ben doesn't get on with his father, that they are completely different people. Ben always

72

says he doesn't want to be like him: flashy, brash and showy. He doesn't even own an expensive watch, though he could afford ten. Anyone meeting him would have no idea of his background, and Kate finds that incredibly attractive about him. But here, in this house of decaying decadence, if you are *somebody*, you are somebody to them. Kate had been allowed into the fold because she was an oddity, a smart, quick-witted girl from the council estate that somehow ended up at their door. Kate worked hard to ensure they maintained that view of her; she didn't want it to slip, she didn't want them to tire of her and find someone else to entertain them. Kate always felt as if she had to keep Susanna's interest piqued. She got an adrenalin kick when she made her laugh.

Kate fiddles with her necklace. Now she's just Kate, a boring teacher who doesn't even drink. Maybe the most exciting thing about her is Ben, and she has no idea why he chose her. She looks around the table and feels a cascade of inhibition as they ponder the information. Are they thinking that too? Are they thinking: why did he choose her?

Susanna claps her hands together. 'We must have some champagne! We need to have a toast!' She stands up excitedly. 'Maria! Maria!' she calls. When she doesn't get a reply, she hurries out of the room.

The others sit in silence. 'Seems a bit silly to toast someone who doesn't drink,' Alexa mutters. 'No wonder Daddy didn't want to come back from Oxfordshire for this.'

Susanna comes back into the room. 'Well, we only have a warm bottle, I was sure there was some in the fridge,' she tuts.

73

'You probably drank it . . .' Becky mutters under her breath.

'What?' Susanna asks.

'Susanna, really . . . we don't need to toast . . .' Kate says.

Susanna looks over at her. 'Don't be ridiculous, it's not every day that one of my daughter's best friends marries into American aristocracy!'

'Mum, Kate doesn't even drink,' says Becky.

'Yes, well, we must celebrate for her! It's bad luck. I've put it in the freezer. Which is sacrilegious . . .' Susanna says.

'And Alexa is pregnant,' Becky continues. 'William, didn't you drive here?'

'What is life if you can't celebrate things, Rebecca?' Susanna snaps at her.

'OK, Mummy, it just seems a bit silly . . .' Becky says.

'Silly! Silly!' Susanna's voice becomes pitchy, her eyes, which were glazed with impromptu fun, turn with a disgusted glint. 'If Rebecca actually pulled her finger out and found a boyfriend like the rest of you, we might actually think there could be something to celebrate round here. But no, instead here she is back at home after . . .'

'Mummy!' Alexa shouts.

Becky's face is redder than Kate's ever seen it. She looks like she is hanging on, hanging on before she crumbles. As though the new persona she has fortified around herself is peeling back and she is tender, like the skin after a plaster has been pulled off. Susanna stumbles on the spot.

Becky stands up and throws her napkin on the table. 'Fuck you, fuck the lot of you!' she shouts, and looks over at her mother. 'I'm not going to celebrate your birthday, and it will probably be your last if you keep drinking like that.' Becky marches out of the room.

Susanna huffs, takes another sip of her drink, and sits down. She actually looks rather pleased with herself. Kate wonders if Susanna's denial will allow her to feel guilty for this in the morning, or if she will find a way to justify the outburst to herself. She remembers that feeling well, of being so sure she was in the right, as if they were lucky to have someone like her finally being honest about their faults . . . and then waking up the next morning, not able to comprehend her behaviour, it was so alien to anything she would do sober. She has a sudden sense of relief that she isn't that person any more. How odd to think she used to look up to this woman.

Kate stands. 'I might just . . .' She rushes out after her friend, not bothering to finish her sentence.

Kate finds Becky in her bedroom, and she hovers at the frame of the open door. Becky is sitting on the same bed she had when she was a teenager, crying into her hands. Her posters have all come down, dots of Blu-Tack are left on the walls, half-scratched-off Hello Kitty stickers adorn her old pink-and-white desk. There are cardboard boxes piled high against the far wall.

'Hey,' says Kate quietly. 'Can I come in?'

Becky looks up. 'Yeah, sure,' she whispers. 'I just don't know why she hates me so much.' She looks down at her shaking hands.

'She doesn't hate you.' Kate sits down next to Becky on the bed. 'She's got a drinking problem, she's not well.'

'Alexa can do nothing wrong, but she barely even notices I'm here. She never has.' She's wiping the tears from her face miserably. 'It's like she wishes I didn't exist.' Kate holds Becky's hand and it is squeezed back.

'How long has she been like this?'

Becky snorts. 'Forever?' She looks at her friend oddly. 'Don't you remember?'

Teenagers are so clumsy in their observations; they are so black-and-white and selfish. She had always seen Susanna as eccentric, exciting even, the kind of parent every six-teen-year-old wants. She let them drink and smoke in the house, she even shared a joint with them once. Kate always thought that Becky was ungrateful for taking her mother for granted when she was all Kate had ever wanted. But she got it all so wrong. Susanna was ill. Her behaviour must have felt familiar to Kate, because she saw herself, or someone she wanted to be. And that sort of familiarity when you feel lost is more important than anything.

And it suddenly makes sense to Kate why Becky would choose a best friend like her, allowing her to treat her the way she did. They say you crave the love that you understand.

'She's why I wanted to get away in the first place, and then Alexa guilt-tripped me into coming home because she wants to continue producing her football team without the extra burden.' She sniffs, then turns to Kate. 'Part of me thought maybe I'd got it wrong, you know? That maybe she wasn't really such a bitch to me, or maybe her feelings towards me would have changed. But people like her don't change.' She snarls slightly. The comment takes Kate's breath away. She wants to shout: *yes they do, look at me!*

'I feel like I'm going mad,' Becky whispers. 'I need to get away from her.'

'Maybe some space would be a good idea,' Kate says. 'How is the house hunt going?'

'I haven't really started, to be honest; I've been so wrapped up in job hunting and catching up with everyone,' Becky says. 'I really think I've got this job I interviewed for last week,' she sniffs again, 'so the bank will let me have my mortgage soon. I really don't want to erode my deposit . . . I was thinking of renting something short-term . . .'

Kate thinks of the spare room in their flat in Newington Green. It suddenly occurs to her, an opportunity to help Becky has arisen. A way to really make amends, not just to say words, but to actually prove she is no longer selfish or self-seeking. To prove people like Susanna really can change.

'Come and stay with us for a little while,' she says. 'Just while you find something temporarily?'

'No, I couldn't,' Becky hurries. 'I didn't mean . . . It's fine, there'll be a short-term let I can jump into, I'm sure.'

'But Becky, you don't want to accept something shit because you have to get away from your mum.'

'I really couldn't,' Becky says.

'I won't take no for an answer.'

Becky pauses, looking out of the window. 'What about Ben?' she murmurs.

Kate hasn't even thought about Ben. 'Oh, he'll be fine. He's away most of the week anyway, and it's not for long.' Ben is so easy-going, he won't mind.

'I really shouldn't impose on you,' Becky protests again.

'I want to do this for you, Becky,' Kate says. 'It would mean a lot to me.'

Becky wipes her hand with her face, she looks pained in thought. 'OK, but only for a few weeks.'

Kate nods excitedly. This is perfect, exactly what is meant to happen. She can't wait to tell Clare, she'll think this is some sort of Higher Power magic shining down on her, allowing her to make her amends properly. This was why she had that nagging feeling that there was unfinished business. Sometimes talking isn't enough, she has more work to do repairing this. It isn't just how she treated Becky, but how she idolized her mother – she even took advantage of their difficult relationship to gain favour. Her priorities were all wrong. This is how she can redeem all that. Soon the old version of Kate will be wiped out of Becky's mind, and the new responsible and caring one will replace it forever.

6

'Man, that was a long week.' Ben puts his arms around Kate and lets his case drop to the floor. He smells of outside. Of cold pavements and tart evening air. She hasn't realized how much she missed him until now. Her week has been an emotional assault course, but, as he envelops her, all the anxieties about Becky and school dissipate, and she remembers why she doesn't need to worry about anything any more.

'I feel like the countdown to summer is taking forever this year.' Her lips brush the fabric of his coat as she speaks. She takes another deep breath of his calming scent.

'It'll soon come,' he murmurs and moves her hair to one side, kissing her neck.

'We've got some paperwork to fill out from the town hall,' she tells him as he lets go.

'Shall we have dinner first?' He rubs his face wearily. 'I don't think I'll be much use to you until I've had some food.'

She looks over at him; he does seem tired. He is usually full of energy, sometimes annoyingly so. 'Are you OK?'

'Sorry, I didn't want to be on a downer as soon as I walked

through the door.' His eyes are slightly bloodshot and his face is dry and stubbled.

'Are you really hating it there?' she asks, the feeling of guilt creeping in.

He looks over her shoulder, avoiding her eyes. 'No, it's fine.'

She knows he isn't telling her something. 'But . . . ?'

'It's nothing. I just got offered that job in Philadelphia again.' He pauses. 'I told them I wasn't looking to relocate at the moment.'

Headhunters have been snapping at his heels all year, throwing up exciting opportunities and perks. Kate gets that dull ache of a feeling when she wants to please the other person, but all her instincts are screaming at her not to do it. 'Oh babe, I'm sorry, I just can't leave the kids and the school . . .' She starts with her usual argument.

He raises his hand. 'No, honestly, I wasn't angling . . . It's not like I even want to go back to America particularly.'

'Maybe let's see how we feel next year? Maybe I'll feel differently after the summer,' she says, knowing she won't.

When they started dating, it had been a relief that Ben said he never wanted to live in America again. He said he liked it here, away from his dad who wants him to join the family business. His family terrifies her. When he proposed, in front of everyone, all she could see was the look on his mother's face. She was disappointed – Kate could tell she thought she wasn't good enough for her son. Kate doesn't blame her; sometimes she thinks the exact same thing herself.

That trip away, meeting his family, was one of the hardest

weeks sober she's had. If she thought that Becky's family was from another class, then Ben's wealth was something else entirely. The family's beach house was a cascading white wooden villa – she'd never seen anything so well maintained, with its lush manicured gardens and huge infinity pool. It even sat on its own private beach. It was more like a hotel or country club than a home. Ben's mother fiddled with a neat row of pearls every time she spoke. She wore large sunglasses that Kate often imagined concealed a look of contempt. Kate would stumble on words, unsure what conversations to start. Ben's father was the opposite of his wife, he was loud and booming; he's the star of the show and makes sure everyone knows it. She remembers Ben clenching his fists a few times in his father's presence, the look of horror on Ben's face as his dad flirted with the staff. Kate saw him touch one of the server's bottoms once. He pretended it was an accident, but it obviously wasn't. Ben was furious, he hates behaviour like that. Ben is a gentleman.

But then, there is a part of him that idolizes his father too. Kate watched him work hard to impress the man; it was quite difficult to watch the show he put on. He obviously craves his respect. She witnessed his disappointment when Mr Hamilton changed the subject halfway through Ben discussing his current project at work. He looked crushed. Mr Hamilton Sr brought out a very different side of Ben. When they left his parents to go back to the city he was uptight and brooding, and this didn't end until they landed back at Heathrow.

Maybe, actually, this has all just been a daytrip into how

the other half live and, when it comes to buying houses and having children, Ben still wants to be part of the fold. That would mean their quiet happiness would be pulled and yanked by all the other unresolved family ties that Ben struggles with. And then, maybe, he wouldn't want her any more.

What does that Larkin poem say? That your parents fuck you up. She wonders what they will pass on to their children – it is nearly impossible to be completely unscathed. Will her sobriety be enough to protect them from the pain of addiction? She thinks about her mother, how she left. She understands why she did it. She didn't want Kate to see her like that. Kate has always wondered what her life would have been like if her mother had stuck around. Is the pain of her leaving worse than the pain of watching her slowly drink herself to death?

She is staring out of the window thinking when he speaks again. Her mind has wandered to Lily and the smell of alcohol on her breath, and the worried look on her mother's face from the window.

'Anyway, enough boring crap. How was your week?'

Kate moves away and sits back on the sofa with a huff. 'Oh God, not great. That girl, Lily, hasn't turned up all week.' Kate is starting to worry she won't turn up for the exam.

'Oh, I'm sorry, K,' Ben says. 'I'm sure she'll come back, you've worked really hard with her this year.' Kate is surprised how quickly Ben has picked up on what she is talking about, she must talk about Lily more than she realizes.

Ben sits on the sofa next to her. 'Look at us, a couple of

hopeless cases.' He puts his hand over hers. 'At least we have each other.' He jumps up. 'Right, I'm going to cook, and we'll have a nice meal and can pretend the outside world doesn't exist.' She laughs as he takes off his jacket as though he is about to perform a striptease.

'Oh nooo! Stop,' she giggles, peering through the holes between her fingers.

'I'll save the rest for later.' He wiggles his eyebrows suggestively and goes through to the open-plan kitchen. He clicks his tongue in the back of his mouth as he leans into the fridge, wondering what to cook. She follows him over and perches on one of the stools at the kitchen counter. He pulls out a bag of celery and gives her a knife and chopping board.

'Finely chop, please.'

'Yes, Chef.' She takes the knife and begins to line up the sticks.

'How was that thing the other night with Becky's family?' he asks, his face still inside the fridge.

She lets the knife fall and slowly pick up a satisfying rhythm. 'Oh God, Becky's family is fucking weird.' She bites her lip and stops; she has been so sure that Ben will be relaxed about having a housemate for a few weeks. But now, with his worn face and his excitement about getting away from everything, she isn't so sure.

He clips the fridge door shut, holding some mince in one hand. 'Oh yeah? How come? I thought you got on with her mom.'

'Yeah, so did I.' She swallows and thinks of the look in

Susanna's eye when she shouted at Becky. 'I guess I thought she was someone else, or maybe I was someone else . . .'

'What do you mean?'

She wants to explain, to say she thought this glamorous woman saw her, when she felt no one else knew she was there at all. He wouldn't understand. 'She's an alcoholic, completely untreated.'

'Shit, poor Becky.'

'She had this massive go at her in front of everyone, it was actually quite disturbing.'

'Jesus.' He starts chopping. 'Can you help at all, with your experience?'

'I don't know . . . she's in complete denial. Looking back, the stuff I thought was cool, or charming, was actually quite strange for a parent,' Kate adds. 'I just really feel for Becky, she was so upset.'

'Families are so tricky, believe me, I know! At least she won't have to stay there forever, didn't she say she's going to buy somewhere?'

'Yes, and she accepted a job yesterday!'

'That's great! See, it will all work out,' he says. 'Can you pass me the salt and pepper?'

She reaches to her left and passes them across the counter. 'The thing is, she really wants to get out of there now. And it will take her a few weeks to sort out a rental.' The knife hovers over the board.

Ben looks up. He knows. 'Mmm.'

'And we have a spare room,' she says.

'Right . . .' He's still looking at her. His pupils bore into her as he waits for her to finish.

'So, I said she can have it until she finds somewhere,' she states flatly.

'Wait, she's moving in here? When?'

'Tomorrow,' she says.

His smooth forehead creases. 'Right,' he says thoughtfully, without moving a muscle.

'It won't be for long,' she adds. 'She's so easy-going . . .'

'And you didn't want to run this past me?' he asks, looking over, perplexed.

'I . . . I didn't think you'd mind.'

'I mean, I don't but, Kate . . . I live here too.' He puts the wooden spoon down and washes his hands in the sink. He squirts the soap from the dispenser and turns his head in her direction.

She feels deflated. 'I'm sorry, I should have checked first, it just all happened . . .'

'She's a nice girl, I'm sure it's fine. I'm just so busy with work, and then to put on airs and graces when I'm back when all I want to do is have some time with you . . .' He rinses off the soap and then adds another squirt. He always does that when he's agitated, washes his hands twice. She watches him thoroughly rub them together. It's ritualistic. 'I'm more worried about you, Kate, you get so stressed, you've got your exams coming up. I don't want you to burn out.' He shakes off the excess water and dries his hands on a carefully peeled-off piece of kitchen roll. Ben loves being clean, he likes folding things and piling them up neatly.

'I'm fine,' she says. 'I really want to do this for her.'

'But why?' Ben asks. 'You barely know the girl any more. You saw her for the first time in ten years just the other week and now she's moving in?'

She looks down. 'I feel like I owe it to her.' He looks confused. 'I wasn't very nice to her when we were younger, and she put up with a lot from me.'

He walks around to where she is sitting at the kitchen counter. 'We've all done stuff we're not proud of growing up, don't beat yourself up about it. You weren't well.'

'I did my Step Nine amends with her this week.' Ben knows about the AA steps; she likes that about Americans. They don't see alcoholism as a taboo subject, and, in a similar way to how therapy was normalized in their society way before it caught on here, attending AA meetings is another form of becoming the best version of yourself you can possibly be.

'Oh,' he nods, understanding.

'I don't know, I just feel saying sorry isn't enough. There is more I have to do.'

'OK, well, if it means that much to you . . .' he says supportively. 'It will be fun.'

'Really?' She peers up at him. 'I could tell her it's not great timing.'

'If it makes you happy.'

'Really?' Kate claps her hands together.

He nods and she beams at him. She is so lucky she found him, or actually, that he found her.

*

The next morning they get up early, and Kate tidies the spare room. She puts on fresh bed linen and makes sure there is space in the wardrobe, which she's been using as overspill. There is a wicker picnic basket on the top of the unit with old photographs inside. She steps onto a chair and yanks the strap forward, then hops onto the floor. The weight flops onto her arm like a body dropped in a noose.

She hasn't looked inside for years. In fact, there was a point when she almost burnt the thing. Laying it on the bed, she undoes the leather fastener and opens the lid. Hundreds of prints are loosely splayed inside. She touches their sheen – she can't remember the last time she had a photograph developed. It is as though they are relics of another time now, not just memories, more than that. The clothes they wore, their hair-styles, and their basic mobile phones. It was a simpler time. She often worries for her students, the way they are constantly checking social media, looking at how many 'likes' their pouts have earned.

She gasps and picks out a photograph. It is of Kate and Becky on their prom night. Kate had worn a black satin nightie dress and a leopard-print fake fur coat with smudged red lip-stick. Her hair was messy and wild. She was boiling but refused to take off the coat, because it would ruin the look she was aiming for. Becky was wearing a red Topshop dress that she'd tried on about fifty times in Oxford Circus. It was tight and hadn't done her figure any favours. Kate stares at Becky's hair in the photo, remembering how she'd tried to mimic a look Alexa had in a magazine. Her hair hadn't taken to it, and

Susanna had laughed at her, saying she looked like a scarecrow, just as they were leaving.

Behind Kate's confident carefree smile lay a constant white noise of despair. They thought they were so streetwise, but actually they were vulnerable and stupid. The scrapes they got into make her shudder now. She was so lucky she didn't walk into the road drunk and get hit by a bus. Her sponsor said to her once that every time she took that first sip she was playing Russian roulette with her life. Drinking on its own wouldn't kill her for years and years, it was all the consequences that might. She hadn't thought about it like that before.

Kate lets the photograph flop out of her hand. It should have been such a fun night, finishing school with a big blowout with everyone she'd shared the last five years with. Instead, it is a night she wishes she could forget. She'd stolen a bottle of whisky from her dad's cabinet. Because the truth was, behind the bravado, Kate was hiding something. She was actually painfully shy. Big social situations terrified her and the only way she could deal with them was to get drunk. Flashes of memory bombarded her the next day: shouting at a teacher who had been kind to her, arguing with Becky on the night bus home. Her dad found her on the front steps passed out in the morning. He'd slapped her face to wake her up. She remembers the terror in his eyes. Don't worry, Dad, I just mixed my drinks, she'd said . . . He'd gone to his room, shutting the door with a bang. And she spent the morning throwing up, the black satin dress wet with sweat, her mother's chain knocking against the porcelain toilet. Her dad didn't speak to her for a week.

She shuts the basket. That moment had been one of the first things she'd written about when she started her Twelve Steps with her AA sponsor. Step One involves answering a worksheet of questions which aims to give you a myriad of examples of how you are powerless over alcohol: nights out gone wrong, things you regret, extreme situations that occur more than regularly. All proof that once you have that first drink, all bets are off.

One question asked how her drinking had affected her relationships with her family and friends. The examples tumbled out and she finished A4 page after A4 page. She couldn't stop crying when she read them out to her sponsor – she couldn't believe she'd done all of that stuff. Clare calmed her. She told Kate that all of these anecdotes, all of these sad and twisted stories full of personal shame, could be put in a box, but to think of them if she ever had the urge to drink. She told Kate that, if she got a good Step One, she'd never want to drink again.

She smooths out the duvet Becky is going to sleep under and plumps the pillow. She looks over at the basket again. Instead of climbing on the chair and putting it back on the wardrobe, she takes the basket full of photos into her room and hides it under her bed. Like old dirty secrets, she wishes she had forgotten them, and she hopes that Becky has.

7

Kate is standing in front of the full-length mirror in their bedroom, methodically massaging moisturizer into her skin. She is listening to the radio; a song that mimics the cheery blue sky is playing. Smiling softly to herself, she starts to hum. She's excited; today is the day Becky is coming to stay. She has imagined scenes of them laughing over Sunday roasts, teasing Ben together, of cosy evenings giggling nervously as they watch a horror film. She has already pictured the day that Becky leaves. It will be bittersweet, they'll cry and talk of what a special time it has been and wish it wasn't over. They'll brazenly look each other in the eye, and there will no longer be any pain there. The old Kate, the drunk, selfish version, won't be the default image Becky invokes when thinking of her friend. Instead she will think of the happy time they shared together before Kate got married.

Kate smiles to herself as she thinks of what is to come. She strokes the cream into her leg. Her foot is perched on the side of the bed, and a shard of sun warms her calves. She can feel his presence before she sees him. She doesn't mind that he is watching her, she quite likes it. She turns her head. He is smiling at her, slightly biting the side of his lip in the way that he does when he's lost in something. He's holding two mugs with steam softly flowing. His head is cocked to one side as he enjoys the view.

'Oi, perv,' she says with a wry smile.

'Is a man not allowed to perv at his future wife?' he asks. 'Anyway, I brought you coffee. I think that's a pretty good trade.' He settles the mugs on the bedside table and lies back on the bed.

She walks over and takes a sip. The liquid is so hot she gasps and rolls some cold saliva around in her mouth. She sets it back down on the bedside table to cool and bends down to kiss his forehead. Her mother's pendant dangles in his face, glistening in the sun. People always say when you meet the one, it's easy. They return your texts, they call you back, there are no games. When she met Ben, it was nearly impossible to be cautious, he always seemed so sure she was the one.

'Yum,' she says, climbing on the bed and straddling him. His hands are either side of her thighs, and she can feel him stiffening beneath her. She bends down again for another kiss.

'When's she arriving?' he murmurs.

'Any minute now.' She rocks slightly on his crotch, enjoying the power.

He grabs her and throws her onto the bed. 'Stop it, you minx, I can't have a hard-on when she gets here.'

'Oh, OK,' she says. He can be such a goody two-shoes sometimes.

'Well, it was your idea to have her here, our peace is about to be wrecked!'

'Hey.' She playfully hits him. 'You said you didn't mind.'

She pulls on jeans and a basic white T-shirt and smudges some shiny lip balm onto the top and bottom of her lips. Her eyes flicker up to the top corner of the mirror. She can see his face in the reflection as he scrolls through his phone. Does he look annoyed? Is this a terrible idea? He says he's fine about it, but is he really? *Look at the facts, Kate*, she reminds herself. *You can't trust your brain to be unconditionally honest, the majority of the time it tells you lies.*

The doorbell rings before she can dwell on it longer. Her stomach fizzes with anticipation, she looks up at him and claps her hands together, smiling.

He raises his eyebrows and jumps off the bed. 'Here we go.'

'Come on.' She runs off excitedly. Flinging open the internal door, she rushes down the next set of stairs to the main entrance. Stopping, she composes herself.

Just as she pulls down the latch, Ben's hand covers it. 'I'll do it,' he says. Pulling the door back, he opens his arms. 'Welcome!' he says warmly. Kate reminds herself that she doesn't have to worry about Ben, he's straightforward. All he wants is for her to be happy.

'Hi,' says Becky, handing Kate the huge bunch of flowers she is holding. 'Thanks so much for having me to stay.'

'Not a problem at all!' Kate says, looking down breathlessly at the gorgeous array of blush roses she's been handed. She looks up and peers over to Becky's old blue VW Polo that is sitting in front of their building. 'You still have it!' laughs Kate, amazed.

'Oh God yeah, I look like such a north London princess in it,' Becky says dryly.

'All the posh girls had Polos when we were at college,' Kate explains for Ben.

'Yeah, but not many had hot-rock burns all over their upholstery thanks to their best friend,' says Becky. There is a bite to the end of the light-hearted comment that causes Kate's laugh to catch in the back of her throat. A memory of blazing a joint out of the back window, Becky waving her hand in front of her face and moaning, 'For fuck's sake, Kate, please don't do that in here.' And Kate just carried on. God, she was awful when she was younger, poor Becky.

'Oh God, I'm sorry,' she says, wringing her hands. She feels as if the excitement of having Becky to stay has been winded out of her a bit.

Becky reaches out and squeezes Kate's arm. She must have noticed the look on her face. 'Don't worry, this thing belongs at the tip-yard anyway, look at it!' Her manner shifts. 'I feel like I've come home and I'm eighteen again, I've got so much catching up to do.'

'What are you talking about?' Kate says. 'You've been living a glamorous life in NYC while I've been bumbling around north London.'

'There is nothing wrong with north London,' says Becky.

'Hear, hear,' says Ben. 'Right, come on, ladies, enough gabbling on the doorstep, get upstairs and I'll grab the rest of the bags.' He coaxes them inside before jogging towards the car. He looks back at them with a big, toothy American grin.

'He is too sweet,' says Becky. Kate nods, watching him for a moment. He really is. His dark, floppy hair has fallen into his eyes, and he sweeps up his glasses onto his head like an Alice band as he shifts Becky's belongings about in the boot of the car. He takes out a case and pretends to find it too heavy. The girls laugh.

'You didn't have to bring your gym equipment, Becky,' he shouts over, joking.

Kate tries to see Becky how Ben must be seeing her: she is wearing sleek black leggings with a mesh panel on the back of the calves and a sports bra with an off-the-shoulder slouched jumper over the top. Her hair looks as though it's just been blow-dried. She really is beautiful now, much more beautiful than Kate. She stops herself. Jealousy, there it is. A personality defect she has to stop herself indulging. She shakes her head, reminding herself that her disease tries to make everyone else the enemy to separate her and get her alone, so that she will drink again. It can parachute in under any guise – she must be vigilant.

Their flat is on the top two floors of a Victorian terrace. They've been renting it ever since they moved in together two years ago, six months after they met. Ben could easily afford to buy a large house in London, with not just his salary but his family money too. But they aren't in a rush to move, and Kate doesn't want the responsibility of a whole house while Ben is away during the week.

Becky puts down the large shoulder bag she is carrying as she walks into the open-plan lounge-kitchen.

'Oh Kate, this is lovely,' she says, touching the marble counter and opening and closing the white Smeg fridge with admiration. 'I love this area too.' She takes a look out of the window as she speaks.

'Thanks, we've been really happy here,' says Kate.

Becky turns and touches the fitted shelves on one side of the room. 'These are beautiful, did Jonny make them?' she asks as her fingers brush along the wood. Stopping at a framed photo of the pair, she picks it up and studies it carefully.

'Yes, the first time he came over and saw the space he drew the plan on the back of an old receipt and went out to buy the wood immediately. The man downstairs owns the whole building, and he was more than happy for the improvement to be made.' The shelves are made of thick, dark wood and run up and across the space either side of the old fireplace. What her father lacked in words and communication, he made up for with creating and building. Kate often thinks that's what must have frustrated him the most, that he couldn't fix her with a hammer or a drill.

'Take a seat, I'll make you a tea.' Kate points to one of the large sofas in front of the fireplace. Ben was appalled that she'd bought second-hand sofas, but once she'd expertly strewn throws across any evidence of previous abuse he couldn't dispute how comfortable they were.

'You can tell, there is so much love in them,' Becky says, running her fingers across the shelves before walking towards one of the sofas. 'I can't imagine my dad doing something like this for me,' she says wistfully. 'Have you been to Margate to see him much? Since your grandma passed away?'

'I haven't had the chance yet,' Kate says, knowing she should have gone to visit him by now. There are just so many memories in that place. And being around Jonny is hard. He is so kind and thoughtful, but no one else understands why she finds his meekness infuriating. Why does he get to play the good guy all the time? She wants him to stand up to her, but he never will. She is the only person who can mend their relationship, but it's so bedded in, it is who they are to each other now. To change that would mean she has to admit to things she just isn't ready to face.

Ben comes into the room with two bags. 'I'll pop these upstairs for you.'

'No, really, there is no need. I can . . .' Becky moves towards him.

'It's fine.' He marches ahead, taking the stairs two by two.

'Is he always like that?' Becky asks.

'What do you mean?'

Becky shrugs, and laughs. 'I don't know, just so gentle-manly! And chirpy!'

Kate's eyes look up to where he disappeared. 'Yes, I suppose he is.'

'So, he's perfect then?' Becky asks, and it's as if she is fishing for something.

Kate nods, refusing to fall into the trap. 'I suppose he is. Though I'm sure someone else would find his endless optimism and obsession with war documentaries unbearable.' She laughs.

Becky just nods and watches her, then takes the flowers into the kitchen and starts to undo the rough undyed string. She reaches above the standalone fridge and picks off a vase before opening and closing drawers looking for scissors.

'I met so many trust fund kids in New York. They're up to their eyes in money, but have very little purpose. He's a complete anomaly, Kate,' she says. 'I don't know how you found him! And kept him here!'

Kate watches as Becky turns her head from side to side arranging the flowers, lost in the correct way to structure and prop. She probably learnt how to do that from her mother. Kate never knows what to do with a bunch of mixed flowers, other than chop them down and stick them in. Becky will be a good wife for someone, especially someone from a family like Ben's. She realizes she's never known Becky to have a boyfriend. Kate always thought of Becky getting crushes, rather than actually plucking up the nerve to follow through on anything. She wonders if she's ever really had a proper relationship at all.

'What tea would you like?' Kate asks.

'Have you got herbal?' Becky replies.

Kate nods and pulls open the drawer. 'I've come to the conclusion that relationships are all about timing. Ben wouldn't have looked at me twice six years ago.'

Becky nods. 'Yes, you're right.' She takes out a stem and snips it shorter, pausing before saying, 'Maybe my guy has to get over someone and then he'll be ready for me.' She places the flower in the vase with a flourish.

'Yes, exactly!' says Kate.

Becky nods without responding. She picks up the vase and walks over to the coffee table, placing the feature down on the glass with a clink. 'There,' she says, satisfied, touching a petal gently. 'Perfect.'

As Kate watches steam collect on the window above the kettle, she wonders if Becky is actually quite timid when it comes to men. She may come across as confident, but maybe she isn't when it comes to putting herself out there with the opposite sex. She certainly found them terrifying when she was younger. Kate turns with an idea, clapping her hands together with a bang. 'I know, let's have a girly evening next week when Ben's in Scotland, we can make you a dating profile!'

'I don't know, Kate,' says Becky. 'Everything is so up in the air at the moment.'

'Come on, it will be fun.' Kate laughs.

Becky is wary. 'Maybe.' She walks over to the large bay window that looks down onto the street, and folds her arms across her chest. 'We'll see,' she says mysteriously.

Kate studies her profile; anything clumsy or endearing about her has gone. What's left is something sorrowful that she's never noticed before. Becky used to have a warmth about her, but this has disappeared and what is left is cold and slightly detached. Kate is at a loss on how to continue the conversation. She dips the teabags into the hot water and tries to think of something else to say.

Luckily Ben returns. 'What are you guys up to?'

Kate turns to see him leaning against the wall, an easy smile upon his lips. She's relieved he's back.

'Kate's trying to persuade me to start online dating.' Becky laughs as if she finds it amusing, but she hadn't been amused when Kate suggested it.

'You should. What have you got to lose? You're really attractive . . .' He stumbles on his words. 'I mean you'd get snapped up.' His cheeks redden.

Both of the girls look over at him. Kate's lips part as she wonders what to say. She looks across at Becky who is also confused. What makes it worse is the guilty look that's washed over Ben; his cheeks are flushed red and he's put his hands in his pockets, unsure what to do with them.

'I'm going to go check my emails,' he stammers and walks up the stairs, his hands still in his pockets.

Then the girls are alone again. Kate hands Becky her tea. There is an awkward pause. Kate's still thinking about what Ben said. Her brain wants to turn it over and inspect it some more before she lets it scurry away.

'Thank you so much for saving me from my awful family,' Becky says, changing the subject. 'That scene Mum caused . . . It was outrageous.'

'Are you OK?' asks Kate, pleased to be offered a line of exchange.

'I'm used to it. I've always known she has a problem, but it's as if Alexa has only just realized. She's been locked in her own denial over it. My dad basically washed his hands of her, they've been living in separate houses for years.' Becky pauses and sighs. 'I read that they call alcoholism a family disease, have you heard that?'

Kate nods. 'It affects everyone, not just the person with the addiction.'

'Even friends?' Becky asks, looking at Kate.

She nods sadly. 'Especially friends.' Kate goes to say more, but is interrupted.

'Your mum . . .' Becky starts.

Instinctively Kate's hand goes to her pendant. She knows what Becky is asking her. 'Yes . . . she was . . . from what Jonny says.'

'At least she wasn't around,' Becky says. The comment is so peculiar and hurtful that Kate wants to scream.

'Sorry . . . I didn't mean that!' Becky jumps up from her seat. 'I just mean it's hard watching someone you love do that to themselves. Even if she does hate me.'

'Becky, she doesn't hate you . . . and all you can do is be there for her when she asks for help,' she says weakly. Kate feels as if she's caught in a tangled web all of a sudden – the layers upon layers of their relationship and history. It isn't as simple as she'd thought, she'd been kidding herself. She wants to run and hide to catch her breath again, but Becky is here, in her home, inside her usual retreat.

Becky is staring at the bookcases again. 'You're so lucky to have your dad, Kate. He was always on your side, no matter what you did.'

Kate stiffens at the comment. Becky doesn't know what

happened with her dad, that their relationship is no longer what it was. 'Yes, I suppose,' she says, frowning. 'I can talk to Susanna about AA if you think it will help.'

Becky nods, looking down at the mug settled between her hands. She dunks the bag in and out, the string twisted around her finger. 'Thanks . . . I'll bear that in mind. Maybe she'll listen to you.' She looks up at Kate, a serious look upon her face. 'You always were her favourite.'

Kate detects a note of venom, so subtle she has no way of knowing if paranoia is playing a part. Their eyes meet and Becky smiles sweetly, as if to mask it. Kate smiles back, confused. They both take sips of their tea at exactly the same time. Kate remembers when they used to finish each other's sentences, or just give a look that the other would be able to decipher in a second. There is nothing about this girl, sitting in her living room, drinking tea, that she can read. Her body language and mannerisms are alien to Kate now. Kate is suddenly baffled by her decision to allow this relative stranger into her home. Has she taken this amends thing too far? *The facts, Kate, look at the facts*, she reminds herself again miserably. But everything is so jumbled and convoluted, she has no idea what they are any more. Becky seemed genuinely appeased by her the other night in the pub. Kate licks her dry lips in thought. She must be paranoid – why on earth would Becky want to move in with them if she hadn't forgiven her?

8

Kate's eyes open to the sound of Ben's wheelie bag flop, flop, flopping down the steps outside the front of the house. She blinks, a car door opens and closes, the engine revs and he drives away. He's gone. She places her hand on the crumpled sheets on the other side of the bed. She won't see him for the rest of the week. She feels quite sad that he didn't kiss her goodbye, but then she remembers her fitful night – he probably wanted to let her sleep. She wonders how she'll manage without him at home this week, on her own, with Becky.

She rolls onto her side and takes three deep gulps of water from the glass on her bedside table. Today is meant to be the hottest May day on record. She looks up, watching the curtains move along to the breeze flowing in through the window. She sighs; sleep has never come easily to her. Last night her head was so crammed full of threads of thought that she barely slept a wink. She's already decided to go to an AA meeting tonight. It's been too long, and when she doesn't look after that side of herself she is prone to overanalysing and unnecessary stress.

She sits up and rests back on the cushioned headboard.

Rolling her head on her shoulders, she thinks about last night. She has the urge to push the problem away, but it's too late for that. Becky's here, under her roof. Taking another sip of water, Kate tries to calm herself.

She is probably catastrophizing this whole situation. Becky's behaviour has been odd, but maybe Kate is being hypervigilant and overscrutinizing. Besides, if Becky isn't in a good place then Kate needs to give her a break. She has no idea what Becky's gone through over the last ten years and, of everyone, she deserves Kate's patience.

Clare would say that Kate needs to have empathy for everyone, even people she doesn't really like or get on with. Otherwise these emotions can easily build up into resentments her mind will obsess over – they will grow and grow until she does something she regrets. Then, ultimately, the only person who will suffer is herself. Clare would remind her that it's fine for other people to behave a certain way, but that's because they aren't like her, they aren't alcoholics. For her, a resentment could become so painful she could relapse, and that could kill her. It sounds melodramatic, but that's the truth.

Kate sighs and reminds herself that it's OK if having Becky to stay doesn't work out, but she needs to make the best of it now she's here. It's not forever.

Then she hears the familiar sound of the floorboard creaking outside her room.

'Becky?' she calls.

The door is tapped gently before the knob is jiggled with

103

and opened. 'Hey.' Becky pokes her head around the door, looking sheepish. 'I'm going to go and check out a yoga class.' She is already dressed in leggings and an exercise top. 'I'm trying to get into a routine before I start my new job.'

Kate's eyes wander down to Becky's waist and then to the gap between her thighs. She'd always thought, if she stopped drinking, she'd be one of those people who'd be up at six doing a class before work, maybe even running marathons on weekends. But no, she still loves her bed and needs two coffees before she feels like talking to anyone.

'That's impressive.'

'Look, I'm sorry if I was being a bit intense yesterday,' Becky says quickly. 'I'm just in a weird place at the moment.' She looks as if she had to build herself up to saying that. 'I'm really happy to be here, with you.'

'Honestly, you weren't being weird at all!' Kate instinctively pushes the apology away.

'Are you sure?'

'Totally.' Kate nods profusely.

'I just feel so up and down at the moment.' She looks at the floor.

'I'm going to an AA meeting straight after work and then how about I cook dinner for us?' Kate asks.

Becky nods, thinking. 'That sounds lovely.'

Kate pauses, and then asks her, 'Hey, if you wanted you could come to the meeting? Find out a bit more about what they involve? It might make you understand the stuff with your mum a bit better?'

Becky looks up in surprise. 'Really? Am I allowed? Isn't it some sort of secret cult?' she jokes.

Kate laughs. 'Ha, no! A lot of meetings are open to visitors, you'd be really welcome.'

Becky pauses, and then nods. 'OK, yeah. Sounds interesting.'

Kate watches her leave, suddenly regretting the invitation. She's bringing Becky into all her safest places. She hopes the pull to do the right thing after all these years isn't clouding her judgement.

School is unbearably hot. She is uncomfortable in her top, the sleeve holes are tight under her armpits and she keeps getting paranoid that there is a semicircle of sweat for all to see. Her classroom is probably the warmest in the building; the sun streams in through huge glass windows for the majority of the day. None of the kids can concentrate, and her voice rises as she tries to capture their imagination, but watching them stare out of the window, she can see she's lost them to daydreams of summer holidays and parklife.

During her second lesson, as she attempts a class on *The Catcher in the Rye*, the fire alarm goes off. 'Is it a drill, Miss?' asks Skye, a fifteen-year-old who loves any sort of drama.

Kate hasn't seen an email about a drill, but there are so many emails that take her away from actually doing her job that she occasionally misses something like this. She walks to the door of her classroom and opens it. She sticks her head out; another teacher has done the same and their eyes meet.

'Is this a drill?' they ask each other.

'Doesn't look like it,' says Kate. She goes back into her class. 'Right, everyone, line up next to the door.' There is excited commotion, their prayers have been answered.

'Miss, if the school burns down will we get time off?' asks Skye.

'Don't worry too much about your things.' She ignores the question and claps her hands together. 'Quickly, come on, everyone.'

She marches them down the main corridor and out into the playground. There is a designated meeting point which is pooled in sunlight. 'Right, line up, come on, Mr Skinner has to do a register.'

She crosses her arms and looks up into the sky. Not one cloud. The girls remove their ties and hike up their skirts to allow more light to creep up their bare legs. Kate remembers being that age and the initial taste of summer. During the holidays they became vagrants, devoid of any responsibility. All she had to worry about was how to manipulate Jonny into giving her another twenty quid for a ten bag of hash and a packet of cigarettes. Kate and Becky would hang out at the house in Belsize Park, getting tipped off about various house parties and free yards, hanging out in the park getting stoned and drinking beers in between. Everything they cared about was so insular and unimportant, but so completely all-consuming at the same time. She watches the girls hold up their phones to the sky, pouting and taking group selfies, the excitement that freedom is closing in palpable.

'Is everyone here?' Mr Skinner arrives at her group of

students. He is holding a clipboard and wearing a hi-vis vest that says *Fire Marshal* on the back.

'Yes. Is this a drill?' asks Kate.

'Well, someone broke the fire alarm outside the science lab,' he says, looking down his list and then out at her line of students. 'So, we are treating it like one anyway.'

Kate uses the flat of her hand to cap the sun from her eyes as she looks over at the gaggle of girls in her Year 11 English class. She can't see Lily. As Mr Skinner marks off her kids she walks over to where they are standing.

'Hi, Miss,' says Emma, looking up from her phone for only a brief moment.

'Hi, Emma, did Lily come in today?' Kate asks.

'Nah, I haven't seen her,' she says, her thumb scrolling her screen.

Kate squints painfully at the news. 'OK, thanks.'

Her kitten heels clip with disappointment as she returns to her queue of students, though the line is now more of an imperfect circle. That's another important class Lily has missed, and the exams start soon. She feels a flutter of panic in her chest – she has to do something. She sees Mrs Wells, who is in charge of Pastoral Care, and decides to have a quick word.

'Mrs Wells!' she says loudly, waving.

Mrs Wells spots her and wanders over. 'Miss Sullivan. How are you?' She is wearing a flamboyant skirt with a colourful print and her hair is wrapped in a turban of the same fabric.

'I was just wondering if there is a reason behind Lily Johnson's absence? It's her exams in the next few weeks.'

Mrs Wells thinks for a moment. 'Oh, yes, she's been truanting recently, I've spoken to her mother a few times.'

'These exams are so important to get onto the course she wants . . .' Kate can see Mrs Wells's eyes are darting around, watching the other kids. Kate is frustrated that Mrs Wells isn't more focused on the problem, but knows it's not her fault. There are constant conversations about budget cuts, and Mrs Wells has taken on the Head of Maths role as well this year.

'Russell, get down from there this instant,' she shouts roughly. 'Sorry?' She turns to Kate.

'Lily, she's missing vital classes just before the exams. She's so talented,' Kate says.

'Russell, don't make me come over there!' she shouts, and the boy quickly jumps off the wall he was climbing. Mrs Wells turns back to Kate. 'Look, why don't we organize a meeting with her mother, maybe face to face would be better? You could join us and talk about how well she is doing with her work.'

'I don't know if I need to . . .' Kate starts.

'No, it's a good idea. You have first-hand experience of her abilities. It will be good for you to be there,' Mrs Wells says.

Kate smiles and nods. 'OK, sure. Thanks,' she says. 'I appreciate it.'

She's never met Mrs Johnson, she's only seen her from across the street. She wonders what she will be like in the presence of her daughter's teachers. Parents seem to go one way or the other. Defensive and angry with the school for their child underachieving, refusing to take any responsibility at all, or sitting with straight backs and tears in their eyes asking what they've done wrong. She understands why people care so much about where fault lies – often the solution is hidden between those pages.

People often excused Kate's behaviour because of her mother; they pitied her for it. It gave them a label to put on her and a box to file her away in. It is something that has always bothered her. Is it as simple as that? Other people have similar experiences but don't drink to excess. She's been told a million times that it's a disease, a lottery you lose at birth. A war draft consigned at the moment of conception. But maybe she was just a silly little attention-seeking girl.

She shakes the thought out of her mind and walks back to her students feeling numb, thinking of Lily, and what or who is to blame for her downfall.

Later; Kate takes her bike out of its shackle and starts to mount it. The front wheel skids unhealthily on the hard ground. She bends down to look at it. There is a clean incision a few inches long. She touches the wound and brings the two fingers to her face. They are black with dirt. Owning a bike in London is a ticket for heartbreak. At least they didn't steal anything this time.

It's too nice an evening to spend in the bike shop. She decides to walk home and pick up some food for dinner later. She's nervous about taking Becky to a meeting even though she is the one that offered. It isn't the first time she's taken someone, but usually it's others who think they have a problem with alcohol. This can go either way, depending on whether that person is ready to take help. Ben came once, just to get a better understanding of her recovery. He found it inspiring. Even so, it makes her nervous that Becky may come away thinking it's stupid or weird.

Kate's thinking about Becky and the apology she gave that morning, as she presses avocados and pulls out packets of rice in the grocery store. She can't help but ruminate on the fact there seem to be two versions of Becky: a sad girl with the weight of the world on her shoulders, and an easy-going, unaffected version. She appears to flit between the two. Maybe she has some sort of depression – she did say she was feeling up and down.

Kate comes out of her daydream in the alcohol aisle. The wine bottles gleam as they regimentally poke out their chests. She turns her head left and then right. She reaches out and takes a bottle off the shelf, holding the weight in one hand. She looks around – everyone is oblivious to the woman holding the bottle of wine in aisle five. They have no idea. They don't rush over and pull it out of her hand screaming for her to stop. It will be easy to drop it in her basket, run it through the till. She's not underage, they wouldn't refuse the purchase.

Hurriedly, she puts the bottle back in the empty spot on the shelf where it belongs and turns away. *How quickly everything could unravel*, she thinks. How, if she had one sip of that, everything could slip away. Maybe not today or tomorrow but, like a bullet that's left a barrel, she wouldn't be able to avoid hitting something and smashing into pieces.

Kate stands outside the shop and breathes in the warm,

balmy air, trying to ground herself. She wonders what brought it on. She must be more stressed than she realized. It always spooks her when her willpower is tested – it would have been so simple to go into autopilot and then be standing there in the street with a bottle of wine inside her bag. She leans against the lamp post before bending down and picking up her bags, relieved that she stopped herself.

Then Lily walks out of the store with a boy Kate doesn't recognize. He looks older than Lily, more hardened than the boys at school. He is wearing a baseball cap and low-slung jeans, and his sleeveless T-shirt shows off a riddle of tattoos across his shoulders and arms. Kate knows the type; there isn't a good reason why a young man like this would be hanging out with a schoolgirl. Kate watches as Lily takes two bottles of beer from inside her jacket and proudly shows him. He laughs as she hands him one.

Kate has been on edge, waiting for Lily to turn up at school. Now she is standing in front of her with someone like that, a fiery rage builds up inside Kate and before she knows what she's doing, she shouts Lily's name and rushes towards her.

'Lily!' Kate calls. The girl sees her teacher and starts to hurry away, pulling at the boy's hand. 'Lily, stop!' Kate walks faster. 'Don't make me chase you!' she says with more urgency. 'I just want to talk.' The girl's step slows to a halt in defeat.

She turns to the boy. 'I'll meet you there.'

The boy looks over at Kate, confused, but he nods and marches ahead. Lily watches him hurry off down the street, and then she turns to Kate.

111

'What the fuck, Miss!' she shouts. Kate gasps as she sees a dark-purple blemish under Lily's right eye. She has tried to cover it with make-up but it's still visible under the concealer. It looks sore. 'What do you want?' the girl asks, angrily.

'I . . . I just want to know if you're OK,' Kate says, suddenly unsure why she has meddled. 'You haven't been to school, it's your exams . . .' She coughs. 'Lily, what happened to your eye?'

The dark purple glistens in the light. Lily looks away. 'It was an accident.'

'It looks painful.'

'It's not, it's nothing,' Lily murmurs forcefully.

'I'm worried about you.'

'Why?' Lily asks abruptly, annoyed. 'Why do you give a shit? Why do you keep on my back, can't you just fuck off?' The gold of her chunky rings flashes as she gesticulates wildly.

Kate's cheeks flame red, she's knows she's overstepped the mark.

'I'm sorry.' She looks around. People are watching, wondering what the heated exchange is about. 'I guess I just want you to be happy. And I don't think you are.'

The girl gives her teacher a peculiar look. 'I am,' Lily says unconvincingly. 'I just don't think school is for me.' Her tone has softened.

'But Lily, it is. All this . . .' Kate motions in the direction her friend walked off, '. . . will be meaningless in a few years' time. I know it's hard to comprehend but you'll look back at this as a crossroads moment, and you'll kick yourself.'

Lily brings her long acrylic nail to her mouth and chews.

'It's too late, Miss.'

'No, it's not,' says Kate firmly. 'You just need to pass – I know your work, and you could easily achieve that. Why haven't you been coming in?'

'Had a lot on,' Lily says, kicking the kerb with her shoe.

Kate nods slowly and decides to change tack. 'Mrs Wells is going to call your mother in for a meeting. I'm going to be there. Does she know about the accident?' Kate asks.

Lily shifts on the spot. 'Yeah, she was there when I fell.' She shrugs, Kate can tell she's lying.

'Why don't you come in this week? Then . . . then that meeting will go better, don't you think? I won't have to worry her so much,' Kate suggests.

'Look, I'll come to your stupid lesson, OK? You don't need to bring this up with my mum.'

Kate nods. 'OK, we could maybe do a one-on-one catch-up after the lesson. You haven't missed too much.'

'I'll come to the lesson,' Lily says.

'Lily, if you need help . . .' Kate starts.

'I'll come to the lesson and I'll stay on after like you wanted,' she says, looking across the street to where the boy ran off.

Kate nods and thinks. 'Come in and we'll talk, yeah?'

Lily nods vigorously and then backs away and runs off down the street. Kate watches her and thinks of all the accidents she had herself when she was a drunk teenager, and all the boys she let take advantage of her. She feels the small scar she's got by her eye. She doesn't even remember how

113

she got it, she probably should have had stitches, but she would have been too hungover to care. She bends down and picks up her bags. She needs to get into town, Becky will be waiting for her.

9

Kate went to her first AA meeting in her early twenties. By then, any delusions of fun had been completely eradicated. She could no longer kid herself that she was a party girl within a thriving scene. She'd been sacked from her job at the Vulture, and Camden had lost its sparkle again. Life was a grind, a lonely, desperate groundhog day.

She'd lived in a seven-bedroom house-share in Finsbury Park. She rarely spoke to anyone else living there, and she would only leave her room to cling on to her shitty job in a shoe shop. She was always late, and she would spend the eight-hour shift doing as little as possible, staring at the clock, waiting for it to end. Every morning she would promise herself she wouldn't go via the off-licence on her way home, then every evening she would find herself there. She just didn't have the tools to stop. She would drink and drink until she woke up in her clothes on top of her bed, the telly playing early-morning cartoons, the sun berating her with its cheery bright light.

A French girl, Colette, moved into one of the rooms in

Finsbury Park. Kate hadn't liked her one bit. Colette didn't drink and was self-assured and happy. Kate watched her, wondering how she could smile like that. Then one day Colette found her on the floor in the bathroom, passed out, her knickers around her ankles. She helped Kate to bed. The next morning, she gently knocked on Kate's door. She'd told Kate what she was like when she was drinking, and how she got sober. Kate listened – she was too tired and embarrassed not to. She couldn't remember the last day she hadn't had a drink, and she couldn't remember how to function without it. She was stuck between a life unlived and a life not worth living. She was desperate, and that made her one of the lucky ones. Colette took her to her first meeting. Kate owes her life to her.

She remembers being new, sitting in one of those dank basement rooms on a plastic chair for the first time. The relief of listening to someone tell their story eclipsed all the anxiety she felt, and, for the first time since she could remember, she felt hope. These people understood how she felt when she thought no one in the entire world could. While her 'normal' friends were enjoying life, cooking roasts, having healthy relationships, or getting exciting new jobs, Kate just hated everything. If someone smiled, she wanted to grab them by the ears and scream in their face: *how are you smiling, don't you understand how terrifying everything is?*

When she listened to that first person speak, she realized that, although they came from completely different backgrounds and all the details were different, the feelings, oh, the feelings were exactly the same. The constant darkness gently lifted as she attended meetings daily and gradually clocked up sobriety time. She went for coffees with other people in recovery, she got a sponsor and worked the steps. And then, slowly, all the things that kept her isolated, alone and drunk, didn't feel as all-consuming as they had before. Before she knew it, she was smiling and laughing, and it wasn't alcohol-induced – she was actually happy. Maybe it was the steps, maybe it was finding out that she wasn't alone, maybe it was the support of her sponsor. She doesn't really care how or why it worked – it just did. She lost the obsession with alcohol, something she had worried she was stuck with for life.

Kate had arranged to meet Becky at the end of the road where the meeting is held. She can see her waiting. Becky is wearing a light denim jacket and jeans with black boots. Her hair is down and tempered into obedient waves – the kind Kate has seen in adverts for shampoo that even her hairdresser can't replicate on her locks. If Kate hadn't been meeting her, she would have walked past with an admiring, slightly jealous, look.

'Hey,' Kate says as she approaches.

Becky turns. 'Hi.' She smiles widely.

'You still want to do this?' asks Kate nervously. She only wants to take Becky if she is sure.

'Yes, definitely. I'm really intrigued,' says Becky. She looks genuinely excited.

'OK . . . cool. Just to warn you, there's lots of talk about God, especially written on the twelve steps. But it's not religious or anything, it's not about that,' she explains. 'The best thing is to have an open mind.'

'Yes, of course,' says Becky, 'I mean, if it saved you, there must be something in it!' she jokes. Kate is relieved it is this version of Becky with her tonight.

The meeting is in the basement of an old church. A huddle of people smoking cigarettes, or clutching mugs of tea, are laughing by the front door. Kate takes Becky's hand and pulls her through the entrance. Everyone says hello and smiles at them. They walk into a large room with a low ceiling. The floor is tiled with olive-green carpet, and the glossy white walls are peeling and worn. They hover at the back deciding where to sit.

Becky looks behind her at the old corkboard where various notices and posters are pinned. *KEEP COMING BACK, KEEP IT SIMPLE, FIRST THINGS FIRST* . . . Becky looks at the slogans, the simple sayings that are repeated over and over at meetings like this. When someone first gets sober, they need everything to be simple, just a few lines they can roll over in their heads to calm them and keep them on track. Just so they can do the next right thing, rather than think of everything in their life that needs mending.

'My favourite is: If it works . . . don't fix it,' Kate whispers as she points to a few free chairs near the back. She can see Becky is taking it all in, probably imagining what her mother would make of this dingy room. 'You'll be surprised at the clientele.'

The girls watch the room slowly fill. The majority of people are well dressed and well groomed. Kate sees Becky relaxing in her chair, probably relieved they aren't in a room full of tramps. She remembers thinking the same thing when she sat in her first meeting – she was completely deluded then. If anyone had looked like a vagrant it was her: she hadn't washed her hair all week, her clothes were dirty, and she stank of last night's booze. It took her a while to realize that everyone was well presented because this worked – they were well again because of this place.

'Everyone looks . . . so normal,' Becky whispers across to her.

Kate nods with a smile. 'Yep. That's because they are – well, as normal as anyone can be,' she whispers back.

Two men take the front seats. The smattering of people chatting across chair backs turn to listen. The older man checks the clock, which has just hit the hour mark. He is wearing a pinstriped suit, and he has a beautiful vintage leather briefcase by the side of his chair. Kate wonders if anyone at his office knows where he spends his spare time.

'Hello, everyone. I'm Peter, I'm an alcoholic.'

The whole room murmurs hello.

'This is Michael; he's very kindly agreed to share his experience, strength, and hope and then he'll invite you to share back by raised hands. Please keep it to three minutes. If it goes over this, I'll raise this yellow card.' He holds up a piece of paper as an example. 'Right, over to you, Michael.'

Kate casts her eyes across to Becky. Her mouth is open, and she is looking ahead with keen interest. Michael, the man about to speak, is in his late twenties. He's wearing a beanie hat and a boxy white T-shirt. He looks like he works for a trendy streetwear brand or a tech start-up in Shoreditch.

'My name is Michael and I'm an alcoholic,' he starts. 'I've been sober two years . . .' He takes a deep breath, then suddenly his eyes well up and his cheeks burn red. He bows his head and his fingers cling to the hem of his hat, as if he wants to pull the wool down over his face. 'Sorry . . .'

The room waits. No one bats an eyelid at the man with a neck tattoo who is visibly emotional in front of them.

'Sorry, I was actually going to cancel today. But then I thought, fuck it, maybe this is what I need. And my Higher Power knows what I need more than I do . . .'

He looks at his hands and shakes his head, forcing himself to continue. 'My mum's been diagnosed with cancer. And all I want to do is get off my face, run into oblivion with open arms and think fuck this, fuck dealing with these emotions, fuck looking my mother in the eye, knowing she might not be here much longer.' He pauses and coughs into his hand. 'I was such a shit to her when I was drinking. I kind of got a kick out of hurting people. Because I hated myself so much, it was just another way to self-destruct. It was a form of self-harm, making people hate me, pushing them away.' He sniffs and looks up at the ceiling. 'I just can't help but feel like this is karma, that I hurt her, and now I'm better and I've fixed that relationship, she's going to die and it's my fault.'

He takes another breath; the whole room sits patiently. Then, all of a sudden, he smiles.

'Man, I'm so glad I've said that out loud, it's completely

zapped the power out of it. That would've eaten me whole, that would . . .' He breathes out deeply again and wipes the side of his face and sniffs. 'My brain tells me lies, and that thought would have got me down the pub if I wasn't careful. It would've eroded through me and I would've drunk on it. But that's the disease, isn't it? Instead of helping my mum, being with her at hospital visits, looking after her when she has chemo, I would have been another thing for her to worry about. Fuck that, I don't know what will happen, but I'm going to make sure I'm there with her, being the best son I can be, to make up for the shitshow I was before.' He sits back in his seat, satisfied. 'Thanks for being here, I'll leave it there.'

Kate looks at Becky; she's visibly moved. She looks as if she might cry.

Peter, the secretary, begins to speak, 'Thanks, Michael, that was really honest and powerful. I think we can all relate to feeling like that, to getting bad news and using it as an excuse to drink again. We are so pleased you came here and shared it with us instead of acting on your own will. In my experience it is helpful to reflect on your own recovery and how fragile it is, no matter how many years you have under your belt. One piece of bad news can floor you. You need the strong foundations of this programme to ground you when the shit hits the fan.'

The group is then invited to share back. Becky looks around at those who raise their arms; she seems lost in the activity, as if she's completely immersed in this new world that she's found herself in. Kate is relieved that Becky isn't smirking or rolling her eyes, but then she always forgets the power of something like this. Groups of people with a shared problem helping each other to overcome it.

The next forty-five minutes are filled with short vignettes, other people sharing their own experiences similar to Michael's, and what they have learnt from it. Everyone is eloquent and has something unique to say.

Peter calls time on the session and a pot is passed round for people to leave a donation. Becky reaches for her purse, but Kate stops her. 'It's only for members.' She dashes a couple of pounds inside the tin. They then say the serenity prayer together. Becky pretends to move her lips as the others repeat the words with vigour. They leave and walk up the steps to street level and wander in silence to the bus stop.

'Do you think you'll ever drink again?' asks Becky.

'I really hope not, but you can't predict the future.'

'What? So, if something awful happened to you, you might drink again?' Becky asks, her brow furrowed with concern.

'I hope that I've got a good enough support network to stop that happening. My meetings, my sponsor, Ben . . .' Kate smiles.

Becky smiles back, nodding. The air is cooler than it had been when they arrived, and Kate digs inside her backpack for a cardigan.

'I mean . . . it happens, I'm not immune. I've heard of real old-timers falling off the wagon after decades of sobriety. And I get it . . . I've had really shit times sober . . . during teacher training I started hermiting myself, I wouldn't pick up the phone to Clare or anyone else in the rooms. Everything got really dark in here.' She points to her head. 'I nearly did something really stupid.'

'What stopped you?' Becky asks.

Kate takes a deep breath. 'Well . . . It was Ben.' She turns to Becky. 'He saved my life.'

Becky looks confused for a moment, and then chuckles. 'I thought the whole point is that you're not meant to let someone else save you, that you have to do it yourself.'

Kate swallows thickly and stops walking. 'When I met him on Waterloo Bridge, I . . .' Becky continues a few steps before realizing Kate has stopped, and she turns to face her. 'When I met him on Waterloo Bridge . . . I was about to jump off. I would have if he hadn't stopped me. He literally saved my life.'

Becky's eyes blink in shock. She looks as if she doesn't know what to say. She shakes her head and takes Kate's hand in hers, and they walk down the road together, their fingers intertwined.

10

Kate's eyes flick open, and she wonders why. And then she hears a distant scream. She waits – she hears the noise again, louder. Confused, she sits up. Her eyes search the darkness for some sort of clue. It takes her a moment to remember where she is. She turns to push Ben's shoulder to wake him, but there is just an empty space. Then she remembers, he's in Scotland. She hears a call for help, and a rush of sickening adrenalin freezes her to the spot. *Becky*, she thinks. Somehow, she manages to cut through the fear and untangles herself from the sheet, rushing to the door, yanking it open. She crosses the dark hallway and finds the handle to the spare room from memory. There isn't time to think of any potential consequences.

Inside the room, Kate flicks the light. She's expecting to find more than one person, but all she can see is Becky's body flailing around on the bed like an eel out of water.

'Help!' she moans. 'Please, no!'

Kate charges over and grabs her shoulders, pinning her to the bed.

'Becky! Becky, it's OK!'

Slowly, the movement stalls and Becky shudders to a stop. Her rigid limbs become slack and she weeps uncontrollably, holding onto Kate for dear life. After some time, gently, they move apart. Becky's breathing is heavy, she swallows and looks around.

'Was I dreaming?' Strands of hair are stuck to her face from the moisture of her tears.

Kate nods. 'I think you were having a nightmare.'

Becky's face bunches up with confusion. She looks down, ashamed. 'I'm sorry. Was I screaming?'

'You sounded like you were being attacked, Becky,' Kate tells her.

'I'm sorry I woke you up.' She looks around the room as if she's still in shock.

'That's OK. Do you get these dreams a lot?'

'Only sometimes,' Becky replies, hugging herself.

'Do you know why?' Kate's brow is furrowed with concern.

Becky isn't looking at her, she is looking at the dark space between her crossed arms and folded legs. 'I think I'll go back to sleep, Kate. Can we talk about this another time? I'm really tired.' Her voice shakes as she talks.

Kate steps back, away from the bed. 'Yes, sure.' She watches Becky lie back down and turn to face the wall.

'Can you get the light?'

Kate pauses before she leaves. 'Becky, if there is something you need to talk about . . . It helps, you know.'

'Thanks Kate,' she says to the wall. 'Don't forget the light.'

Kate moves away and snaps the switch as she backs out of the door, shutting it carefully. Her whole body is reeling from the sudden burst of action. She puts her hand on her chest; she can feel her heart beating in hard thrusting motions.

She slowly walks across the landing back to her room and climbs into bed. Kate folds her knees under the light summer duvet and brings them close to her chest for comfort. She's rattled. It takes her a while to get back to sleep; she keeps lifting her head, thinking she can hear shouting again, but it's only the memory echoing over and over as if she is in a tunnel or down a well. All Kate can think is: *Becky, what happened to you?*

It is tweeting birds that wake her the next morning. She finds the cheerful noise piercing, it makes her wince. Sitting up, she slams the window shut. She hears the door to the spare room open and footsteps quickly patter away down the stairs. The front door slams. Becky must be embarrassed, but Kate doesn't want her to be.

Over the last six years she has met many people in distress, getting over some of the worst kinds of trauma. She has sponsored a few girls and listened to their Step Fours, which have been full of painful experiences she's helped them come to terms with. A thought occurs. Maybe that's why Becky is here, why she's reappeared in her life – so that Kate can help her, using the tools she's obtained getting away from her own demons. The thought pleases Kate. She takes out her phone and composes a text. *I'll cook us dinner again tonight, I'll be back at 6. K x*

*

Later, her phone rings just as she unlocks her classroom. She's in a rush and isn't planning on answering. She checks the screen: it's Jonny, her dad. She hasn't spoken to him for a couple of months, or is it longer? He rarely calls her. Her thumb hesitates over the cancel option before the feeling of guilty obligation forces her to change her mind.

'Hi, Jonny,' she snaps. She's always called him by his first name, ever since she was a little girl.

'Hey, kiddo. Are you at work?'

'Yes, I've got five minutes before my first class. Is everything OK?'

'Yeah, all good . . .' He stops.

Her dad hates the phone, he would only have called for a reason; he's not one to chat. It irritates her that she is the one who has to instigate the conversation, even though she isn't the one who made the call.

'Is there something . . . you wanted to talk about?' A pause. She looks around at the room. She left it in a state yesterday, she's got a lot to do in five . . . four minutes. 'Jonny? What's up?' she says again, annoyed already.

'The wedding, I wanted to ask you if you needed any help,' he says, sounding defeated.

'I told you, Jonny, it isn't really even a wedding. Just the town hall. We don't want it to be a big deal.' She picks up a balled-up piece of paper off the floor, and her knee creaks as she stands up again. 'It's just admin.'

'What about flowers? You'll have a few flowers, won't you?'

127

She hasn't really thought about it, aside from picking up a bunch en route. 'I think there will be,' she says with a sigh.

'Let me buy that, yeah? Your bunch . . . the bouquet.'

Kate thinks about what Becky said about Jonny walking her down the aisle. 'Sure, Jonny.' She scrunches the paper in her hand. 'Sure.'

'I'm coming to London this weekend on a buying trip, are you around in the morning if I swing by?' Jonny asks.

Kate wants to say no, but can't think of a reason to deny the request. She wishes he would just stay in his box in Kent and not meddle in her life. She hates feeling like this about him, but he reminds her of all the stuff that happened when she went to stay in Margate that year after Becky left. Going back there . . . she shudders. It would bring it all up again and remind her that she can't change things. Decisions were made and she can't take them back.

Clare is under the impression that Kate hasn't done a vocal Step Nine with Jonny because she's fulfilling a living amends, being the best daughter she can, to make up for all the shit she put him through. But that's not actually the case, and, whenever they are in contact, she's reminded that she's lying to Clare. You shouldn't keep anything from your sponsor. If she's really honest with herself, she isn't ready to make the amends because she's still furious with what he made her do.

Kate was a daddy's girl growing up; she'd run into his arms, and he'd pick her up and twirl her around. There was nothing he could do wrong, he even learnt how to braid hair – he's good with his hands, her daddy. But that was all before, before her adolescence descended and she suddenly realized how terrifying the world was, and how he couldn't really save her from anything at all. And then when he tried to help, his meddling made it all worse. She wonders if it can be repaired. She bites her lip; for that to happen she knows she'll have to forgive him.

'Jonny, I've got to go, that was the bell,' she lies. 'Yes, pop by in the morning. We're around so we can talk about the flowers.'

'OK.'

Kate puts the phone down, sighing. She wonders if she should message him a lie, that they are busy and she forgot. He just doesn't fit into her life any more. Also, she finds time spent between Ben and Jonny unbearable. They are so different. Jonny is not a natural socializer, and Ben's been brought up to charm everyone. She finds it painfully awkward watching Ben flatter Jonny and then watching Jonny try to keep up. She'll stand on the edge, eagerly filling any silences. She balls up her fists in frustration; why does he always have to ruin everything? She has enough on her plate with all this Becky stuff and getting the kids through these exams.

She throws the scrunched-up piece of paper towards the bin and misses. Bollocks, she whispers. The bell rings, preluding the familiar rumble of action as the kids leave assembly.

Kate's got her Year 11 English class later. She wonders if Lily will turn up, if their chat last night had any effect at all. The outcome will determine whether Kate returns home elated or depressed. She takes a deep breath and looks up at the ceiling, trying to balance herself – she has been so stuck inside her feelings recently. Her ability to 'watch the movie' – another helpful term she has learnt – rather than take part in it has eroded with everything that's been going on. She should just let things happen, watch them from afar, question emotions that pop up and analyse their presence, rather than getting heavily involved and allowing her mind to project future scenes and outcomes that then cause her unnecessary anxiety. She needs to 'hand it over' – let what will be, be. She murmurs a line of the serenity prayer: *Grant me the serenity to accept the things I cannot change.* It calms her instantly.

She watches her second period troop out of the classroom and breathes air into her cheeks so they blow up like taut inflatables. When no more can fit inside, she opens her mouth with a satisfied *oomph*. If Lily doesn't turn up today there is a high chance she's given up completely and won't take her exams. Kate will have done her best, but it won't have been enough. She will have failed the girl, and the whole reason she asked for that class was to ensure Lily gets the grade she deserves.

To distract herself from everything, Kate pushes her earphones into her ears and places a pile of Year 8 essays on the desk. She peels off the top sheet and nods her head to the beat, intent on getting through the pile within the lunch hour. She gets lost in the red ticks and crosses of the work. She smiles at their innocent mistakes and naively poignant explanations as she flicks her pen on her bottom lip.

She suddenly thinks of last night and Becky shouting; the

thought makes her stop and look up, out of the window. Her sweaty body, her legs and arms scrambling to get away from nothing at all. Kate's mind starts to walk through a door, a memory, a distant memory of something like that happening before. Like déjà vu, something so intangible, like a bitten-down nail trying to scratch an unreachable itch. What is it . . . why has she heard what Becky was yelling before? Another flash, Becky pulling her arm, pleading with her that she wants to leave, and Kate wanting to stay on and party. *Please, Kate, I feel weird, I don't like this . . . we should go . . .*

'Kate!' Her name is shouted through the pumping beat. She looks up, shocked. It's Gus, the teacher who trained at the same time as her. She pulls out her earphones.

'Hi!' she says, blushing.

'You in the zone?' He looks at her with a mix of bemusement and disorientation.

'Sorry.' She twists the earphones wire around her handset. 'Ha ha, yeah, totally in the zone,' she replies, embarrassed.

'You were meant to be on lunch duty . . . I covered for you. You owe me one.'

'Oh . . . shit, sorry Gus . . . I . . .' She looks at the work in front of her – she's been so distracted.

He laughs. 'Hey, it's no biggie. Anyway, see you later.' He shuts her inside her classroom again.

Kate is tearful by the time the bell rings for the final lesson. It's been hard to concentrate. She's had to continually ask pupils to repeat questions and stop mid-sentence to remember the point of what she is saying. She's become quite the perfectionist since getting her life back on track, so not giving these kids her very best self gives her that familiar feeling of failure. Clare says it's a control thing, and she needs to watch herself around it. No one can ever be perfect, Kate, she says, but you can die trying. It sounds extreme, but for someone like Kate, who might let herself wallow in these failures, they could ultimately make her so unhappy she would drink again.

She feels exhausted when Lizzie comes swaggering through the door. 'Miss? Can I charge my phone, please?' she asks urgently.

'Yes, no problem,' Kate says, pointing to the power source on the wall.

'Yeah, and then he posted that she was a slut . . .' She's chatting to Emma, as usual. The others troop in and find seats, twirling pens and fiddling with hair and phones.

'OK, enough screen time, away please!' Kate shouts. They moan, but do as she asks.

Kate looks at the open door, willing Lily to come through it. She doesn't even care if she gives her a hard time today, she'll take it. The students look up at their teacher expectantly, and Kate begins, defeated.

'Right, did everyone do the questions on "Human Interest" that I asked you to do last week?' she calls out to the room, as she turns away from the class to hide her face, busying herself by wiping the board clean. Her cheeks have heated up and her throat feels swollen and tight – she bites her teeth together to stop herself from crying.

Then she hears the familiar screech of a chair being pulled back and spins around. Lily sits down. She has hidden the bruise better than the night before, you can't even really tell it's there. Her classmates smile at her and she smiles back. Kate can't quite believe she's sitting there.

'Lily, I'm so happy you could join us,' Kate says, breathless.

Lily shrugs and tries not to look as though it's a big deal. She pulls out a pen from her bag and sits poised, ready to work. She looks brighter than she has for a while; her eyes are clear, her hair is neat. She doesn't look as if she has been up all night partying. There is a special energy for the rest of the hour. Lily is one of those people who determine the atmosphere in a room; today she is concentrating and studious, so the others take their lead from her.

'Does everyone feel confident they could answer exam questions about the poem? Has anyone got anything they want to ask me before we go back to Shakespeare?'

She scans the room, but they stay silent.

'Right . . .' She turns to pick up another textbook.

A voice pipes up. 'It's really sad,' says Lily, almost as an afterthought. She's looking wistfully out of the window. 'Do you think she did cheat?'

Kate looks down at the poem, which is about domestic abuse, and then at Lily and the patchy concealer by her right eye. 'It's not really the point, is it? Even if she did, you don't kill someone for it. A healthy relationship isn't made out of jealousy and violence.'

Lily nods thoughtfully.

133

'My uncle went to Pentonville for beating up his wife,' Lizzie pips in. 'But she was asking for it; she slept with his best mate.' She cackles, looking around the room to check for a reaction.

'A lot of people believe it's never OK to hit a woman, Lizzie,' Kate says.

'Yeah, I know that,' she says, before turning to her friend. 'She was asking for it, though,' she sniggers in her ear.

The bell rings and they hurry to leave. Lily stays behind. When they are finally alone, Kate gets out some textbooks and sits at the table with her. She takes the opportunity to lean in and silently sniff. All she can smell is apple shampoo.

'Miss, I can't stay long.'

'That's OK,' says Kate softly. 'Shall we just go through everything and work out a plan? If we find a couple of hours in the next week, it will really help before the exam.' Kate pulls out her diary and they find a couple of study periods to meet up.

'Do you really think I can pass, Miss?' Lily asks.

'Yes, Lily, if you just focus for this last week.' She pauses. 'The way you write is beautiful.'

Lily blushes. Then she looks up at the time and stands. 'I've got to go, Miss. When are you seeing my mum? Will you tell her I came?'

Kate sits back in her chair and sighs. 'She's coming in tomorrow. It's great that I can talk to her about today and the plan we've come up with.'

Lily smiles. 'Great.'

Kate watches her leave. She's happy Lily came, but she has an underlying feeling of unease about the girl's lifestyle choices. There is so much about Lily she can relate to. She wants to march her home by the sleeve and lock the door, make her cups of tea and toast and talk to her about everything she's going through. But she can't, all she can do is watch from the periphery and hope something she says sticks. Mrs Wells often has to remind her that they aren't their parents, and there is only so much they can do.

11

Kate feels as if a missing piece of herself has returned when she picks up her bike from the shop. She tests the new wheel by bouncing the front against the pavement, holding the bars. It boings up and down happily, like an excited puppy knowing its owner is about to take it home. She climbs the frame and slowly eases herself up onto the pedals, riding off towards Newington Green. She hopes that Becky isn't in – she just wants a few moments of peace to recharge before she has to deal with something else. The day has been stressful, and even though things went her way in the end, the inner turmoil has taken it out of her. She just wants half an hour to herself. She walks across the threshold and is met with comforting silence.

'Becky?' she shouts into the dim space. Not a word. She is flooded with relief.

Her muscles ache as she climbs the stairs. She goes into the bathroom and turns on the hot water. As she removes her clothes, the room steams up, the sweet smell of bath foam diffusing within the wet plumes of mist. She wipes a hand across the moist mirror to see her reflection. She looks worn.

Kate is in her late twenties, and she normally thinks she looks OK. Her mind wanders to the way Ben looked at Becky the other day, when he commented on her attractiveness. She pulls at the skin on the side of her face to stretch out the tiny wrinkles collecting by the corner of her eye. They are the same age, but Becky's skin is radiant and taut, and her lips are perfectly plump. Maybe Kate needs to try harder, she can't take her looks for granted any more or assume her face does things it used to on its own. She hasn't had her eyebrows tinted in a while, and she should probably have a facial before the wedding. The thought of Ben's mum, and the disapproving look she'll give her this summer, makes her shiver. She knows what she'll be thinking: Why her? Why did my golden boy choose her?

Kate shakes the thought out of her head. Clare says her mind plays tricks on her; it makes her say things to herself that she wouldn't say to her worst enemy. Clare says alcoholism isn't actually about drinking at all, that's just what is used to self-medicate from the pain of how her brain is wired. And once she put the bottle down, it took time to unplug and reroute all the old behaviours. Kate has learnt she must ignore that mean-spirited voice and focus on the good one. Over the last six years the latter has certainly overridden the one she gave too much worth to previously. Well, most of the time.

She lights a small candle and puts it on the lip of the bath and switches off the main light. It feels calm, and peaceful. The only sound is the slow drip, drip, drip of the tap. She lies back in the bath, her hair piled on top of her head, letting the bubbles soak the back of her neck. She sighs with pleasure and closes her eyes. It's moments like this that she tries not to take for granted, just lying still and feeling content. Not having to keep moving and consuming and talking and reacting . . . as though if she stopped for one moment she would be in agony. It used to feel as if she needed to keep the ball rolling because if she ended her tornado of destruction, all the feelings she was trying to avoid would come at her with pointed knives.

She hears someone on the stairs and opens one eye. Becky must be home. There is a pause at the top of the landing, but instead of turning left and walking across the bathroom entrance to the spare room, she turns the other way, towards Kate and Ben's room. Confused, Kate doesn't move a muscle, she waits for more. After a few minutes of silence, she slowly climbs out of the bath as quietly as she can and pulls her robe off the hook, silently wrapping it around herself. Gently opening the door, she is careful not to let the knob click. She doesn't know why she doesn't want Becky to hear her approach, it is just an instinct.

Her bare feet touch the landing carpet; she can see her bedroom door is open, and the light is on. Someone is rummaging around quietly in there. Moving her hand onto the body of the door, Kate pushes it open.

She stands there motionless as she watches Becky search through a drawer in the large chest on the other side of the room. It is the one full of Ben's personal things: certificates and photographs, notebooks and old diaries. Kate looks at

Becky's hand. She is holding a bottle of his aftershave which usually sits on the surface.

'Becky?'

Becky turns. Her mouth hangs open and gabbles with silent words before murmuring, 'Kate.' She looks down at her hand holding the glass bottle and scrappily puts it back where it belongs. 'Kate, I'm so sorry.' She walks towards her.

'What are you doing?' Kate asks, her brow furrowed.

'I . . . I was looking for something,' she stammers.

'What?' Kate asks, tilting her head to one side.

'I was looking for one of those books, those blue books that you have in AA,' she says in a rush. 'I wanted to take one over to my mum.'

Kate watches her features; she looks innocent with her wide eyes.

'Sorry, I shouldn't have . . .' She wipes her forehead. 'I should have waited for you . . .'

Kate walks into the room and pulls out the drawer of her bedside table. Inside lies a blue hardback book, about the same size and weight as a Bible. She picks it up. 'You just had to ask,' she whispers.

Becky grimaces nervously. 'Sorry . . .'

'Hey . . . It's OK.' She walks over and touches Becky's arm. She hates to see other people crippled with embarrassment; she knows that feeling too well. 'Becky . . . about last night,' she starts.

'Kate, I'm sorry, I haven't done that for a long time,' she rushes to say, her face flushing.

139

'Did something happen to you? You know there are people you can talk to if you are suffering in some way?'

Becky looks up at her and tenderly reaches her fingers to the side of Kate's face. 'You still have the scar,' she whispers.

Kate jerks her head back in surprise, and Becky moves her hand away. Kate touches the side of her eye; there is the small scar, about two centimetres long. 'Oh God, the amount of accidents I had.' She pauses, thinking of the flashing lights and the disapproving looks from doctors and nurses. She's been such a drain on society.

Becky watches her as if she is looking for something.

'What?' asks Kate, mystified.

Becky shakes her head. 'Never mind.'

'What?' Kate asks again.

'It's nothing, really.' Becky twirls around and manoeuvres herself to the door frame. 'I'm cooking you dinner tonight, to say thank you.' She turns to walk down the stairs. 'It'll be ready in an hour.'

And just like that she's gone.

Kate stands in the room, confused at the whirlwind of action. She looks down; the book is still in her hand. Becky forgot to take it. She goes over to the drawer that Becky was looking inside and yanks it open. It is full of dollars and discarded coins, his American driver's licence and a few old Moleskine notebooks with the elastic wrapped around. She picks up his aftershave. Ben always wears it, she could recall the smell from memory if she had to. She sniffs; it's like coming home. Gently placing the bottle back down she looks toward the open door Becky walked through a few moments before.

Once Kate is dressed and her hair is dry, she pads down the stairs. The sweet exotic smell of curry greets her as she enters the kitchen. 'This smells amazing. You didn't have to go to all this trouble.' The kitchen is a hive of activity. Chopping boards out, used knives, bowls with wooden spoons resting inside.

'It's a curry, butternut squash,' says Becky proudly. The steam from the food has made some of her natural loose curls shrink up around her face. 'In New York I'd sometimes eat out five nights a week. My kitchen was about a third of the size of this.' She looks around. 'I can't wait to get my own place and start cooking again,' she says. 'It's one of the things that made me homesick. Imagine that! Missing a Tesco Local.' She looks excited and impassioned; there isn't a glimmer of the sweaty, anxious girl she shook awake the night before.

'It's home,' Kate shrugs. 'I guess no matter how glamorous your life is, home is always home.' She notices a bottle of wine on the counter; it's red, the label looks expensive. 'Want me to pour you a glass?'

'Oh, don't worry, I was going to have a glass while you're out with Ben on the weekend . . .'

'Becky, I don't have a problem with people drinking around me. Ben drinks at home all the time.' She doesn't want Becky feeling awkward about drinking in the house. It's another way she can show her how well she is now.

Kate removes a corkscrew from the drawer and uses the

pointed edge to cut around the foil on the top of the bottle. She then starts to twist the device slowly, enjoying the ritual. Once eased out, she looks at the purple-red stain at the end of the cork. She has the sudden urge to put it in her mouth and suck.

Once they've eaten, they take their glasses over to the sofa.

'That was delicious, thank you so much, Becky.'

'It could have been better,' Becky says. 'But what was that saying at the meeting the other night? Progress not perfection!' She laughs.

'Oh God, what is it about being a grown-up?' Kate scoffs. 'You realize all the bloody clichés are true. You should see the kids at school roll their eyes at me when I spout that shit.'

'Well, we used to do exactly the same,' Becky reminds her.

'True.' Kate thinks back to them in their school uniforms, tucking a note under a desk with a wink. Taking turns to play with each other's hair while they listened to a lecture on the floor in the music room. Sharing a cigarette in the alleyway behind the lunch hall, taking turns to be lookout. Everything was shared and everything was exchanged.

Kate looks over at Becky, sitting by the window, the street light streaming in, her glass in one hand tilted ever so slightly. She looks ethereal. 'We should do you a dating profile like we said!'

Becky immediately starts to shake her head. 'I don't know, Kate, I'm just not sure I can, everything is so up in the air right now.'

'Come on, that's just an excuse. You've got to be in it to win it!' Kate laughs. 'Please? Can we just choose a picture?' This could be just what Becky needs, someone to push her to get out there and meet someone special.

Becky shakes her head again.

'Oh, come on, I have to live vicariously through you now.'

'Kate, I really don't . . .' Becky says again.

'I promise I'm a better matchmaker than drinker,' Kate jokes. 'You need to get back on the horse.' She giggles at the saying.

'I really don't feel ready, Kate,' Becky says again.

'Oh, come on, it will be a bit of fun,' she pleads. 'Or maybe Internet dating isn't for you . . . I could ask Ben if there are any eligible bachelors at work?' She wiggles her eyebrows.

Becky face grows dark and heavy. 'I said I'm not ready! For fuck's sake, Kate, just leave it,' she says, tearfully.

The phone starts to ring in Becky's hand, and she looks down. 'It's my sister, I'll go and take it upstairs.' Becky walks away and puts the phone to her ear. 'Hi, Alexa.' Her footsteps are heavy and punctuated as she climbs the staircase.

The moment turned from jovial to testy in a matter of seconds. Kate has no idea what she's done wrong. She sits back in her seat, feeling like she's been slapped. All she can hear is the floorboards creaking upstairs as Becky walks from one end of the room to the other, pacing. Dumbfounded, Kate goes back to the kitchen. She picks up the half-drunk bottle of wine by the sink, pauses, and then tips the rest of the contents away, watching the red liquid run down the plughole like blood, and disappear.

12

Kate walks her bike down the road, the spiralling spokes make a clicking noise as she pushes the frame forward. She wipes her face and shakes her head, trying to wake herself up. She needs another coffee, and she desperately needs to talk to Clare before going to work. She walks to the small square of green that gives the area its name. The café kiosk is open, and she orders a flat white and looks around while she waits for it to be made. Birds dive between branches which shake loosely above her head, calling out happily in the early morning sunshine. She takes a deep breath. London smells sweeter in the summer – not so dank and rotten, the city seems less weary. She closes her eyes, trying to just listen to the birds' happy chirping and to filter out the beeps and skidding halts of the morning traffic. It is important to do that in London sometimes, pretend the dirt and chaos isn't there and focus on the little patches of nature that keep everyone from suffocating.

A sudden scream jolts her head to the right. There is a little girl in a green dress, her thin blonde hair in pigtails on either side of her head. She looks as if she's just mastered running and is moving quickly away from her shouting mother who is chasing her and calling for her to stop before she gets to the road. Just before the girl approaches the wrought-iron fence, the woman catches her from behind, and she wraps her arms around her, bringing the child in to herself.

'Miss?' the man in the kiosk says.

Kate takes the small cardboard cup that is handed to her. 'Thank you.' She looks over again at the mother clutching her daughter and bites her bottom lip.

Along the path that runs through the square she finds an empty bench. She leans her bike against it and removes her phone from her pocket. She sits down and takes a swig of her drink as she listens to the phone ring.

'How did it go?' The phone is picked up almost straight away. 'Have you seen her?' Clare asks, intrigued.

Kate realizes she never updated Clare on how the Step Nine went. 'Oh, well . . . she's actually staying in our spare room,' Kate says.

'Oh.' Clare sounds surprised. 'So, well then, I guess.'

'Yes, it did go well.' She thinks back to the evening in the Vulture. It feels like months ago, so much has happened. 'But now . . . I don't know, I think I'm being paranoid.'

'Did she talk about what happened that night?' Clare gets to the crux straight away.

Kate clears her throat. 'That was the other thing, she said nothing of importance really happened, just that she'd had enough.'

'OK, well, that must be a relief, you've worried about that for years,' Clare says kindly.

Kate looks up at the blue sky; the green leaves have turned luminous reflecting off it. 'It's not . . . it's not a relief.' She chokes, 'I keep thinking about that night . . . and . . . I know she said nothing happened, but I just have this sick feeling that something really bad happened to her . . . and then, she had this nightmare the other night . . . and it reminded me of something . . . I don't know . . .' She pauses; she can't finish, she doesn't know what she is trying to say.

Kate waits, she knows Clare will say something helpful. 'So, you think she's hiding something from you, and is still angry?'

'She had this massive go at me last night . . . she's so up and down, I can't work her out at all.'

'Mmm . . . Kate, this all sounds really intense. Is there a reason you asked her to stay? Because if it was your guilt wanting to reimburse her or something, that's not what the programme is about. All you had to do was keep your side of the street clean, Kate; you've apologized, and she accepted that.' Clare pauses and sighs. 'You don't have to take her in, try and fix her. That's not your job.'

'I just feel like I owe her,' Kate says miserably.

'Kate, you weren't well . . .' Clare starts.

'I know, but . . . when does that just become an excuse for past behaviour?'

'It's not an excuse, you had, you *have*, a disease,' Clare says. 'So how long is she staying with you for?'

146

'A few weeks? While she finds something temporary. She couldn't stay with her mother,' Kate explains.

'What about her sister? I'm sure she has other options. Just remember, Kate, just because you hold this guilt, you don't owe her anything,' Clare says. 'Don't you have exams coming up? And the wedding?'

'Yes.'

'You are doing amazing things, Kate. She also chose to hang out with you, to be treated like that, so she must have been getting something out of it too.'

'I suppose . . .' says Kate.

'Just remember, OK? You are enough,' Clare adds, knowing this is Kate's Achilles heel.

'Thanks, Clare.' A tear has collected in her eye; she blinks, and it runs down her face. She quickly swats it away. 'Thanks so much.'

'Maybe now is not the right time to have a house guest? Especially one who brings up so much stuff for you. You are trying to fix something, Kate, and it's not for you to fix, so you might end up making it worse.'

'I just want her to be OK.'

'I know, but that's up to her. I've got to go feed the baby, but call me any time, OK?' They say their goodbyes.

Kate pushes herself off the bench and throws the empty cardboard cup into a nearby bin. She needs to call Clare more often, she's been keeping her, and the whole of her programme, at arm's length. When Kate started Alcoholics Anonymous she had regular meetings she went to nearly every night, she had commitments, where she made tea or greeted people as they arrived. Ever since she went through that dark period and met Ben, she's not been as involved in her recovery, she's just been so happy and busy. Life got so full of good stuff that it became easier to pretend the bad stuff never happened.

She often wonders what would have happened if she hadn't met Ben that night. Was she really going to jump? Or was she just scaring herself into getting help again? Whatever the case, her Higher Power obviously led her there for a reason, and she can't help feeling that it was so she met Ben. Relief swells in her chest when she remembers he is back from Scotland later. He'll help untangle this for her, he always knows what to do.

Swinging her leg over her bike, she cycles in the direction of work. She thinks about the day ahead. She is meeting Lily's mother today. She has often wondered about Mrs Johnson, and what it must be like to have Lily as a daughter. Waiting for her to come home at night. Trying to reach her at four in the morning, listening to the phone ring and ring, looking up at the clock in the dim early morning light as it ticks and ticks. She thinks of Jonny, and how she let him down again and again, but didn't know how to stop. Hating him because he didn't know how to fix her. A warm cup of cocoa and a bedtime story didn't work like it used to.

Mrs Johnson is sitting on the chair outside Mrs Wells's office as Kate approaches. Her head is cocked to one side, staring ahead, looking both bored and worried. Kate hasn't seen her like this, dressed ready to impress. She has short brown hair and is wearing a fashionable, asymmetric white blouse, expensive jeans and neat black ballet pumps. Her make-up is expertly applied, and although she must be fifteen years older than Kate, there is a dewy, fresh quality to her skin. It would be easy to assume Lily came from one of the many council estates in the area, not a beautiful terrace on a recently gentrified street. Kate wonders where Mrs Johnson works . . . in finance, or maybe something more creative like a magazine? Mrs Johnson would never have picked this school for her daughter, but she didn't have much choice once Lily got expelled from the area's preferred state school two years ago.

'Mrs Johnson,' Kate says as she approaches, reaching out her hand. The woman stands up quickly and shakes it. 'I'm Lily's English teacher, Miss Sullivan.'

'Nice to meet you, Miss Sullivan,' Mrs Johnson says politely. 'I'm so sorry Lily is causing all these issues. Teenagers,' she adds with a quick shrug of her shoulders, trying to make light of the situation, which is obviously weighing heavily on her.

'Don't worry, Mrs Johnson, we're here to see if we can help at all,' Kate says warmly. She knocks on the office door and Mrs Wells shouts through it, 'Come in!'

Kate opens the door. The office is piled with paperwork, the keyboard barely visible under layers. Mrs Wells starts moving the disorganised piles around, looking for the file that holds her notes for the meeting. Kate notices a file with Lily's name on it so picks it up and hands it to her. Mrs Wells smiles gratefully.

'Thanks for coming in, Mrs Johnson,' she says.

'Thank you for taking the time to see me.' She takes her seat in front of the two teachers. She rests her hands together in her lap and leans forward, as if she is in a job interview. She obviously wants them to see her in a good light, to ensure they see Lily's waywardness doesn't stem from her parenting.

'We've called you in because of Lily's truanting and lack of motivation so close to her final exams,' says Mrs Wells. 'To see if, collectively, we can do anything to get her through these last few weeks.'

'Thank you . . . I don't know what to say, really. I've been trying to get her to revise, to keep her from going out . . .' Her voice cracks and she has to stop and compose herself. Kate takes a tissue from a box on the windowsill and hands it to her. Mrs Johnson shakes her head, refusing the gesture. 'She's got this awful boyfriend. I've tried talking to her, but she just won't listen.' She looks over at the two teachers, 'She's just so headstrong. I can't lock her in her room, can I?' Her voice falters. She stops and puts her hand over her mouth, trying to hold it together.

'That all sounds very stressful,' says Mrs Wells. 'I'm sure you are doing your best. Kids this age can be very stubborn.'

'She goes out all the time, sometimes not coming home till the morning. I stopped giving her money, I tried taking her phone off her. She still doesn't seem to get the fact she has her GCSEs in a few weeks . . .' Then she lets out a little cry and looks down at the floor, trying not to let the small outburst turn into a full-blown sob. Has she been holding this in for a long time? She probably isn't used to failure.

People probably assume she has the perfect life, until they hear about her daughter. Kate hands her the box of tissues again; she takes one.

'I always wanted a daughter . . .' she says. 'I just wish I knew what I could do to make it right.' This often happens, worried parents cracking in situations when someone finally asks them if they are OK.

'She is so talented, Mrs Johnson,' Kate says, trying to give the mother hope. The woman looks up at Kate; her watery eyes blink in surprise.

'Really?' she whispers.

Kate nods. 'And she turned up yesterday, and has agreed to a few extra lessons with me.'

'Has she?' Mrs Johnson sniffs. 'She doesn't tell me anything.'

'She'll come back to you again,' Mrs Wells says. 'Teenage girls always hate their mothers; believe me, I've had two of them, they always come back.' Mrs Wells laughs.

It makes Kate think of her own mother, and how she never got the opportunity to hate her, or to go back to her.

'Another thing . . . it has been reported to me by a teacher that she's been walking around with a black eye,' Mrs Wells adds. Kate looks over at her in surprise. Mrs Wells is the Designated Safeguarding Lead, the person Kate should have reported it to.

Mrs Johnson nods. 'Yes, she told me it was an accident. I don't know what to believe any more.' She sniffs and looks up with a thought. 'Do you think that boy could have something to do with it?'

Mrs Wells shakes her head. 'I don't know, Mrs Johnson, I think it's something we really need to keep an eye on and, if anything else crops up, we may have to escalate it further,' says Mrs Wells. 'It is good you've come in, so we can all be on the same page and have an open line of communication about her. Please feel free to ring me with an update whenever you want.'

Mrs Johnson looks awash with relief as she stands up. 'Thank you,' she says to them both. 'I'm so relieved she is turning up again. Whatever you did, thank you,' she says to Kate, her eyes shining with gratitude.

She looks around for a bin. Kate picks it up from the corner of the room and holds it out to her. Mrs Johnson smiles warmly, throwing the tissue inside.

'I'll walk you out,' says Kate.

The two women walk in silence for a moment. 'You really think she's talented?' Mrs Johnson asks, proud.

'She is, she shouldn't be in bottom set at all. If she applied herself, Lily could be in the top.' Kate checks her reaction, and Mrs Johnson looks thrilled with the comments. Kate takes the opportunity to ask her a more personal question. 'I hope you don't think I'm out of line, but has she ever had therapy?' asks Kate tentatively.

Mrs Johnson fiddles with her handbag strap. 'Yes, she used to. She stopped going, she didn't even tell me! I only realized because the cheques I'd been giving her weren't being used.'

Kate nods, understanding. That kind of therapy never worked for her either. 'Do you think she has addiction issues?'

she asks, trying to keep her tone light. 'She's come in a few times smelling of alcohol and I know you said she sometimes doesn't come home after a night out.'

'What?' Mrs Johnson says. Her head swings over to Kate; her demeanour has changed completely. 'She's sixteen! Everyone experiments at that age,' she spits.

Kate instantly regrets bringing it up. 'Yes, of course, I was just . . .'

'Look, she's got some issues at the moment and has got in with a bad crowd, but she's certainly not an addict.' Mrs Johnson looks cross, as if she's called her daughter a prostitute or something.

'It's nothing to be ashamed of, Mrs Johnson, it's just another mental health issue that can be fixed,' Kate says.

They are standing at the main doors, and Maureen is peering over to see who Kate is talking to. 'I really think you should concentrate on teaching rather than making outlandish accusations about students that could end up going on permanent records. Have a good day, Miss Sullivan,' she says crossly, storming off out to the car park.

Kate watches her huff as she bundles her bag into the passenger seat. She wonders what she would think if she told her that her daughter's teacher was one of them, an alcoholic, a dirty addict. Turning, she walks back into the school. She shouldn't have said anything; it's not Mrs Johnson's fault, the stigma around addiction is so ingrained. It often annoys her that alcoholism is seen as an older person's issue. She's met plenty of teenagers who attend meetings. They are the lucky ones, they've saved themselves years of agony by finding a solution so early.

As she marches back down the corridor, she starts to feel wretched; maybe she's taken this too far. Maybe Lily isn't an addict; just because she turned out to be, doesn't mean Lily is. Maybe she is pushing too much of her own experience onto the girl. Mrs Johnson could be right, she could just be going through a rough patch. Kate wishes she hadn't said anything at all.

Kate has that feeling of dread when a conversation with another person hasn't gone well and that person has walked off thinking bad things about her. She tries to shrug it off, remind herself she can't control what happens in Mrs Johnson's mind. She used to think she could hear what people were thinking about her. If she was drunk, she would imagine the adjectives were pleasant and agreeable, but as soon as she sobered up, they were full of hatred or ambivalence. Clare once said, no wonder you drank, it must have been so much easier to be around other people when you didn't think they all hated you.

She feels tired of everything all of a sudden – of school, of the old friend she's got staying with her, of the fact that she has this painful inner neurosis that other people don't have. It's so unfair. The only thing that gets her through the rest of the day is knowing that Ben is home that evening, and he'll envelop her in one of those all-consuming hugs that will put everything into perspective again.

*

Kate takes her keys out of her bag and walks into the main house. The smell of Ben's aftershave lingers in the hallway, making her stomach flip with excitement because he is home. Smiling, she walks forward. Halfway up the stairs her smile falters as she hears the soft sound of laughter, and then some excited shouting too. She turns her cheek to their door and listens. Ben and Becky are conversing vigorously, there is laughter and even the occasional cheer. Kate stands there a moment, too nervous to interrupt. She shakes her head: stop being stupid, she tells herself. This is her home and her fiancé. She puts her key in the lock and pushes just as another cheer rings through the air.

Ben is on his knees on the floor, his arms are punching towards the ceiling. Becky is standing on the sofa, her arms bent into her sides, her fists clenched, the same look of climax on her face. There is a basketball game on the flat-screen television.

'Hi,' Kate stammers. Becky's hair is a mess, but she looks nicer than she did the other night when she was wearing a faceful of make-up.

Ben gets off the floor. 'Babe!' he shouts. He gestures to the screen. 'I recorded it a few days ago, I know how much you hate basketball. Becky got really into it while she was out there, isn't that cool?'

'Oh my God, I love everything about it! The cheerleaders, the huge hunky men.' She laughs, she is lit up like Oxford Circus at Christmas. 'You guys should go watch the Nets while you're there over the summer.' Becky flops back onto the sofa and stretches out like a cat. She looks very comfortable.

'Kate hates sport,' says Ben.

'Even just for the spectacle, it's really amazing, Kate. Are you going to be in the city much?' She looks at Kate innocently.

Becky seems to have completely changed from the stoic, ghostly figure that Kate's been living with the past week. She is chirpy and happy, a similar demeanour to the cheerleaders that are bouncing around on the television. Something doesn't feel right.

'We might pop into Manhattan for a few nights out and to do some shopping,' Ben says. 'We could definitely check out a game . . . if you want, Kate?'

'Sure,' Kate says shrugging, putting her bag down on the floor.

'Ben was telling me about the party his mum is organizing for you guys at the beach house. It sounds incredible!' Becky says, stretching her arms as she takes herself off the sofa.

'Oh, I don't know, it's all pretty terrifying if you ask me,' says Kate. 'All of his friends and family, most of whom I haven't met, in one place.' She looks at them standing next to each other. They are really good together.

'I bet they love you, you're an English rose, Kate,' Becky says.

'They love her!' Ben says, nodding aggressively, labouring the point, which makes it seem if he's trying to believe it himself. *Stop it, Kate.* She digs her nails into her palm as she tells herself not to listen to that voice in her head.

'So exciting! What are you going to wear?' Becky asks.

Kate bites her lip. She has to buy some new clothes for the

trip, she just hasn't had a chance with everything that's been going on. 'I'm not sure yet, I have a few things in mind.'

Becky claps her hands together. 'Oooh, I can feel a shopping trip coming on!'

Ben nods encouragingly. 'You should! You can take my card, you haven't bought anything new for ages, Kate, and Becky's got great taste.'

The comment burns.

'Yeah, maybe,' she says softly. 'I'm going to go get washed up, I've had a long day.' She doesn't like it in that room, all that energy – she can tell they have been clicking. It makes her feel isolated and alone.

Kate puts her hands flat against the cool tiles as the hot water runs over her. She closes her eyes as she raises her face into the stream of water. She still feels tied up in knots when her feet step onto the mat.

Ben is already in their room when she comes in and closes the door.

'Hey, are you OK?' he asks.

She shores up the knot at the top of her towel. 'Yes. I'm fine.' She walks over to the wardrobe and takes out a trusty pair of jeans and a light-grey cardigan. Then she thinks of Becky downstairs and puts them back and takes out a jersey dress she hasn't worn for a while. It is black with a low neckline, and the shape has always just felt right – she knows she looks effortless in it. She puts on some black underwear and fights it over her head.

'That looks nice,' says Ben, his head cocked to one side. 'You look gorgeous.'

'You think I have good taste, then?' she asks, feeling brave.

He throws himself back on the bed. 'Eurgh, I knew the second I said that you'd be annoyed,' he groans.

'Well, why did you say it? Do you know how demeaning that sounded?' she asks, trying to keep her voice low.

'I'm sorry, I didn't mean it like that. You have great taste,' he says. 'You always look wonderful.'

'You know she used to copy me at school. If I came in with low-waisted jeans one day, guess who had the same ones on Monday. If I decided Dr Martens were cool, guess who had a pair all of a sudden,' she whispers, knowing she sounds crazy.

Ben is laughing. 'You're being mental.'

She lets her arms hang down by her side and takes a breath. 'I'm sorry. It's been a long week.'

He nods and pats the space next to him on the bed and she plonks herself down and curls herself under his arm. 'That's OK, I'm sorry I made you feel inferior to Becky.'

Inferior. To Becky. That's not how he made her feel, he couldn't make her feel like that. She bites the corner of her lip. 'I actually don't know if I want her here any more.'

'What? Every time I've spoken to you this week you've said you were enjoying having her here,' he says. She has barely spoken to him this week, he'd worked late most evenings, and sounded so busy she hadn't wanted to launch into what she was really worrying about.

'She's just really up and down, Ben, it's exhausting being around her,' she says. 'I don't know, I think we are really different people now.' She lowers her voice again.

'Well, I did say, it has been a long time.'

'I'm worried about her.' She pauses. 'There is something just not quite right.'

Ben nods and looks at the door. 'She seems pretty normal to me. Are you sure you're not just being paranoid? You know how you get sometimes.'

The comment hits her in the throat.

'How I get sometimes?' she manages.

He waves his hand in the air. 'Sorry, sorry.' He sighs. 'Look, I never wanted her here in the first place,' he whispers. 'You told her a couple of weeks, right? That will fly by.'

Kate nods slowly, disappointed. She really wanted him to do something that would fix this whole problem for her. He looks over at her and must have noticed that wasn't enough.

'Look, if it's really getting on top of you just let me know and I'll have a word with her, OK?'

'No, you don't have to do that . . .'

He leans forward and kisses her. 'I just want you to be happy, OK? So, if giving Becky the heave-ho will do that, then I'm game.' He gives her that cheeky smile, and Kate's shoulders relax.

She starts to feel better then; there is a solution to the problem if she needs it. Ben's back and he'll make everything OK. And he's hers, no one else's. He's in her corner, not

Becky's. But then the voice creeps in and paints her a picture from memory . . . his eyes running over the shape of Becky's breasts, and his cheeks heating up ever so slightly.

13

The next morning Kate is sitting up in bed, scrolling through her phone, waiting for Ben to bring her a coffee in bed. She is so relieved it is the weekend; she doesn't think she could cope with another day at school. Chewing on her bottom lip, she thinks of Lily's black eye. Kate chose to trust a wayward sixteen-year-old, instead of doing the right thing and reporting it to Mrs Wells. She wanted to get her on side, gain her trust. Was it that bad? It had worked, after all, she came into school and stayed on for an extra session.

A knock on the door ends the line of thought.

'Come in,' she calls.

Becky's face peers round the door. 'Hey.'

'Morning,' Kate says, nervously.

'I haven't had the chance to apologize for the other night.' Becky drums her fingers against the wood; her long, manicured nails tap like metal against the door frame. 'I shouldn't have spoken to you like that. I know you were just trying to help.'

'No, I'm sorry,' Kate says. 'I shouldn't have pushed that on you.'

Becky smiles sweetly, and blinks. 'I seem to be making a habit of these early morning apologies.'

Kate smiles back at her. 'Don't be silly, it's my fault too.' Becky shrugs lightly and turns away. Kate hears her walk steadily down the stairs.

Kate's sweet smile dissipates as she listens to Becky and Ben conversing downstairs. Light patters of laughter float up to where she is sitting. Her teeth grit together in annoyance. She wishes she had never accepted the invitation to dinner, that she'd never invited Becky to stay. She can feel something stirring, a feeling of lacking control, like something is slipping through her fingers.

Kate turns to the framed photograph on her bedside table and picks it up. It is one of her favourites of her and Ben, it's her Facebook profile picture and the screen saver on her phone. She often looks at it in the middle of her day when things get a bit much. It brings her back to the present, and reminds her of everything she has to be grateful for, when everything seems overwhelming. Her expression in the picture is the closest she's come to bliss, her smile is a mile wide and her eyes are gleaming with emotion. It was a moment she barely dared to dream would happen to her. The day Ben proposed. People say a man can't fix you, and there is no such thing as a knight in shining armour. And the feminist in Kate agrees, but like any girl with daddy issues, secretly, she had always hoped a dashing young man would appear who would make everything OK. And he did.

A calm smile finds her lips as she lets out a relieved

sigh. She's being stupid, her mind is just feeling around for something to worry about, the way that it does when she's overloaded herself. Clare was right when she said she'd taken too much on, this is just a blip. Soon Becky will have moved out, the exams will be over, and she'll be wearing her wedding ring. She'll look back at these few weeks and laugh at herself over what a palaver she's made of everything.

She settles the picture back down as Ben returns with a mug of coffee; he places it next to her and kisses her forehead. His hair flops in his face and he pushes it back with one hand. He looks easy, calm, and happy.

'Here you go, light of my life,' he says, laughing. 'Would Madame like anything else?'

'Shhh . . . too much talking.' There is a running joke about her daily morning malaise.

Kate often thinks what it must be like to be someone like Ben. To find life so easy, to be so self-assured and able to unhook himself from any fear thrown his way. He begins to organize his clean shirts from the dry-cleaners and put them away, in colour order. As he hangs one up, the old grey T-shirt he is wearing allows a flash of his muscular side. She wonders if Becky admired him like that, as they chatted downstairs.

'Becky just came in here and apologized.' She lowers her voice to a conspiratorial whisper.

He shrugs. 'Maybe she was out of line, it is intense living with other people, babe. Don't give yourself a hard time.' He walks over and moves a strand of hair from her face. Kate tries to keep a frown from forming; why would she give herself a hard time? She can't help feeling that Ben is siding with Becky, rather than her.

'What do you want to do this morning? Becky is going for a run in Victoria Park. She asked if we wanted to go. I could do with stretching my legs.'

She can tell he wants to go. Kate imagines them running together, their pace in sync. Becky will do some stretches against a low wall and tell a funny story about something to do with New York that Kate wouldn't understand. She puts her hand on the side of her face: *stop it*, she thinks.

Looking over at the clock, she says, 'Jonny's coming soon, I want to have a bath and start cooking some brunch. You guys go.'

'Are you sure? I can stay and help.'

'No, you should go,' she insists.

Kate watches him change into his exercise gear. She feels as if she needs to let him go to prove to herself that she isn't some sort of paranoid, untrusting girlfriend. He runs downstairs and after a short lull the front door slams. She pulls the sheets back and stands up, groaning. 'Stop being such a grump,' she tells herself in the mirror. Kate needs to remember she's helping Becky because she wants to do something nice for someone she owes it to. And anyway, Becky's just a house guest, why does Kate need to overcomplicate everything? Her behaviour is letting her down, she needs to stop reading into every little thing and making wild assumptions. Her head is hard-wired to search constantly for negative outcomes. It creates problems that don't exist, so she fiddles with things until she breaks them anyway. She needs to go to a meeting tonight and share about this before it starts taking root in her mind. If she talks about her thought process, the power of it will evaporate, she is sure of it.

Kate walks to the bathroom naked, enjoying the freedom of an empty house. She takes her time in the shower, trying to stay present and ignore the images in her head of the perfect couple jogging in unison around the park. Just as she's getting the food out of the fridge the doorbell goes. Jonny is early. How annoying, he's always early.

Opening the door, she tries to mimic her father's warm smile. He looks dishevelled and dusty, as if he's just come off a building site.

'Come in, Jonny,' she says, turning back up the stairs, not allowing any time for a hug or a kiss hello.

'All right, darlin'?' he asks as he brushes his shoes against the doormat. 'Want me to take these off?' he asks when they get to the top. She looks down at his torn and blemished workman's boots and nods.

'Sure.' She watches him bend over and untie his laces. 'How's the trip going?'

'Not sure yet. Going to Billy's after this, he says he's got all the timber I need. But you know what he's like.'

Kate walks into the kitchen and puts the kettle on. Jonny will want coffee, a really strong one with three sugars. He stands awkwardly at the kitchen counter as she makes his drink.

'How is the house going?' she asks, without looking up.

He nods. 'Well, still very much at the taking everything apart stage, but we'll get there.' There is a pause. 'Are you going to come to see it, Kate?'

The kettle clicks and she pours hot water into a mug. The thought of going to Margate, with all the memories she has there . . . 'Yes, Jonny, I said I would, didn't I?' Her tone is defensive, she wishes she could take it back. 'I've just got so much on at the moment,' she says, her manner more measured and relaxed.

Jonny nods sadly. 'I understand.' He looks around the apartment. 'The flat is looking nice, anything need fixing?' he asks. His hands are moving around, as if they need a purpose. Kate's eyes rest on a few posters she's had framed that need hanging.

'Would you mind hanging those? Next to each other above that sofa?'

Jonny jumps up willingly. 'I'll go get my things out the van.' He rubs his hands together, eager to start.

As she prepares the food Kate watches Jonny measure and carefully pencil each spot before drilling and hammering in wall plugs. For a man in his sixties he is agile. She wonders what he'll do when his body will no longer allow him to do what he loves. The thought makes her sad. He looks over and catches her staring. He gives her a smile. She turns and continues to whisk the eggs.

All she wants to do is walk over and hug him, to get lost behind his shield-like embrace. But there is this invisible thing that stops them from being able to get close to one another. Like opposing magnets forcing them away. That thing that happened, long ago, which lies discarded in a crevasse, unaddressed. Something that hurts so much, she hasn't even told her sponsor, the person she is meant to offload everything onto. It's like she put a map pin in it and stuck it way up high, so she never has to go there. No one knows she hasn't really completed her steps, that she's fudged them, she did only the work she wanted to do. Not the work she needed to do.

The front door opens just as she is easing the scrambled eggs out from the saucepan with a wooden spoon. She looks up at them, both red and sweaty, as if they've just had hot, vigorous sex. She shakes the mental image out of her head.

'Perfect timing!' she says. 'Food's ready.'

'Great, I'm starving!' Ben says, eyeing up the spread.

'Me too!' Becky has her arm pulled up behind her head, stretching.

Behind them, Jonny jumps off the chair he's been using as a ladder and dusts his hands against themselves. 'Hi there,' he says, self-consciously.

They turn to see him awkwardly standing there. 'Mr Sullivan!' Ben says, walking over and shaking his hand robustly. Kate takes a deep breath and grinds the back of her teeth. 'It's great to see you.'

Jonny nods. 'And you,' he says, unable to match Ben's enthusiasm.

'Jonny!' shouts Becky. 'It's so good to see you, you haven't changed a bit.'

'Hello, Becky, that's very nice of you.' He pats her back as she throws her arms around him. She used to come to their house sometimes too, though less frequently and usually only when Kate needed a bit of cash from Jonny.

'Kate said you are doing up a place in Margate. Sounds incredible,' Becky says.

'Well, hopefully it will be.' Jonny is nervous; he finds it difficult when attention is focused on him. He turns back to the pictures he's just hung and starts to adjust them, even though they don't need adjusting at all.

Becky continues, 'I bet you can't wait for the wedding?'

Kate's head turns. *Fuck.*

Jonny doesn't say anything. He starts to put his tools back in their box. 'Well, you see, Becky, we're just planning on pulling some witnesses off the street,' Kate says. 'It's really just a bit of admin.'

Becky looks over at Ben, and then at her. 'Oh right, so Jonny isn't going to be there?' she asks, confused.

Kate can't see Jonny's face but knows it will be wrinkled with sadness. She clenches her teeth. It's his own fault, don't feel sorry for him, she thinks.

'I'd better be off,' he says. 'Billy is waiting for me.' He grabs his bag of tools and starts to tie his laces by the door.

'But I made food,' says Kate.

'I'm sure you lot can polish that off,' he says. 'Bye, have fun!' And he is out of the door in an instant. Kate sighs, she is relieved. Which makes her feel guilty.

'Is he all right?' asks Becky, turning to Kate, confused.

'Yeah, he's got a lot to do today.'

'You know, we could invite him, Kate – he seemed really put out,' Ben says. He looks concerned.

Kate is irritated Becky brought it up. 'But then your parents might be annoyed they weren't there too.'

Ben shrugs. 'Not if we say it was a last-minute thing.'

'Yeah, maybe.' Kate nods, hoping it will be forgotten.

'Oh great, he hung those pictures.' Ben looks up at Jonny's handiwork.

'Right, come on, let's eat!' Kate shouts, changing the subject.

'I'm just going to change my top.' He wipes his wet face on the front of his T-shirt and leaves the room without looking at her. She bites her lip, he's annoyed.

Becky walks over to the kitchen. Kate is counting out cutlery. 'Is something going on with your dad, Kate?'

Kate shakes her head. 'No, what do you mean?' she asks, feigning innocence.

'I don't know, you and your dad always used to get on, I thought.'

'We do,' says Kate, annoyed to be questioned over it.

'Then why isn't he coming to the wedding?' Becky asks.

Kate feels het up. 'Look, Becky,' she says, turning. 'I'm really happy you are back, but honestly a lot has happened since we last saw each other. And maybe you need to respect my boundaries, OK?'

Becky looks at her strangely. 'OK. I'm sorry.'

She feels awful that she snapped. 'No, sorry. I shouldn't have . . . I'll tell you about it another time.'

169

Becky watches her. 'Only if you want to,' she replies. Kate wonders if she would ever confide in Becky about this.

A few minutes later Ben comes bounding down the stairs, his hair wet from the shower. He takes a plate from the pile and starts to help himself to food. 'After this, want me to look at that computer problem, Beck?' he asks.

Becky smiles sweetly at him. 'That would be amazing, if you wouldn't mind, Ben.'

They sit next to each other and start to eat. Kate watches them, feeling anxious. She wishes Jonny had never come. All he's done is make her feel guilty and ashamed. And now Ben thinks she's mean, and he doesn't understand why. She feels out of place, in her own home. It shouldn't be her; it should be Becky who feels like the gooseberry. Kate puts a forkful of food in her mouth and chews; all at once she is filled with jealousy. Becky, the girl who has everything: the family, the money, the ease with which she's found herself a new job, her beautiful face and perfect hair, the way she can just slot herself into any situation and easily become part of the furniture without even trying. She doesn't have to go to AA meetings just so she can be 'normal'. *Stop it*, Kate tells herself again.

The silence starts to become uncomfortable. Ben looks up from his meal and then between the two girls.

'Hey . . . did that girl turn up?' he asks Kate, looking pleased he's found a new talking point.

'What?'

'That girl, the one from school you were worried about?'

'Oh. Yes,' Kate says. 'And she's agreed to come for some extra tuition before the exam next week.'

'See, I told you,' Ben says, popping a piece of bacon into his mouth. 'Kate gets far too stressed about these exams, it's almost like she's got to take them.'

'It is not,' she says stubbornly.

He throws his napkin down and walks over to her. 'You're so clever,' he whispers in her ear. Kate's eyes drift over to where Becky is sitting, concentrating hard on her plate of food, as if she is the spare part. This pleases Kate, which then makes her cringe. This isn't her; she isn't jealous, she isn't paranoid. These are all old behaviours that have come back to haunt her because she hasn't been looking after herself enough. She really needs to go to a meeting. She really needs to talk about what she's putting herself through.

'We should celebrate tonight!' Ben says.

'Get a takeaway?' Kate suggests.

Becky looks up. 'Let's go into town!' she suggests, an excited smile on her face.

'Yes!' shouts Ben. 'Let's properly celebrate. I'll get us a table somewhere in Soho.'

'I don't know, guys . . .' Kate starts.

'You're not allowed to say you have loads of marking to do,' Ben says. 'We can get dressed up. I'm going to treat us.'

'I don't know . . .' Kate tries to think of a reason. The thought of a whole night trapped with the two of them makes her feel anxious.

'Kate! Come on! Remember when we used to drop everything for a night out . . .' Becky is eager.

Kate stands there, looking at both their faces. She doesn't want to be a party pooper. 'OK, let's do it,' she agrees. Ben whips out his phone and starts looking at restaurant options, Becky shouts over some tips she's been given since she's been back. Kate nods along agreeably with the possibilities, pretending to be excited, pretending to look forward to the evening ahead. Then she remembers that she was going to go to a meeting tonight. She'll have to go tomorrow instead. One night won't make a difference.

14

They stand outside the front door checking each number plate that passes, waiting for their taxi to arrive. Kate feels exhausted by the events of the afternoon. Her mind has remained in overdrive, trying to second-guess each comment, each hand Becky put on Ben's arm. The two of them shared a bottle of wine while they all got ready, now they're giggling together over a stupid story Becky is telling about a cab ride in Manhattan where she forgot her wallet. The story isn't funny, but Ben is laughing as if it is. Kate is trying her best to join in, she mimics their facial expressions and copies the noises they are making. She hasn't done this for a long time: had to act in a way that is different to how she is feeling. It brings on the worst kind of nostalgia.

She's frustrated by the situation and herself. Why doesn't she want to go out? What's there not to want, a night out at a posh restaurant with your fiancé and old friend who seem to be getting on really well? *Too well.* Kate shakes the creeping thought out of her head, *stop it.* She should be having a lovely time, why isn't she having a lovely time? She presses her nails into the palms of her hands in exasperation as she pretends to laugh along with the others.

Clare's voice rings inside her head, singing 'comparing is despairing' at her as she watches Becky in full swing. She looks stylish, her eyes are smoky, and her outfit is boxy, simple and sexy. Kate feels overdone with her bright-red lipstick and the short dress Ben wanted her to wear. She feels like a teenager and Becky looks like a woman.

They arrive in the centre of buzzy Soho and Ben and Becky charge out of the car, leaving Kate to lift herself out. She pulls her short skirt down awkwardly and thanks the driver. She watches them rush ahead, conversation flowing, their heads tilting back as they laugh. Becky touches Ben's arm as she giggles. It is so overtly flirtatious that it makes Kate feel sick. What the hell does Becky think she is doing? Kate's steps quicken. They haven't even checked that she's following. Kate's eyes narrow as she watches Becky grab Ben's wrist and scream, 'No! That's hilarious!' in his face as he tells her something. He looks at her nods; his eyes shine admiringly.

Becky and Ben are about the same height; their long legs and excited chatter have escalated their pace. Kate has to walk in a near jog to keep up. They weave in and around clusters of people, tourists with maps, the queues outside gay clubs, couples on dates holding hands. That's what Ben and Becky look like, the voice says, they look like they've hit it off on a first date. *Look at them, he is having a better time with her than he has with you.* Stop it, stop it, stop it, she whispers, wanting to scream.

*

At dinner, Kate's smile is plastered uncomfortably on her face. She is nodding eagerly and laughing where she's meant to. But all she can really concentrate on is the image of Becky's hand on Ben's arm, and the way they finish each other's sentences. She feels utterly miserable and confused. And the worst thing is she can't work out if she's being ridiculous, or if a line has been crossed somewhere.

'I bet you were in the best fraternity at college,' Becky says, poking him.

Ben holds his hands up. 'Well, my dad did pay for the library,' he laughs, pulling a face.

'Shut up, he did not!'

'Well, only part of it,' he says modestly.

'Gross, I bet you were the top dog there.' She narrows her eyes, 'I can imagine what you guys got up to,' her mouth turning in mock disgust.

'They probably played beer pong and video games.' Kate knows what a geek Ben can be.

'Kate, you are far too innocent nowadays,' Becky sings. 'Those guys do so much gross stuff to each other.' She turns back to Ben. 'I hate to think how much piss you've drunk. Have you ever docked another guy?' She leans in.

'Hey, I'm not like that . . .' He laughs.

'Becky, Ben is such a loser, I bet he never missed a class for a night out.'

'Oh, come on . . .' Becky darts back at Ben, a playful smile on her face. 'I can tell you used to be a bad boy back then.

What about girls? You must have a pretty impressive number if you used to head up an Ivy League fraternity.'

'Hey! I never said I headed one up. Come on, let's change the subject.' He's started looking around, removing himself from the intense bubble of conversation. 'I want to hear all about Kate as a teenager.'

'Oh God, no.' Kate puts her head in her hands and then looks back up at Becky; please don't, her eyes plead.

'Kate was . . .' Becky starts, lifting her wine glass in thought. 'Kate was the naughtiest girl in school. Hanging out with Kate was like going on safari with the roof down. It was exhilarating and exciting. But . . .'

'Becky . . . please . . .' Kate says, her heart thudding.

Becky's smile fades and she looks over at Kate, who watches nervously. 'Kate was her own worst enemy, and she got us in trouble more times than I can remember . . . certainly more times than she can,' she says. Is that a dig? Kate can't work it out.

She looks at Becky questioningly; there is something eerie about her manner. And then the moment is lost.

'Would you like to see the dessert menu?' the waiter asks.

'Yes, why not, we'll have a look,' replies Ben.

'I'm going to pop to the ladies.' Becky gets up, taking her bag with her.

'Are you OK?' Ben asks Kate once they are alone. 'It's nice here, isn't it?'

Kate looks around, it is really nice here. What people who've never had any sort of mental health issue just don't get is that she could be in the most wonderful place: the best restaurant in the world, the most glamorous hotel. She could be looking at the view from the tallest building or floating in the Mediterranean on a yacht. But that doesn't mean she isn't herself, trapped, listening to her head telling her lies.

'Yeah, it's lovely,' she whispers.

'Becky's on good form. I think you probably were being sensitive the other night, babe,' he tells her. Kate nods in agreement, hoping her faint smile doesn't give her away.

'Hey!' Becky is back, she plops into her seat and looks down at the dessert menu the waiter has left, before tossing it aside. 'You know there's a dive bar in the basement, don't you?' she says, leaning her elbow into the table, her face gently resting in her hand.

'I never knew that,' says Ben.

'Well, you are the tourist,' Becky teases. 'Shall we go?' She looks over at Kate. 'You want to get home, don't you?' She gives her a sympathetic look.

'No! Not at all, let's definitely go check it out,' Kate says, nodding furiously, wishing she could run away.

They step back out into the hustle and bustle. Soho is alive with after-show crowds. Laughter and shouts reverberate against the starless black sky. They loop around the pavement and descend the wrought-iron steps into the basement. Kate's teeth press together in annoyance as Becky trips and falls into Ben's back, laughing. Ben laughs too and helps her to her feet.

They are more than tipsy now. Kate hasn't seen Ben this drunk for a while. Maybe he's been craving this night out, she thinks, maybe he's been holding back for her sake. Maybe he's been missing these crazy, drunk, spontaneous nights that he doesn't get with her. She sighs and wishes there was a button she could press that would stop her mind thinking of anything at all. She thinks about what Clare would say, she'd tell her just to go home, she doesn't have to prove anything to anyone. But Kate wants to stay, she wants to show them she can be fun too, Becky isn't the only one.

It is a shock to enter the basement bar after the sophisticated tone of the restaurant above. Music is banging, people's arms are in the air, their bodies gleam with sweat, they are shouting into each other's ears to talk. As soon as the door closes behind her, Kate feels trapped.

'I'll get a round in,' Becky shouts. She scans the room and points. 'It looks like they're leaving, why don't you grab that table while I'm at the bar.'

Ben takes Kate's hand and pulls her across the room. They hover and pounce as soon as the space becomes available. Kate slides into the booth and places her clutch on the table. She stares out into the crowd, refusing to look at him, she is too annoyed. But how can she be annoyed with him for having a good time? Is this just her disease? Angry that they get to drink when she can't? Is she actually angry that Becky's getting all the attention? Her mind rushes through the possibilities . . . her defects of character are running wild on this night out: jealousy, ego, fear, resentment . . . they're having their own party in her head while everyone else is having a good time.

'Hey, are you OK?' Ben asks, putting his hand on her leg, touching her for the first time since they got out of the taxi.

'Yes, of course.' She starts swaying to the music and mouthing the words as if she is just as lost in the music as everyone else.

Becky approaches the table with three drinks between splayed fingers. She looks around, excited. 'I'm glad some things don't change.' She puts the drinks on the table. 'I got you a virgin mojito, he seemed offended when I asked for water. Yours is the one with two pieces of lime,' Becky tells her.

'This is such a good find!' says Ben, shouting over the music.

'Wonderful, isn't it? I found it just before I moved to the States. I was working round the corner, and we used to come here if after-work drinks got out of hand.'

For a moment the music stalls, then an intro they all know whips the small but invested crowd into an excited hysteria.

Ben's leg starts to jiggle. 'Ah man, this reminds me of school.' He pulls at Kate's hand. 'Come on, I wanna dance.'

Kate looks over at the crowd. She's had some of her best nights out sober and dancing. That feeling of freedom when you lose your inhibitions and you're not thinking about how much drink you've got left, or how long the queue is at the bar, or the fact you need the loo again because you've drunk so much liquid you need to pee every ten minutes. When you don't have all that to think about, you can just dance joyfully, and after a little while, you feel drunk and giggly too. But Kate knows tonight won't be like that. She's too involved in the commentary in her head about Ben and

Becky. She'll never be one of those people over there losing themselves to the music.

'I really don't feel like it,' she says. 'I'm fine here.' She nods her head to the music again to show she's content.

Becky jumps out of her seat. 'I'll dance!' she cries. 'Come on, you Yank, let me show you how it's done.'

Ben looks at Kate to check that's OK. Kate nods profusely and watches them run into the crowd like excited teenagers who've just had their curfew waived. Kate takes a deep breath; she spreads her hands on her knees. *Come on, Kate, this is just your illness, making you sabotage your night, making you think crazy thoughts to push people away so that you're alone and vulnerable. And then it's got you right where it wants you.*

She looks down at the three drinks in front of her. What did Becky say? Two limes or two straws? There is an option for both.

Kate picks one of them up; she'd usually ask Ben to take a sip to check. But he's across the room, with Becky. *It must be this one, they usually put two straws in the non-alcoholic one.* She picks it up and raises it to her lips. She takes a straw between her teeth, her lips fasten themselves around it, and she sucks. It stings her tongue, and she swallows. She knows immediately it is the wrong one. She feels the familiar relax of her shoulders, like the first gasp of breath after holding it in for so long. She doesn't move from her spot, she doesn't unpress her lips. She stares over at Becky and Ben jumping around shouting words to a song into each other's faces. Ben's hand is on Becky's shoulder and he's saying something to her. His

180

lips are practically touching her ear. Becky stands back and hits his arm in jest and then, laughing, they return to jumping around. Ben looks as if he's having the time of his life.

Both Kate's hands are clasped around the cold glass. Put it down, she tells herself. It was an accident, you made a mistake, if you take another one you will have knowingly drunk. It will be classed as a relapse, all that time, six years, will be gone in a swig.

She can't stop watching them dance. Lights flash against them in short bursts so moment to moment they are lost to the darkness. It is jarring, as if they are one of those flipbooks she used to make as a child: Becky's arms around Ben's shoulders, Ben taking her by the hand, Becky twirling, laughing uncontrollably. It all comes in short, sharp surges of pain. Then her head is on his shoulder, his eyes are closed, she looks up at him and smiles, his eyes flutter open and he smiles down at her too. Kate realizes – in a flash of what feels like clarity – that Becky is actually *trying* to steal Ben from her. She is attempting to seduce him right in front of Kate's face. The glass shakes in her hand.

Kate takes another sip. For a moment she doesn't care about anything, all she cares about is that drink in her hand. She takes another, and another. This is going to fix her, it will stop the constant babble, it will take her away from this awful place, thinking these awful thoughts. It will stop her hating herself, and everyone around her. She takes another sip, and another.

Suddenly, the good voice inside pips in, forcefully pushing

181

past the one goading her. She looks down at the drink and realizes what's she's done. The pooling alcohol swirls around in her stomach; it feels rotten as it churns against her pristine guts. She puts her hand over her mouth and tries not to retch. She stands up quickly, eyes searching for the toilets, bashing against bodies as she runs. She knocks her shoulder into the door and falls into an empty cubicle, the wet tiled floor hard against her bare knees. She sticks her fingers down her throat and gags; vomit rushes out as if it were desperate for an escape route.

'Kate? Kate!' She hears her name being called.

She retches again. A lone, hot tear cascades down her face.

'Kate, are you OK?' There is a knock at the door.

'Yes,' she calls back feebly, wiping her face as she looks down into the toilet bowl, a view she hasn't seen for the longest time.

'Can I get you some water? Was it something you ate?' calls Becky. 'Oh God, you're not pregnant, are you?' She laughs.

Kate scrambles to her feet and opens the door. 'I drank some of the wrong drink,' she says, wiping her mouth with the back of her hand.

Becky's hand goes to her mouth. 'Oh God! ... oh my God, Kate, I'm so sorry.' She looks genuinely upset. 'Are you OK?' She puts her arm around her, and Kate wants to push her away.

'I want to go home.'

The words come out with such force Becky is taken aback. 'Yes, of course. I'm sorry, we should never have come,' Becky stammers.

'Why?' Kate turns and shouts, 'I can come to a fucking bar.'

'I know, I didn't mean . . .' Becky starts, and then gives up. 'Come on, let's go home.'

She gently steers Kate out of the toilets as if she is damaged, and Kate wants to shake her off. This isn't who she is any more, she doesn't need looking after. She feels a sense of déjà vu, as if they've done this many times before. And then she realizes, they have. She looks up at Becky, there is a look on her face Kate cannot decipher. Is it pity, or is it guilt? She can't help thinking that Becky reappearing has begun to erode everything she's worked so hard for.

15

Kate sits between Ben and Becky in the taxi, looking straight ahead. They are staring out of their respective windows, silently watching the streets roll past. The journey is the opposite of the ride out, where they were each eagerly waiting for the other to stop talking so they could speak. Kate wonders what everyone is thinking, which is a well-trodden but pointless process. You can never know that; everyone's motivations are completely different. And for the first time, Kate really feels as if she has no idea what everyone is aiming for.

She looks over at Ben; his lips are parted slightly, his jaw clenches and the shape of his profile changes. He takes his glasses off and rubs the part of his nose between his eyes and then places them back and blinks a few times. She puts her hand on his knee to test his reaction. He looks down at it and then up at her. He gives her a tired smile and puts his hand on top of hers. She is relieved.

Once back at the house the girls take off their heels so as not to irritate the downstairs landlord and creep up the stairs into the flat. Kate looks at the clock in the kitchen; it is past midnight. Before, there would be birds tweeting as they exited an all-night rave. Or cocaine nights that turned into days. But in the last few months of her drinking Kate barely socialized, it became too exhausting to monitor herself around others while she was drunk. It was easier to remove herself from an occasion at about ten-thirty, just before she tipped over the edge of sanity. And besides, then she still had time to go to the off-licence before it closed, and she could drink to her heart's content in the privacy of her bedroom. She would wake up fully dressed, a scattering of empty bottles on the floor and an ashtray full of cigarette butts by the windowsill. Her mouth would taste rotten. She would look down at her phone as if it was a smoking gun, terrified of whom she might have contacted and flirted with or ranted at.

One of the gifts of sobriety is never waking up with that dread. The feeling that someone else has taken your life and drawn all over it like a toddler with a big fat red marker pen. It was like being on a treadmill: getting drunk, doing something awful, then drinking to get over the shame. She was stuck in some sort of sickening loop, trying to blot out everything and everyone. But most of all herself.

Becky is filling a glass of water at the sink. 'I would suggest a nightcap, but I think that would be a bad idea.'

Ben looks over at Kate. He has a look of deep concern on his face. She hasn't seen him look at her like that for a long time. Not since he nursed her back from the brink when they first met and he encouraged her to go back to her meetings again. Clare says it probably wasn't him, that she was just ready to come back, and he was just there saying all the right things. But Kate knows she was meant to be standing on the bridge that day, because that's how she met Ben, and he is what she gets for staying sober.

Just as the thought processes, she swallows. *I drank*, she thinks.

'Yeah, I think we've had enough.' He rubs the back of his neck.

Kate looks over at Becky; her make-up is slightly awry from the heat of club, her hair is ruffled, she looks like a hot mess. Her long, sweaty neck rises to the ceiling as she gulps a pint of water down. The tap is still running and she refills the glass to start swallowing again. Kate would never do that when she drank, she would never know how to end the night tipsy, she wouldn't be able to get into bed after washing her face and drinking two pints of water. She only knew how to drink to oblivion.

Becky walks over to the stairs and pauses. 'Night, then.'

'Night, great dancing,' Ben adds.

'Told you I'd teach you a thing or two,' Becky jokes.

'Night,' Kate says softly.

'Night, K,' Becky says, sort of sadly, before proceeding to walk up the stairs.

They stand in silence until they hear the door to her room close. Ben turns to her. 'God, Kate, you drank?' he says in disbelief.

'No . . . Ben, not really, I just had a bit.'

'Enough to make you throw up,' he reproaches.

'Honestly, it was just my body reacting to it . . . I . . . I . . . I didn't mean to. It's not a big deal, it's not a relapse or anything,' she says, knowing that's not true.

He looks relieved. 'Kate, I'm worried about you.'

'You honestly don't have to worry; it was an accident,' she repeats. 'It was nothing.'

'You were acting weird tonight, you didn't seem like you were having much fun,' he says gently.

'I had a great night,' she says defensively. 'I told you, it was an accident, I didn't mean to drink it,' annoyed that he thought she didn't have a good time, when she had tried so hard to pretend that she was enjoying herself.

'OK . . . well . . . It just seems like you're not really here, that your head isn't in the room at all.'

Kate can feel anger rising within her, she can't contain it. How dare he see through her, how dare he manage to articulate exactly what she is trying to hide? 'It's your fault,' she bursts out.

'What?' he asks, spluttering.

'I was watching you and Becky dancing, it wound me up,' she says, checking his face for signs of culpability.

'What? You were jealous?'

'It was like I wasn't even there most of the night,' she says, and there is a needy quality to her voice she hadn't intended.

'Are you kidding?' He looks at her in disbelief. His mouth has turned up in a slight snarl which makes her feel as if she's got this all wrong.

'I'm sorry . . .' She pauses, putting her hand on her face. She looks up at him. 'You just looked like you were having such a good time . . . a better time than you ever have with me.' *Unattractive, needy, pathetic. Stop it, Kate.*

'Shit, Kate, I mean . . .' He moves towards her and holds onto her arms as if he wants to pull her close, but she resists. 'What do I have to do to prove that I love you?'

She relents and allows him to hold her tight.

'I told you, didn't I, the first night we spent together. That you can trust me, that I never want you to feel any sort of pain ever again.' He kisses the top of her head. 'That night on the bridge . . . Kate, I want to protect you from everything.'

'I'm sorry . . .' she says, allowing him to hold her. 'I think I'm going a bit crazy . . . everything that's going on . . .'

He pulls her tightly into him, and she wants to press her face into his chest so hard that she is smothered. 'We should never have gone out tonight, it wasn't very good timing, was it? Your exams are next week and we've barely had time to talk about the wedding,' he says gently.

'You don't have to make excuses for me,' she says, upset.

He holds her tighter. 'Yes, I do, and I will for the rest of my life,' he laughs.

She lets a laugh escape too. 'Let's go to bed. Can we forget about all this? Pretend I never said all that? I'm being stupid.'

'Don't worry, babe, I've got your back.' He kisses the top of her head again.

Kate takes off her make-up, slowly caressing her face with a puff of cotton wool. The mirror is directly in front of their bed, so through it she can see him propped up against the headboard. He is reading, but he hasn't turned a page for a long time.

She slips in next to him and he envelops her, kissing her lips.

'I love you,' he says. 'I never want you to ever feel shit . . .'

'I'm fine,' she lies. 'I'm sorry for acting like this. I love you too,' she tells him, enjoying the intoxicating smell of wine on his breath.

She must have fallen asleep without much effort because she can't remember any frustration. Opening her eyes, she fully expects it to be light outside, but the room is lit only by the moon. Kate presses her phone on the bedside table; it is 3 a.m. She turns over, assuming she'll see the mound of Ben's body with the duvet tucked over. The bed is flat where he should be. She feels the fabric with her hand and then sits up.

A creak turns her head towards the door. It is unlike him to get up in the night, but he did drink a lot, he must be in the bathroom. Her eyes narrow as she listens; she thinks she can hear whispering. Her chest tightens and she stands, wobbling at first. Walking towards the door, she places her ear on the wood to listen. She can hear soft murmurings; an intense exchange is taking place. Her heart is thudding in her ears. It doesn't sound like the light-hearted conversation of two people caught on the landing together during a bathroom trip in the middle of the night. It sounds invested, it sounds urgent and fervid.

Suddenly creaking starts again, footsteps are coming back

towards the room. She walks backwards; tripping back onto the bed, she lets herself fall into it and wraps the duvet around herself, squeezing her eyes shut. The door is opened quietly, and Ben tiptoes around to his side of the bed, climbing in next to her, trying not to let the bed bounce. She hears him sigh.

A tear rolls down her cheek, and she squishes her face on the pillow to blot it away. What were they doing out there? Were they kissing? Her stomach turns at the prospect. *You're being paranoid*, she tells herself, *Ben would never do that to you*. But all Kate can think about is a night out she and Becky had when they were fifteen. There was a house party at Rachel's, a girl they went to school with. Her parents were away, so she had what they called back then a 'free yard'. Becky fancied Rachel's brother, so was desperate to go. Kate had yawned at the thought of the gathering; she was more interested in partying with the boys from the sixth-form college up the road. She never totally committed to going, and Becky would never go on her own. When the day finally came around, there was nothing better on offer, so Kate agreed. Becky was thrilled and made a big thing of getting ready, stealing a bottle of her mother's rosé. They had danced to Kiss FM and Kate helped Becky choose an outfit to wear.

Kate had met Rachel's brother before; he was nothing special, a sweet-looking geek. She'd never thought of him like that. She had vodka in her bag in a plastic Evian bottle, and was drinking heavily from it before they left. She was nervous about the other girls who would be there, the ones who called her a slut behind her back. By the time they arrived she was more than tipsy. The thronging room was full of half-dressed teenagers gyrating against one another. Kate saw Becky make a beeline for the end of the room where Rachel's brother was sitting. She saw the desperation in her friend's eyes to be near him, and something clicked. Kate wanted to be the one he wanted.

Kate slept with Rachel's brother that night. When she woke up, shame rolled over her and she felt sick. She didn't even fancy him. She'd taken it too far. She got the bus straight to Belsize Park, and Becky answered the door, furious. Kate cried dramatically, she said sorry and sorry some more. Those kind of *sorry*s are the worst, the ones in active addiction. Because she'd say the word over and over again, but really, she had no idea how to honour it.

The memory of the anger on Becky's face is all she can think about as she lies in bed. Has Becky really forgiven her? Has she really put those years behind her like she said? Or has she come here to take some sort of revenge and stop Kate from getting the happy ending that she has worked so hard for by stealing the only man she has ever truly loved?

'Wow, an early-morning phone call,' Clare jokes. 'This must be important.'

'I'm still grumpy, so don't take the piss,' Kate says, pulling her cardigan around herself further. It's Sunday morning, and she offered to get everyone croissants as an excuse to get out the house. Really, she wanted to call her sponsor.

'Ha. OK, shoot,' Clare says, as a baby cries in the background.

'Is this a good time?'

'Hang on one sec.' Kate hears shhhhing and the crying slowly comes to an end. 'OK, what's up?'

'I think Ben is having an affair with Becky,' she says firmly.

Clare snorts. 'Are you serious?'

'Yes,' Kate says confidently.

'Perfect, wonderful Ben is shagging your old friend who has recently moved in with you?'

'I mean . . . I don't know if they're shagging . . . yet.' Now she has said it out loud, it sounds quite far-fetched.

'Right, have they had much opportunity to conduct this affair? Is Ben still working in Scotland?'

'They are always laughing at whatever each other says,' Kate tells her. 'They get on so well.' She is running out of steam. 'I heard them talking last night, on the landing.'

'Kate, love, this sounds like you are really searching for something to worry about. Have you talked to Ben about how you're feeling?' Clare asks, concerned.

'Yes. We had a bit of a fight about it,' Kate says quietly, her march slowing down to a stop on the pavement.

'It can be a shock having people from our past lives come back. We aren't the only ones who change,' Clare says kindly.

Kate feels relief surge through her: none of it is actually true. It's just her head playing games with her. 'Oh God, I need to go to a meeting. I'm fucking nuts,' she says to the only person who truly understands.

'Quite possibly,' Clare confirms.

'I'd made up this whole notion about how Becky hadn't

192

really forgiven me for everything and was trying to get revenge for everything I put her through when we were younger or something,' she laughs.

Clare laughs with her. 'Right so, to get back at you for kissing some boys she fancied when you were teenagers, she's trying to steal your fiancé? This is an excellent plot, Kate. Go to a meeting tonight, you'll feel better. And come over and see the baby! He misses you and your crazy ways,' she adds.

'I will . . . and thank you,' Kate says tenderly.

'Always here,' Clare says as she hangs up the phone.

It is only after Kate's been to the bakery and is walking back down their road that she realizes she didn't tell Clare about the alcoholic cocktail. Kate bites her lip and considers calling her back. Maybe she doesn't have to tell her, maybe she can pretend to herself that it wasn't a proper relapse, she didn't get drunk, she threw it all up. Maybe it doesn't count and she can still hang onto her six years. To anyone else that would make sense. But to her, and anyone who sits on one of those plastic chairs in a damp church basement, those small slips are where the rot sets in, and then it's only a matter of time before the whole ceiling comes crashing down.

16

Kate is one of the first to enter the echoing halls of Felix Road Academy on Monday morning. Her shoes click loudly against the floor, and the lock of her classroom door pops like a knuckle. Being inside an empty school is like being in a theme park before it opens, or a football stadium once everyone has gone home. The silence rings with yesterday's noise, and quivers with anticipation, waiting for the next bombardment. She sits at her desk and turns her computer on. She inhales deeply, before letting the thread of air extend out. She frowns at a flashback from Saturday night, of Ben and Becky dancing. It builds and grows and the memory turns into a dark fantasy where Becky looks over to where Kate is sitting and smiles, before pressing her lips against Ben's, kissing him.

Kate tells herself harshly to 'stop it' aloud, and the sound of her own voice surprises her. Shouting at herself in an empty room – great, she is going mad. Kate thinks again of how she shouldn't have gone out, she shouldn't have tried to please everyone else, she should've stuck to her instincts and attended a meeting. Then none of it would have happened, the drink, the argument . . .

There is a tap on the classroom door. Lily is standing there awkwardly.

Kate smiles. 'Great, you made it,' she says, pointing to the chair by her desk.

Lily shrugs. 'I didn't have anything else to do.' She wanders inside and sits down at the table. She isn't wearing any make-up today and looks much younger than her sixteen years.

'What do you want to study first? *Romeo and Juliet* or *Of Mice And Men*? We can save the poem for after the first exam, as that's on the second paper.' Kate picks up the books and places them in front of Lily.

Lily's eyes wander over the textbooks. 'I like that poem, Miss, I never really got poems before.'

Kate studies her face. 'Yes, it's very engaging and thought-provoking, isn't it?' She looks at Lily's eye; there is still a tinge of yellow where the bruise was, but you would only notice it if you knew what was there before.

Lily nods. 'My mum said you told her I was really talented. That I should be in top set,' she says quietly.

Kate nods. 'I tell you that all the time, Lily.'

'I don't know why I find it so hard to focus.' The girl's eyes well up. 'It's like I just want to push it all away.'

'I know.' Kate puts her hand on Lily's shoulder. 'But look, you're here now. You came for an extra session. That's an achievement in itself. All you have to do is focus on right now, don't worry about the bigger picture. And then after this, focus on the next thing and then the next. Slowly, you'll look behind you and you'll have done everything you were too scared to think about before.'

Lily nods and thinks for a moment. 'I can do that, Miss.' She looks at Kate as if the simple piece of advice has clicked somewhere. 'Can we do the play today?'

'Of course!' Kate picks up the book and they start talking about the different themes the exam may focus on.

Later, Kate takes an apple out of her bag and sits back in her chair. She props her feet up on the desk and crosses them at her ankles. The revision session went well, she is feeling good, on track. She takes a bite.

'Ouch!' she shouts. As she sits up, her feet land on the floor with a loud clack. She moves the fruit away from her mouth; there is now a smear of bright-red blood on the spongy white tissue. She sucks the inside of her cheek where she bit herself, and tastes the coppery liquid. Putting her hand around her pendant, she holds the cold metal until it is warm.

Her phone vibrates. She puts the apple down and turns over the handset. It's Ben. 'Hi,' she says softly.

'Hey. It's so hot today!' He sounds as if he's bounding down the pavement.

'Where are you?'

'Just on my way out of Head Office, I'm going to work from home the rest of the day.'

'Nice.' She wants to ask him about his talk with Becky in

the early hours of Sunday morning. But then she thinks about what Clare said, and stops herself.

'Listen, I wanted to talk about what you said about Becky.'

'I know, I was out of order,' she says in a hurry.

'It's just that, I think you might be right. Maybe we should ask her to go?'

'Really?' Kate's surprised, he's completely changed his tune.

'Yeah, I just think . . . it's obviously getting to you, her being here, and what happened with the drink . . . I think she's a bit full on, you know?'

'I thought you said I was being paranoid?'

He clears his throat. 'I think you may have been a little paranoid, but we have so much on, and she's not our responsibility. And ultimately, you're not enjoying having her here, and you're my priority.'

A warm feeling spreads, loosening her tight chest. 'I thought you liked her?'

'So? It's obviously churning up loads of stuff for you,' he presses.

'Ben . . . I thought I heard you on the landing on Saturday night, talking to her?'

There is a pause, he doesn't say anything for a long three seconds. And then he laughs. 'Ah man, I sleepwalked to the toilet, I think. I found myself there. I'd peed all over the floor! Becky caught me. I was hoping I wouldn't have to tell you about my drunken misdemeanour.'

'Oh . . . I see,' she says, trying not to think of the intense nature of the whispering.

'So, do you want me to talk to her?' He changes the subject back. 'It might be less awkward if I do it. I can say I'm stressed or something . . . we get on, it won't be weird.'

'Really? Are you sure?'

'Sometimes it's easier having these conversations with people you aren't so connected with.'

He's making sense.

'I can speak to her when I get home this afternoon,' he says.

'OK, if you're sure.'

Kate puts the phone down. It is a relief; Ben is going to fix the problem. One of the promises of AA is: *we will intuitively know how to handle situations that used to baffle us.* She chews her lip; maybe she should be the one to talk to Becky. Although it will be nice not to have to deal with it. And Ben seems to have been born with this innate quality of reading situations and resolving them in the most diplomatic way, making everyone in the scenario feel validated and happy. The warm feeling spreads through her arms and fingertips. She is marrying a man who can take over. She isn't alone any more; they are a team.

She walks down the main corridor feeling lighter than she has since Becky moved in. Everything is slotting into place. Becky is going, the exams will be over soon, and then the wedding. Soon she'll be Mrs Hamilton. *Gosh, that sounds so important and grown-up*, she thinks. Kate Sullivan, that name is worn and tired. It is tied up in the chaotic, mad, alcoholic, attention-seeking version of herself. It will be cathartic to leave it behind once and for all. Kate Hamilton is going to be someone you can always rely on, a successful teacher, a wonderful wife, a mother . . . she wants to have at least three kids. A big, noisy home far removed from the isolated, quiet flat she grew up in that made her want to shout and scream.

Life is about to begin. Everything she wished for when she was drinking to oblivion is coming true and it's all because she's sober. She thinks about the cocktail on Saturday night, then she pushes it to the back of her mind again.

'Happy Friday!' Gus says.

She is standing in the lunch hall monitoring the kids as they hurl bread at each other, laughing like hyenas.

'You too,' she says.

'Have you got any plans?'

'Think I'm just going to hang with my fiancé, maybe catch up on a box set. We've had an old friend to stay recently, so I think we just want some time together.'

'Fun,' he says, waiting.

'Have you got any plans?' she asks, not really bothered by his answer. She wants to continue daydreaming about their big house: the family dog bounding after a stick Ben has thrown, and all the kids laughing when it lands up a tree.

'Just going to this jazz festival, which should be fun,' he says. 'Did I see one of the girls from Year 11 coming out of your classroom before assembly?'

'Oh yeah, Lily. I'm giving her some extra help. She missed some classes, so I'm just making sure she has everything she needs for next week.'

'Wow, that's amazing that she came in for extra tuition.'

He's impressed. Kate smiles, she is pleased. She's always seen Gus as a bit of a competitor as they have similar targets and experience. 'I think we have an understanding.'

'That's great, Kate, you'll have to tell me your secret sometime!' he says as he runs off to shout at some Year 7s who've started a water fight by the drinking fountain.

Kate stops off at the independent bookshop on her way home. It is one of her favourite places. Her dad would bring her here on weekends when she was a little girl. He didn't always have money for the cinema or McDonalds, but they could happily spend hours together here. She walks in and breathes that familiar musty scent. Then she calmly wanders around for half an hour, selecting books based on the cover, or a tag line, or something she read a review of in the weekend paper. She then sits on a beanbag at the back of the shop going through each of them before choosing three, always three, to buy and take home.

Kate feels centred, rebalanced, whole again by the time she walks up the steps to the house. Just as she puts her key in the lock she stops and wonders how Becky will have taken the news. She hopes there will be no awkwardness or bad feeling. Then she remembers that it's Ben sorting it out, and he's bound to have tidied it away neatly. She doesn't need to worry. They'll be able to go back to normal and focus on each other again, and the fact that they are about to be man and wife, without any distractions.

Before she opens the internal door, she pauses again. She can't hear anything, no chatter or laughter like there has been recently. Letting herself in, she walks into the living room. Ben is in the kitchen. A glass of wine sits between his hunched shoulders, his hands rest on the countertop, he is looking down into the glass.

'Hi,' she says with a hopeful smile.

He looks up, with a sudden burst of energy. 'Babe,' he says. His smile seems too good to be true.

'It's a bit early for that, isn't it?' She looks at the clock above his shoulder.

'It's six,' he says staunchly.

'You just don't normally . . . did you speak to Becky?' she whispers, looking towards her room.

His smile fades. 'Her sister's decorating the spare room, apparently, and she's refusing to go to Susanna's. She said she'll go next week.' He swallows weakly.

'OK. Well, at least that's something.' She's trying to read his face.

There is a creak and she looks up. Becky is standing halfway down the stairs.

'Hi,' she says, not flinching from her spot. 'Ben said that it's probably time I went.'

Kate takes a deep breath. 'Next week is fine, Becky,' she says cheerily.

Becky nods. 'OK.' She looks at Ben warily. 'I'm sorry to have put you out.'

'No, you haven't!' says Kate. 'Not at all.'

Becky nods, and walks towards the front door, taking her coat from the hook. 'I'm going out for dinner with some friends. I'll leave you guys to it.'

'You don't have to go out . . .' Kate feels shitty that she's made Becky feel unwanted. This isn't the effect she wanted Ben's conversation to have at all. She looks over at him, wanting him to extend the same courtesy. He stays quiet.

'See you later,' Becky says quietly over her shoulder as she shuts the door.

Kate clenches her jaw. She really thought Ben would have tackled this better; she is surprised how badly Becky's taken the news. Also, Ben seems stressed, it's not like him at all.

'Are you OK?'

'Yes, fine,' he replies defensively.

'How did the conversation go?'

He shrugs. 'Fine, just like I said. She's going to go; she just needs to wait a few days for the room at her sister's to free up.' He takes a sip of his drink. 'What do you want to eat? Shall we order a delivery? I feel like we haven't been alone for ages.'

'Do you think she's upset?'

'No, she seemed fine,' he says dismissively.

'I thought she looked annoyed.'

'Maybe she is a little! Who cares, she's some old friend, you've done her more than enough of a favour,' he says curtly. 'Come on, what do you want to eat?' He beckons her over to his phone. She gives the door Becky walked out of another glance before joining him in discussing the options. She can't

202

help but feel as if she doesn't know the whole story, and that both of them are hiding something from her.

Becky makes herself scarce for the rest of the weekend. It's nice to have Ben back, just the two of them, but he isn't his usual carefree self, he's troubled. He can't sit still; his OCD has gone into overdrive. He can't stop fixing and cleaning, jumping up to align something or rushing off to wash his hands or to clear a smudge. Whenever she asks him if he's OK, he laughs and says he's fine.

On Sunday night she lies in bed with her eyes open, staring at the ceiling. Her brain has welcomed such salacious pieces of information to obsess over. Tossing and turning, the thoughts tumble into each other, morphing and changing. It occurs to her that Becky may have told Ben something about Kate's past, something that has made him view her another way. After all, Ben never saw that side of her, he's never seen her drunk. He doesn't know what she is capable of the way Becky does.

The front door is quietly shut; she can hear Becky downstairs. Kate looks over at Ben, his chest silently rising and falling; he's fast asleep. She twists her hips to one side and tries not to wake him as she leaves the room. It was wrong of her to leave Ben to speak to Becky. This is Kate's responsibility, Becky is her friend, this is her past that has come back to haunt her, not his.

She pads down the stairs. Becky is drinking a glass of water by the sink, and a bottle of pills sits on the counter. Becky quickly twists the lid back on and puts the container in her pocket when she sees Kate. She looks tired, her sheen has fallen away. She looks more real now.

'Hi,' Kate says.

Becky looks up at her with surprising warmth. 'Hey.'

'I don't know what Ben said to you on Friday . . .' she starts.

'Don't worry, Kate. It's fine. We don't need to have this conversation,' Becky says simply.

'I feel like we do,' Kate begins. 'I'm just so stressed with school, I've started to go a bit mad, all that stuff I went through growing up. It obviously still affects me, I really wound myself up the other day. The cocktail in the club . . .' She's trying to make her understand.

'Kate. It's fine. Everything will be fine,' she says with force. 'I'm going to Alexa's next week. It's no big deal.'

'OK. If you're sure.' Kate tries to work out if she is being genuine.

Becky crosses her arms and shifts on the spot as if she wants to say something else. 'I am. I'm going to bed.' She rocks herself off the counter and walks away from their conversation.

Kate watches her climb the stairs; there is something crushing about the way she moves. She stops midway up and turns. She looks over at Kate, and then, just as Kate thinks she is about to talk, Becky shakes her head and walks up the remaining steps. Kate is baffled. Maybe she tried it on with Ben, and he turned her down. The thought lingers. Maybe, maybe, maybe. *Stop it.* None of it means anything. Clare is right, she's done everything she was meant to do. Nothing else is in her control.

17

Kate bolts up in bed instinctively knowing that today is special in some way. The first English exam, she remembers. Tossing the duvet from her legs, she uncharacteristically leaps out of bed. Just as she finds her balance, she remembers the night before and dread washes over her. She plonks back down. The mattress bounces lightly as it breaks her fall. The shower is running in the bathroom, and the radio is playing downstairs. She looks over at Ben's case by the door; he's going to Scotland, he'll be leaving her on her own with Becky again. The thought makes her shiver.

She wraps the belt of her dressing gown around her waist and bites her bottom lip. She pads down into the kitchen. It is an important day at school. She can't afford to obsess over Becky. Every time her mind strays onto the subject she tells herself to stop, to compartmentalize it till later. Clare would tell her there is no way of knowing how things will pan out, so it is pointless to project an outcome onto it. Her mind wants to play a game of catch, passing each possibility over, before throwing it on and replacing it with another. Testing how it feels in her hands, working out what emotions it will produce, and what consequences will come of it. She has to work hard to stop herself from dwelling on something that hasn't happened yet, so that it doesn't render her useless for her students, who are here now in the present, and who need her on the most important day of their lives so far.

She helps Gus set up the hall for the exam. To stay sane, she repeats the AA serenity prayer in her head over and over: *God, grant me the serenity to accept the things I cannot change, the courage to change the things I can, and the wisdom to know the difference.* Her lips move silently as she repeats the mantra, and it does help. When she first heard the prayer, at that first meeting, the word 'God' made her panic. She thought she was about to be indoctrinated into some weird sect. But people from all religions, and those who follow none at all, attend AA meetings. Kate learnt that 'God' in this context can be anything, it can be the universe, nature, a relative you feel looking down on you. Kate spent the first few years thinking it was all bollocks, but she didn't really care. She just wanted to get better, so decided to fake it till she made it. And then everything started going well, she started passing exams, enjoying nights out sober . . . and suddenly she didn't feel like she was pretending, she felt like there really was something bigger than her, willing her to do the right thing. Saying that, a lot of the time she still thinks it's a placebo. But hey, they do say placebos work.

'You praying Lily shows up?' Gus laughs.

She's embarrassed he noticed. 'Sorry, was I speaking aloud?'

206

'No! Just to yourself.' He is looking at her how he sometimes does, as if he can't work her out.

'Sorry, I've got a lot on my mind.'

'Don't worry, she will.' He gives her a reassuring smile.

Kate smiles back at him, pleased to have the support. The bell rings and the deputy head, Mr Skinner, arrives with the exam papers. He helps them lay one on each desk. Kate whips one open impatiently to look through the questions. She is relieved, she has covered most of the essay question angles in her classes.

'Come along,' Mr Skinner shouts. The line of students at the door walk into the room, with terrified looks on their faces. 'Find your name on the desk, it is in alphabetical order. Chop, chop.'

Kate is checking each student's face as they come into view, they all pause and look confused before finding their places. Kate knows exactly where Lily's seat is, and she is willing it to be filled, hoping that in a few minutes she'll be able to sigh with relief and give the girl an encouraging smile. She sees Lizzie and Emma, they wave at her and pull nervous faces. Kate gives them both a thumbs up. She looks up at the clock; the minute hand shakes precariously near the hour mark. Mr Skinner stands by the main door beckoning in the last few stragglers. He looks at the time. If he shuts the doors that will be it, Lily will have missed the exam.

Kate marches over to distract him. 'The paper looks good,' she whispers. 'I'm so pleased we chose *The Catcher in the Rye* over the other one, aren't you?'

He continues looking up and down the corridor, before saying in a laboured, nasally voice, 'Miss Sullivan, I don't want to argue with you again about text choices, let's save that for next year.' He looks down at his watch. 'Right, we should start.'

Kate looks out onto the corridor sorrowfully. All that work . . . for nothing. It will be difficult for Lily to recover from this. Not taking her exams will be a cold hard fact for the voice in her head to cling onto when listing everything that is wrong with her. When she takes the leap into the darkness, she'll look behind her, and there will be nothing positive holding her back. Kate wants to cry. She imagines Lily in her boyfriend's bedroom, the colours reflecting off the TV onto her face. She'll look up at the clock and think about the exam that is about to start, and then she'll take another toke of her spliff to try and forget where she is meant to be.

Mr Skinner puts his hand on the knob of the door and begins to swing it shut.

'Miss, wait!'

Kate's head turns back out onto the corridor; Lily is running and waving her hand. 'Please, Sir!' Kate puts herself between the doors and coaxes Lily in before Mr Skinner has a chance to think.

'Come on Lily, last one in!' she laughs, and Mr Skinner allows it. She shows her to the desk and whispers, 'Lily, are you trying to give me a heart attack?' She really needs to have a word with her about time management.

Pens are poised, Mr Skinner calls time on the start of the exam, heads bow, and ink is drawn. Kate spends the next ninety minutes trying to stay present, trying to stay in the room, she doesn't want to think about the evening ahead. She looks over at Lily writing profusely, occasionally looking out of the window, thinking. She's so brave, being here. Feeling the fear and doing it anyway, that is the hardest thing of all. Kate is proud of her.

As the hour ticks by her mind can't help wandering to Becky. *The courage to change the things I can* ... she says under her breath, closing her eyes and opening them to watch Lily facing her demons. Kate can do this.

The bell rings and Mr Skinner shouts, 'Pens down, everyone. Please make sure your name is on the front. Don't smirk, Charlie, smarter people than you have forgotten in the past. Right, don't move until all the papers have been picked up by one of us . . .'

Kate starts loading the sheets into her arms. She picks up Lily's, her name is written neatly on the top and each sheet of paper is riddled with pen marks. 'Good work,' she mouths as she walks on.

Once all the papers are collected the students are free to go. Kate walks up to Lily.

'How did it go? It looks like you answered all the questions.'

'Yeah, it was OK, Miss.' She looks as if she is in a hurry. 'I've got to get back.'

'Lily!' She calls, the girl turns. 'I'll see you for that last session? We'll do the poem?' Lily nods and continues rushing away.

Kate texts Ben letting him know that Lily turned up. He texts straight back: *Number 1 teacher x.* It feels good to be good at something, because for a long time she thought she wasn't good at anything at all. Her self-belief had been chiselled away by fear, by mistakes she'd made under the influence, and the consequences. The shame had battered her like a sail in a storm. It was easier to fold away, not to bother, to stay in her room gulping down liquid hoping it would keep the dread from knocking at her door.

She changes into her cycling gear and begins to leave the school, perfectly balanced between euphoria and dread.

'Miss Sullivan.' She turns. It's Malcolm, the Head. 'How did it go?'

'They all turned up,' she says proudly.

'Excellent! You know that three didn't last year.'

'I had heard that.' She's trying to be modest. 'I'm really pleased at the turnout.'

'I'm sure you've done us all proud,' he says. 'One down, one to go!' he shouts as he walks towards the pupils' entrance to have his usual impromptu chats with kids as they leave the grounds.

Before she gets on her bike she flicks through her phone for a playlist for the ride. She needs something positive and nourishing before sitting down with Becky. The phone rings in her hand. It's Clare.

'I don't fucking know, Greg. Google it!' Clare screams at her husband before coming to the phone. Kate pulls an amused face at the altercation. She loves the passionate relationship her sponsor has with her husband, it is so honest. They say you should choose a sponsor who has the life you want. When Kate met Clare she was five years clean, she'd just got engaged, they'd bought a house. She had an important job at a children's charity. She had what Kate wanted. There was no one better to steer her through the steps.

'Everything OK?' Kate asks.

'Well, not really. I need a favour,' Clare says, quite manically.

'What's up?' Kate asks. She doesn't generally see this side of Clare as she has her own sponsor to burden with her neuroses. It is nice to occasionally be reminded that she is only human too.

'The baby's got a rash. I think it's nothing, but Greg's started to stress me out that it's scarlet fever or some bullshit. We're going to A & E, but the thing is I'm meant to be doing a chair in town in half an hour. Do you think you could do it for me?' Clare is out of breath, and Kate can hear her storming around the house grabbing things in a panic.

Without thinking Kate replies, 'Yes, of course. I'm just leaving school, I can go there straight away.'

'Oh my God, you're a lifesaver, Kate.' Relief swims through her otherwise frazzled voice.

It isn't until she puts the phone down that Kate realizes she should be going home to speak to Becky. She wants to finish the conversation that they started the night before. She looks down at her handset thinking about whether to call back and cancel. But Kate can't do that, Clare is relying on her and it isn't often she gets the opportunity to help her out. Becky can wait an hour, she isn't going anywhere.

As she cycles into town, she thinks about the first chair she ever did. She was about a year sober and was so terrified she nearly cancelled. The secretary, the person nominated to run the meeting, convinced her it would be OK. He told her to pretend she was talking to herself at her first meeting, and to say what she needed to hear. From then on, whenever she shares her story, she picks an empty chair and talks to it, pretending she's talking to that scared little girl she once was, convincing her that she's in the right place and everything will be OK.

The meeting is in Soho, in another basement underneath another church. She picks up the pace as she arrives and swings one leg over the frame of her bike as she comes to a stop. This meeting is specifically for young people: everyone is under forty, the majority are in their twenties, there are teenagers and university students too. Kate hurries through the cigarette cloud hanging above the entrance, nodding and smiling at anyone that catches her eye.

Out of breath, Kate takes the seat at the front of the room next to the secretary. 'Thanks for jumping in last minute.' He leans over.

'That's OK,' she replies, suddenly wary. She hasn't had a chance to process what she's about to do.

All the faces look up at her expectantly, hoping she'll say something wise that will hit a nerve and help them. First, there is a reading from the 'Big Book', AA's manual. It is about getting sober before alcohol has done too much damage . . . 'They Stopped in Time'. The first time she heard it, it made so much sense to her: *They realized that repeated lack of drinking*

*control, when they really wanted control, was the fatal symptom that
spelled problem drinking . . . certainly no sane man would wait for a
malignant growth to become fatal before seeking help . . .*

She closes her eyes as she listens to the passage, she's heard
it hundreds of times before. It calms her. When the young
preppy man with thick glasses finishes, he sets it aside. The
secretary asks if there is anyone new who would like to introduce themselves. People turn their necks to see if anyone is
going to speak.

'I'm Pandora, and I'm . . . well, I think I'm an alcoholic . . .
It's my first time to this meeting.' The young girl blushes and
looks down as she talks.

Kate gives her a warm smile and others mutter 'Welcome'
and 'Great to have you here'. The crowd then turns to Kate and
waits for her to begin. She pauses, she hasn't had a chance to
prepare. They say all you have to do is be honest.

She takes a deep breath and starts, 'My name's Kate, I'm
an alcoholic. It's funny, I used to come here when I first got
sober. I felt like a little girl. I was actually twenty-two. Society
would have seen me as an adult. I remember someone telling
me once, that you are emotionally the age you were when you
started drinking or using drugs to push your feelings away.
By that reasoning I would have only been thirteen, and I felt
it. I felt like a vulnerable child. I wanted someone to pick me
up and tuck me away. But as soon as anyone came near me
and offered me any sort of love, I shoved it away, I got angry.
I know now it was a coping mechanism. I was scared that if
they got to know me, they would get there first.'

213

Kate looks over at Pandora, the young girl at her first meeting, her eyes sparkling with emotion as she listens.

'But I should start at the beginning. My mother died when I was five, my dad has never said she had addiction issues, but I think that's what must have happened. She killed herself. She jumped off a bridge. It took me a long time to say that out loud. The pain involved in telling other people that my mother just didn't want to stay with me . . . That she'd prefer to die rather than watch me grow up . . .' She takes a deep breath. 'I drank on that for a long time. The pain kept me in oblivion. I used it to keep myself the victim, it was the perfect poor me . . . poor me . . . pour me a drink. If I'm honest, I still wallow in it sometimes. On bad days, I still tell myself that I'm destined to turn into her and there isn't any point to any of this.'

She takes another breath; the basement air is so stagnant it doesn't feel as if she has dragged any in. 'I grew up in a silent flat making myself cheesy pasta and fish fingers after school while my dad worked himself to the bone to provide for me. But all I could do was look at what other people around me had and I was overcome with jealousy.'

She thinks of Becky, and her mother, and how wrong she got it.

'I had my first drink at thirteen; I convinced my friend we should break into her dad's alcohol cabinet. That first taste, that first release, it was like magic. I'd finally found the answer, the thing that was going to stop me feeling so alone. Her parents found us puking in her bedroom surrounded by her childhood toys. Her father drove me home and told my dad what we'd done. The look in his eyes still haunts me today. That was the first time I felt the shame I came to know so well over the next decade. It became a cycle, drinking, doing something shameful, drinking to block it out. On repeat, over and over, until I couldn't remember why I was drinking any more.'

She looks around, people are nodding, even smiling to themselves in personal recognition.

'I don't like telling war stories when I do chairs, I prefer to talk about the good stuff. I've been sober for six years . . .' She blinks, the words trail off, she thinks of the cocktail. She looks at her hands resting on her lap, she looks over at Pandora, so expectant, waiting to hear how wonderful everything is now.

She coughs. 'These rooms gave me my life back. I'm not saying it's been easy. I've had some pretty dark times sober, but it's given me the ability to do life on life's terms. Go into war prepared to win or lose.'

She thinks about that cocktail again, so recent she can still remember the taste and the desire. She shouldn't be sitting here, she shouldn't be spouting her wisdom to all these faces, what does she even know? She drank more recently than most of the people in the room. She's a joke, a liar.

'I'm engaged to be married in a couple of weeks.' A few people whoop. 'I've got a job I'm genuinely passionate about.' She pauses, she's a fraud, that's all she can think. 'I've got all the stuff that I wanted when I was drinking but couldn't work out how to get,' she says softly. Her mouth is dry. She looks down.

She thinks she hears a noise, a cry for help. Looking up,

there is nothing but silent faces, patiently waiting for her to speak.

'I had an old friend come back into my life recently.' Her voice cracks. 'I got really paranoid that she came back to ruin my life, because, I guess subconsciously, I knew that I'd ruined hers. I tried to make amends – I did my Step Nine with her.' She swallows. 'She hugged me and said not to worry.' She chokes. 'I thought there was something darker that I had to apologize for, but . . .'

A flash of an image comes to her mind suddenly. Of being in the flat above the pub, of stumbling around, of having to be guided. Swaying side to side, someone holding her wrist. She can hear Becky, she sounds upset and her words are echoing through the room. Kate swallows. She coughs, it hurts. She looks up; the faces that had been full of admiration and respect now look concerned. She turns to Pandora; her brow is furrowed. Kate feels hot, unbearably hot.

'I'm sorry, I have to go.' She stands up. 'I'm sorry,' she says to the baffled secretary as she begins to run through the seated crowd and out of the room.

18

She grabs the handlebars of her bike, forgetting to undo the lock. 'Fuck!' she shouts. She looks up to see the people sitting outside the pub across the road staring at her, nudging each other gripping wet foamy pints. Her hands shake as she rolls the numerical combination to the correct position on the lock. She needs to speak to Becky and find out what happened that night. She hops onto the seat and pulls off the kerb. A horn beeps, making her jump. She turns her head over her shoulder, seeing a man in an electric-blue suit curse at her from behind the wheel.

Panting, she rides back to Newington Green. The feelings swimming around her head are big and weighty; she wants to turn around and run away from this. Exit signs flash in her mind, trying to lure her away from this scary reality. Oblivion is tempting. Technically she's already relapsed, she thinks, she may as well do it properly. She locks her jaw and grinds her teeth, trying to push the thoughts away. She hasn't felt in so much danger for a long time.

She opens the door; at first she thinks she's too late. Then she hears a noise from upstairs and she jumps the steps two by two. Softly she knocks on the door of the spare room and opens it. Becky is zipping up her bag, she is already wearing her coat.

'You're leaving?'

Becky nods. 'Yes.'

'Did you take me to the Vulture because you wanted to remind me of something?'

Becky stops what she is doing, pauses, and then nods, 'I guess I wanted to see if you remembered.'

'Remembered what?'

Becky doesn't answer.

Kate moves towards her and grabs her arm. 'What happened that night, Becky?'

Becky looks up, her eyes are red and sore around the lids. She lifts her bag off the bed. 'I can't, I'm sorry.'

'Have you been trying to get between Ben and me?' Kate studies Becky's face, which is sad and brittle. 'To get back at me for something?'

Becky's chin wobbles ever so slightly. 'Do you really love him?'

Kate wasn't expecting that question. 'Yes . . . more than anything.'

Becky looks up at the ceiling, pained, and swallows. 'Do you . . .' Her voice cracks as she talks.

Then Kate's phone rings from inside her pocket. 'Ignore it,' Kate says. She takes it out to turn it off. The name flashing on the screen says *Jonny*. 'It's Jonny. He's probably just wondering how the exam went.' She cancels the call, and then it rings again.

'You should take it.' Becky sniffs. 'It could be important.'

She's right, Jonny would never be so eager to get in touch unless it was something that couldn't wait. Kate picks up the call.

'Hi Jonny, you OK? I'm just in the middle—' she starts.

A woman's voice surprises her. 'Katie, sorry, I'm Ronda, an erm . . . a friend of your father's.'

Kate is taken aback. 'Ronda?'

'I'm using his phone. Darlin', your daddy's had a heart attack, I'm in the hospital with him now . . .' The woman's voice is thick and gravelly.

Kate gasps, 'Heart attack.' She stands.

'I don't want to panic you, love. They're assessing him now. They said I should call you and that you should come straight away.'

'Where is he?'

'The Queen Mother Hospital, in Margate. Let me know when you're off the train and I'll meet you near the entrance. Don't worry, he won't be on his own.'

'I'm coming. I'm coming right now.' Kate puts the phone down. 'Jonny's had a heart attack,' she says robotically.

'Can I do anything?' Becky is concerned.

Kate searches for her keys. Shoving her wallet and phone in her pocket, she doesn't even bother with a bag. She can be at the hospital in under two hours if she's quick. Before she dashes out, she remembers Becky, and turns.

'Will you be here when I get back?'

'I . . .' Becky starts.

'Please don't go to Alexa's, stay here, please, Becky,' she begs her. 'We need to sort this out, once and for all.'

Becky chews on her lip and nods. 'OK.'

Kate walks back into the room and hugs her. 'I'm sorry, I'm so sorry.' Becky freezes, Kate can feel her shoulder bones lock; she doesn't hug her back.

Kate dashes out into the road to look for a taxi. Panicked, she turns her head left and right; the road is abnormally quiet for this time of evening. Just as she is about to give in and order one on her phone, the familiar sight of a lit-up orange rectangle comes into view. She shuts the rattly black taxi door and asks to be taken to St Pancras Station. She sits back in the car and rests her head against the leather and tries not to think about Jonny, with his shirt open, lying on a trolley. Will they be cutting open his chest? Her daddy, her dad, who never meant to hurt anyone. Who just tried to make everything OK the only way he knew how.

It's getting dark. Headlights flash against her face, causing her to blink. She should let Ben know what's happening. She calls him.

'Hey.' Her voice is croaky.

'Are you OK? What's happened? Is it Becky . . . what's she said—'

'Jonny's had a heart attack.' Kate can't believe what she's saying.

'What?'

220

'Some woman called Ronda just called me, he's at the hospital, they said for me to go straight there. I never told him that I love him . . . I never got to tell him how sorry I was for everything . . .' She starts to weep.

'Kate, Kate . . .'

'I should have told him. And now I'm not going to get the chance.' She smears a tear off her face. She catches the driver's eye in the rear-view mirror, a flicker of curiosity evident before he turns back to the road.

'You will get the chance. He's going to be fine. People recover from heart attacks all the time. Do you want me to come down? Work will understand.'

'No . . . no . . . let me find out what's going on.'

'You don't have to do this on your own, Kate. We're a team.'

'I know,' she tells him. 'I'll call you when I know more.'

'I love you.'

'I love you too,' she says back and hangs up the phone.

She rushes into the station and checks the board. There is a train in four minutes. Panic twists in her chest, making it hard to breathe. Fumbling with her card, she buys a ticket and runs to the correct gate. She can see the train by the platform. Legging it through the barrier she runs up to the first carriage and presses the button with quick agitated jabs. She lets out a relieved sigh when the doors swing open.

Once on the train she sits back and half closes her eyes, wanting to give in to the exhaustion that's rattling through her bones. She's barely sat down when the train lurches forward, and slowly the outline of buildings turns into the outline

221

of trees and fields and electricity pylons. They canter down into the east of the country, the noise of the train sounding like hooves pelting down onto clay mud. She looks at her reflection in the glass. She isn't wearing any make-up; her lips have been stung red and her hair has been foraged through. She's so utterly ripe she's ready to rot. Focusing on the sounds around her she tries to empty her mind, concentrate on her breath entering and leaving her body. Finally, she gives in to her heavy lids and closes her eyes, the rhythmic noise of the train rocking her to sleep like a baby. She dreams of someone offering her a drink. It is so real she can feel the anguished abandon as she chokes down the liquid and then the horror when she realizes she can't take it back.

A touch on her shoulder makes Kate jump forward. The ticket inspector laughs. 'Sorry to wake you. Ticket, please.'

In a daze she produces the piece of card. She wipes her lips with the back of her hand. He walks away, satisfied. She rolls her tongue inside her mouth. Her saliva doesn't taste pungent like it had moments before; the memory of vodka stinging the sensitive pores inside her cheeks was so physical she feels as though she's got something to feel guilty for. Relief swims through her like a fish that's found a hole in the net. It was a dream; she didn't really do it. Then she thinks of the other night in the bar and remembers that she did. She tries to swallow the dread down, but it bobs up like a yellow rubber duck.

She rocks her leg backwards and forwards, jiggling it about. The man sitting opposite gives an annoyed look. She stops. She scrolls on her phone. She hasn't had an update from Ronda. She wonders who she is, Jonny hasn't said anything about her before. He's definitely never said anything about a girlfriend.

Kate is tapping the table now: more annoyed looks. She is full of unresolved anxiety, she wants to jump out of her seat and run around, or shake, or dance, or scream or just do something. She stands up and squeezes out of the space between the chair and the table. She needs to walk. Marching forcefully down the carriage, she looks at the commuters on their daily voyage out of the city, eating nuts, updating spreadsheets, drinking pre-made G & Ts out of tin cans. She clicks her tongue against the top of her mouth as she continues down the aisle.

There should be a restaurant car somewhere on this train. She wants to consume something, anything. Whatever will change the way she feels. Putting her hands inside her pockets, she walks. It feels dangerous on a moving object, and she likes the feeling. It's weird travelling without any luggage, she feels like a fugitive, like there isn't anything pinning her down to her usual reality. Kate wonders if Ronda will be able to help her find a pharmacy to buy a toothbrush, or even lend her some spare clothes. She thinks about what will happen the next time she's on the train if she doesn't have a daddy. How lost she'll feel then.

Finally, she arrives at the small café at one end of the train. The carriage flails about, swinging on a limb. A man in front of her is buying three cans of beer; he already looks quite drunk. What is it about trains and planes that makes it OK to shirk usual boundaries? In the rooms, she's often heard people speak about a new-found fear of flying. It's not crashing they're worried about, it's the fear that, hemmed into the window seat with nowhere to run, a nice lady will walk past asking if they'd like a bottle of red or white. And that, out of nowhere, they'll ask for one of each.

'What would you like?' the old man behind the counter asks. She wonders how long he's worked there; he seems too distinguished for the job. Maybe he got sacked from a job at the bank, since everyone uses Internet banking now, so he had to get a job on the jittery train, trying not to burn himself with hot drinks as he pours them into cheap plastic cups. She wonders what he thinks about during his shift. She wonders if he ever thinks about jumping off the back of the carriage.

She looks up at the refrigerators behind him. 'You know, there is a disproportionate amount of alcohol.'

He shrugs. 'Would you like tea? Coffee? Fanta?' He raises his arm to show her the other options.

She looks at the wine, the cheap white wine. It always used to get her a special type of drunk. It would make her cry, and it made her angry. She once threw a shoe at a boyfriend and gave him a bloody nose. Red wine, red wine she never bothered with much. She always wished she could be one of those people who could sip a full-bodied red at dinner. You can't glug red wine very easily, and if you have too much it will slosh around in the bottom of your stomach, which isn't very comfortable when you're trying to get off your face. Beer, oh, she loved beer. She was drawn to it because it's meant to be a man's drink, and she had created a tomboy persona for herself, as though she didn't have real feelings, she wasn't a girl, she could handle herself. She could drink like a man, she could have sex like a man – *it's OK, you can use me, I don't care . . . because, ha! I'm actually using you.*

But not really at all. None of it worked because none of it was true.

'Miss, would you like a drink? Or not?' the man behind the counter asks.

'Can I have a bag of nuts?' she asks.

He looks bored. 'Cashew or pistachio?'

She thinks. 'Both.'

He chucks the bags over and she gives him her bank card to tap. She opens the silver foil bag and throws a nut into her mouth and crunches, then another, and another. A thought creeps in. If the next time she's on that train Jonny has died, then she'll buy some wine off the man in the restaurant car.

She'll be well within her rights. She'll drink all of those tiny bottles of white wine and, once she's off the train, she'll go to the off-licence in the station and buy a litre bottle of vodka to take home. She could hide it in the airing cupboard. She could tell Becky maybe it was for the best she went to stay with Alexa. Maybe Kate never needs to find out what happened that night in the pub, maybe you should let sleeping dogs lie. Ben, well . . . Ben will probably fall out of love with her anyway. Maybe it would be for the best. Maybe Ben and Becky are actually better suited anyway. They're from similar backgrounds. Ben's mum wouldn't give Becky a disapproving look.

She sits down on another seat in a different carriage and stares out of the window. Is it bad that part of her, a really bad, secret part of her, hopes that Jonny will die so that she can drink again?

19

The train speeds off behind her. She stands on the platform hesitant to continue her journey. This place, she never wanted to come back here. It is filled with memories . . . of *her*. The tannoy barks, jolting Kate forward a step, and then another. She can see the sea as soon as she is out of the station. It glistens like black tar. Warm air rustles through the tendrils of her hair, tickling her face. She wonders what Ben would make of Margate, and she winces thinking of him pretending to enjoy a sweaty container of fish and chips, or the confused look on his face when he saw the crumbling arcades with smashed lights flashing like shameless harlots trying to reel him in. He'd look up and grimace at the half-torn British flags brazenly flapping in the wind as though they are looking for a fight. It's a million miles away from the manicured beach towns of Long Island.

She walks towards a queue of people carriers with yellow stickers that say *Taxi* on the side, and she climbs inside one. Rolling the door shut, she composes a text: *Hi Clare, Jonny's had a heart attack. I'm in Margate, was having some pretty wild*

conversations with myself on the train. I'm OK, I'll call you when I can.
I need to tell you something important x

Then she remembers that Clare's baby may be ill, and she decides not to send the message.

Kate feels very alone. The dark voice is getting louder, she can barely compete with it any more. It's scary how close she is to talking herself into a big relapse. She squeezes her eyes shut and searches for the good voice in there. What does it matter if she needs to restart her sobriety date, it's only time. If she doesn't, everything she has worked so hard for could slip through her fingers in a matter of moments. That's what she should care about, not her ego clinging onto a number.

Kate steps out of the dark taxi and into the strobing lights of the hospital. She's been here before, that winter she lived with her grandmother. The electric doors part and she turns left. In the waiting area there are four people dotted around looking bored. A man with a clump of bloody tissue round his hand, a woman with a young boy resting his head on her shoulder. There is a woman in a big furry coat wearing red patent Mary Jane shoes. She is cradling a hot drink and staring at the floor as if she is trying to work out a Sudoku puzzle. Kate knows that it's Ronda.

'Ronda?' She bends down, and the woman's eyes flicker up at her.

She must have put red lipstick on that morning, there are the faint remnants of colour in the deep wrinkles of her lips. 'Katie?'

'Yes . . . Kate.'

'Oh, love . . .' she says, standing and looking for her bag.

'Is he . . . is he OK?' Kate is suddenly panicked.

Ronda tucks her handbag under her armpit. 'They said they'd give me an update five minutes ago. We should tell them you're here; I think we'll get a bit further.' Ronda takes Kate's hand and marches them both over to the reception desk.

Occasionally, at school, Kate will see angry mothers in reception, holding the hand of a worried-looking student. She's watched as they bark at Maureen, banging on the glass raging about some sort of injustice their child has been put through because they've been asked to do some homework or aren't allowed to wear their new trainers. Although this is obviously not brilliant parenting, Kate always watches them with acute interest, noting how a mother is the person who would do anything to fight your corner, your biggest cheerleader and advocate. Kate wonders what her mother would have done that winter she needed her the most, when she was stuck here with her grandmother. Would she have been any help at all? Or would she have been too immersed in her own inner turmoil to care?

They arrive at the reception desk. Ronda, who has a buxom, stumpy sort of build, raises her elbows and crosses her arms at the high counter.

'Here, I've got his daughter with me now.'

The receptionist doesn't bother to look up. 'What's the name, please?' she asks, clicking away at her computer.

'Jonny Sullivan, he had a heart attack. This is Katie Sullivan, his daughter.'

'It's Kate,' she interjects.

'Um . . . I can't find him on the system any more . . . It did say he'd been moved to intensive care, I thought . . .' Kate's heart thuds as the woman speaks to a colleague. Then she checks again, her initial snootiness floundering.

'Ah, that was someone else. Mr Sullivan has been taken through to the cath lab for surgery,' she says, pleased she's found him on the system.

'Surgery?' Kate's worried.

'And where's that?' asks Ronda.

'Through the double doors, turn right and then right again at the water fountain.' Ronda's eyes follow the woman's hand.

'Come on, Katie!' she shouts as she marches ahead.

'It's . . .' She can't be bothered to correct her again. 'What happened?' Kate asks as she rushes behind Ronda.

'That bloody house of his is such a deathtrap,' Ronda rages. 'He can't do it all himself, but he's bloody-minded, that one.' She continues, banging through the double doors as if she has an axe to grind.

'What happened?' Kate asks again.

'We were at his house, the bugger decided to get up a ladder and start pulling a ceiling down. I told him not to, it isn't a one-man job,' she sighs. 'He started clutching his left side and wheezing, he went such a pasty white. I kept screaming "Get down, Jonny, get down."' Ronda is holding her hands to her chest, re-enacting the moment. 'He turned

230

to get down and then his foot got caught on one of the steps and he fell.'

'Jesus,' says Kate. 'Did he pass out?'

'Passed out, knocked out, I'm not sure. I nearly kicked him out I was so angry. The ambulance came quick. And they rushed off with him as soon as we got here. I haven't been able to get much sense out of them since.'

Kate dares to glance at Ronda's round face; it is angry and tearful. Her dark hair is styled in a 1940s victory roll and she has a sequinned pin of a pair of red lips on one side.

They follow the signs to the correct ward, where another woman peers down from another counter. Ronda pushes Kate forward.

'Hi, my dad, er . . . Jonny Sullivan, he's had a heart attack?'

The woman nods. 'Take a seat, the doctor will come and speak to you in a few minutes.'

Kate looks over at the chair she's been directed to, then back at the receptionist's poker face. Did she give her a sympathetic look? Did the look say, you're about to have the dead dad lecture? Kate blinks and turns to Ronda, who comforts her with an arm around the shoulder. They walk over to the wipe-clean chairs, where they sit gripping each other's hands, even though they barely know each other at all.

'Miss Sullivan, and you're a friend of Mr Sullivan's?' An impossibly young man in a doctor's coat comes towards them. He looks stressed and tired, and far too young to be giving out life-changing information like this. Kate and Ronda stand as he approaches.

'He's fine,' he says quickly, a hand out to placate. 'We had to perform a cardiac catheterization, which involves threading a tube to open the blocked artery. He reacted to it well and is now recovering. He's really lucky, we've X-rayed him, and he hasn't broken anything from the fall.' The doctor chuckles and shakes his head. 'That man is made of steel.'

Kate puts her hand against the wall to balance – relief – she can see microscopic stars worming around in front of her. 'Can I see him?'

'He's sleeping it off at the moment. You can check in, but to be honest you won't get much sense out of him until tomorrow now.' The doctor points to a room. 'Bed 22.'

'You go, love,' Ronda says softly.

Kate tears away from the group and walks towards the door. She pushes it open. It's dark inside, sidelights give out small shards of illumination. Bed 22 has a mint-green curtain squared around it. She pulls a corner back and looks inside.

He is on his back, a tube coming out of his arm. His mouth is slightly ajar, and he is pale. Jonny is always outside, painting something or climbing up scaffolding or sanding something down. His face is usually weathered and dark. She touches his leathery skin, she moves some hair off his forehead, she puts her small hand inside his large hand.

They don't have a tactile relationship any more, she hasn't been so close to him since she was a young girl, then she'd grip onto him as if her life depended on it. Slowly as time went on and she turned from girl to woman her grip loosened, she moved further and further away from him. He was once her lighthouse in the darkness, but as she grew the blinking light became so faint, she didn't know how to get back there any more.

Kate sits on the chair by the bed and puts her head on his shoulder, trying not to apply too much pressure. She wants to stay there listening to him breathing, smelling him, stroking his hand. A tear slides out of her eye, and she thinks of what she said to herself on the train. She is a terrible person. She needs to do the next right thing over and over until this is fixed. The first thing is right in front of her. She never did her Step Nine amends with Jonny. It's always been too scary to bring up again. It's blocking their relationship and it's blocking her recovery.

'I love you, Dad,' she whispers, kissing his cheek. 'I'll come back in the morning.'

Standing, she walks away in a daze. Ronda is waiting outside the door.

'Mind if I just pop my head in?' she asks. Kate nods.

Kate leans against the wall. She texts Ben first: *Dad's recovering. He had to have a procedure to unblock an artery. Will know more in the morning x*

She then emails work and lets Malcolm know she won't be in the next day, and she'll need cover for her lessons. Luckily there are no English exams scheduled.

Ronda returns. She looks as if she's been crying. 'Right, well. Shall we go, then?' she says, dipping a finger under each eye to catch the watery mascara that's collected.

'Do you know a hotel around here?' asks Kate.

'A hotel?' the woman replies. 'You must stay with me.'

'No, I couldn't possibly.'

'Jonny would be furious if I didn't give his beloved daughter a bed for the night. My house is round the corner. You can be in bed in ten minutes.'

Kate thinks; it's the middle of the night. She's got nothing with her, the thought of a bed with a friendly face available for tea-making and spare clothes is very appealing.

'Thanks, Ronda. That would be great.'

They walk the dark, empty streets together in silence. Now the adrenalin has dissipated Ronda seems nervous in her presence. 'Your dad says you're a teacher, a very good one.'

'Well, I don't know about that,' Kate answers, surprised Jonny said that. 'But I am a teacher. How long have you known my dad?'

'Since he's been in town.' Her cheeks flush. 'I was hoping to meet you one of these days.'

'I should have visited him. It's all so busy up in London.' Her voice cracks; the excuse is pathetic. She should have come months ago.

Ronda lives in an unglamorous red-brick house, with square plastic windows and a shallow tiled roof. All the houses on the street are exactly the same. There is nothing unique or special about any of them. Not at all like Ronda, who seems very unique and special to Kate.

Ronda puts the kettle on and Kate wanders into the living room. There are two clothes rails lining each side of the boxy space, leaving barely any room for a sofa and a television. Kate slips her hands between the fabrics. They are silky and dazzling, colourful and embellished. She turns to ask what they are for.

Ronda is already standing there. 'It's overspill. I've got a vintage clothes shop on the seafront. Mostly wartime stuff, but I've started to do more Sixties and Seventies.'

Kate comes to a line of the most beautiful silk dresses she's ever seen, and she fingers the glossy fabric, holds one or two up in admiration.

'They're proper Forties,' says Ronda. She takes out the emerald one and holds it to Kate's frame. 'You must have it.'

'It's really is beautiful. I couldn't . . .'

'I'd like you to have it,' Ronda says.

'Are you sure . . .' Ronda's face encourages Kate to be quiet. 'Thank you.'

'Now, would you like something to wear to bed?' Ronda asks. 'I'll get you some water and I've a spare toothbrush I'll leave in the bathroom for you.' She shows her to the spare room.

'Ronda?' Kate calls out just as she's shutting the door.

'Yes, love?' Ronda pokes her head back in the room.

'Thanks. And . . .' She smiles. 'I'm really glad my dad met you.'

Ronda's cheeks flush. She looks down, embarrassed. 'Thanks, love.'

Kate thinks about speaking to Clare and telling her what's happened. She'd always told her that she didn't need to sit down with Jonny and do a proper amends. She'd embellished things, not told her the whole truth about what happened. A living amends would be enough, she said. She'd be the best daughter going forward, to make up for all the worry she put him through. But she hasn't mended anything there, she hasn't even tried. The silence between them echoes louder with each year that passes.

Outside the window the dark sea is visible in the distance. She watches white crests break against the moody night's sky. The reason she can't bear to be in the same room as him is all wrapped up in this place, in this town. She once vowed she'd never come back. Every street and turning reminds Kate of her. And how she blames Jonny for letting them take her away.

Her bones ache as she gets under the covers and gently rests her weary head against the pillow. All she can think of is Jonny, and how close she was to losing him. How she could be lying here, trying to come to terms with the fact her only remaining parent was now dead.

The next morning Ronda gently places a tea on the side table. 'Thought you'd want to get up and go straight to the hospital.'

Kate stretches. She slept like a log.

She showers and borrows a top from Ronda's rail. It has a Laura Ashley print of tiny flowers with short puff sleeves and a ruched top. She wouldn't usually wear something so distinctive, but Ronda persuaded her.

They walk back to the hospital. The previous night the

streets had looked dark and ominous. Today, they have taken on a jolly demeanour in the fresh morning sunlight. 'It's amazing what medicine can do these days,' Ronda says. 'I was sure he was a goner.'

Kate laughs, enjoying Ronda's honesty. 'I thought I was going to get there, and he'd be dead,' Kate says, swallowing as she remembers the ultimatum she gave herself. 'Ronda, when we get there, do you mind if I have a few minutes with him? Just me?'

Ronda nods. 'I'll get the coffees.'

Kate walks back onto the ward. A different doctor is standing chatting to Jonny. Her father sees her and gives a sad, tight smile.

'I'm sorry I put you through that, love,' he says.

'I'm just glad you're OK, Jonny.'

'I'll leave you to it,' the doctor says. 'Good news is that we can discharge him this morning. He's got a twisted ankle, but his heart is all better. We managed to sort the blockage.' He walks over to the next bed.

'I'm glad you're OK,' Kate says. Her hand hovers near his, then she puts it in her pocket, afraid.

'Sorry for the scare.'

Kate takes a seat. 'I should have come to Margate sooner.'

He presses his lips together and shakes his head. 'You're busy, all those kids . . .'

'That's not an excuse, I should have come. I'm sorry.'

His brow furrows. 'You've got nothing to be sorry for!'

Silence settles, like a feather that's floated onto the floor. It would be so easy to walk away, and get on the train back to London leaving all this behind.

Kate has always felt so much guilt around her relationship with her dad. When she was a teenager it manifested itself as anger, raw and livid. Back then, she was frustrated that he wasn't who she wanted him to be. He wasn't charming or rich like the other girls' fathers. And he couldn't sweep in and save her from herself like she wanted him to. Then what happened when she was nineteen, how he did all the wrong things trying to make it right. She takes a deep breath, remembering what Clare said to her once: sometimes people aren't who you want them to be, but are who you need them to be, if you just give them a chance.

'Dad,' she says, and he looks up, surprised she's called him that. 'I've been meaning to say, for a long time. I'm sorry for everything back when I was drinking. For not appreciating you and everything you've done for me. All the sleepless nights, all the shouting, the hospitals, the overdoses. It must have been awful for you, especially after Mum.' She puts her hand over his, and stares at the floor.

'I never thought for a second how you felt when I was doing all that. I was so selfish, I couldn't see past my pain, let alone think of what I was inflicting on everyone else. I'm going to try and be a better daughter . . .' Her voice trails off. 'I guess I was angry with Mum for leaving me, and I blamed you, 'cause you were there. And that's not fair or right.' She looks up, expecting him to be looking the other way, eyes darting

238

around awkwardly. But he's not, he's looking straight at her; his eyes are kind and watery.

'And then . . . when I came here to stay with Granny, and I was really unwell . . . and then I had her.' Kate starts to cry. 'And you said it might be best we didn't keep her as I couldn't even look after myself.' Tears pour out of her. 'And that Granny was too old, and you couldn't do everything . . . and I've blamed you all these years.'

Jonny takes her hand and lets her talk.

'But actually, I have to take responsibility for that. I agreed to let her go, I knew I was in trouble, that once I had her I wouldn't be able to stop drinking again. And that terrified me. And all this time I blamed you for suggesting it, and I blamed you because I went along with the adoption. But it wasn't your fault. I'm sorry.' She weeps quietly. 'It was my fault that we gave her away, because I couldn't see how I could drink and look after her at the same time. I chose alcohol over my daughter. It was me, not you. It was my fault.' Her shoulders shake, the emotion of saying something she never thought she'd be able to say out loud hitting her in the face. She feels as if she has been clinging on to the side of a boat to stop herself from drowning, and the tips of her toes can finally feel something solid beneath.

He holds her hand, stroking it with his thumb, shhhhing her calmly, letting her cry. And then he speaks. 'I have always regretted it, as soon as that woman took her away in that pink blanket. I should have fought for her. I'm so, so sorry, love,' Jonny says. 'I wished I could have protected you better. Your mother would have turned in her grave,' he grimaces.

'No, Daddy.' She shakes her head, sniffing. 'She would have understood, I think. Out of everyone she would have . . .'

His brow crinkles and he looks confused. 'Why do you say that, love?'

Kate wipes the moisture from under her nose with the side of her hand and sniffs. 'You know, because I've got what she had. She left me because she was scared of who she was, and the kind of mother she would be. That's why she jumped.'

Her father shakes his head a few times, a baffled look has struck his face. 'Kate . . . love. Your mother wasn't an alcoholic. She didn't jump off that bridge. It was an accident.'

Kate swallows. 'What?'

'She was knocked off. A car swerved to avoid a cyclist and hit her instead. It was an accident, Kate . . . she never would have left you.'

'But Granny always said she jumped into the arms of God. And you always said I was just like her.'

'I thought you knew.' He shakes his head angrily. 'I'm so sorry. I should have sat you down and explained. I thought that they told you. I was a mess . . . and you were so, so young.' He looks up and out the window. 'Love, I meant she was just like you. Beautiful, and funny, and full of life. She loved you more than anything.'

'All this time . . . I thought I was pushing against something I was destined for . . .' Kate whispers.

'What, love?'

Kate looks down at her dad, lying in the hospital bed. 'I never let you talk about her, did I? I shut you down every time you brought her up.' She looks at her hands; her fingers are curled limp. What a mess. What a mess she's made of everything, hurting this man who loves her so. 'I promise, I'll never be something you have to lie in bed awake at night worrying about again. All that is in my past.'

'I'm sorry I let you down, your mother would be so proud of you. I am so proud of you.'

Kate whips a tissue out from the box by his bed and holds it against her cheek, blotting the moisture away. Her mother didn't leave her, she didn't decide she'd rather die than be there for Kate. She has clung on to the layers of pain over the years – as if she needed that to justify her behaviour and explain it. She feels as if something has unlocked within herself, as if she can step out of the cage now. The voice that was holding her back, telling her she was a certain way because of something outside of her control, and that eventually, no matter what she did, she was going to end up the same way because of an intrinsic link – the voice can't say that any more. She can hear it calling desperately for attention as it falls further and further away.

She blinks and looks at Jonny. She always said to herself, if she had this conversation with him it would be uncomfortable, the words wouldn't come out how she wanted, and he wouldn't reply with what she needed to hear. But actually, the opposite is true. The only thing that has kept her from a relationship with her father is herself. She put these barriers up; how could he possibly talk to her about anything when she didn't want to hear it?

'You didn't tell me you had a girlfriend!' She hits his arm lightly.

Jonny's cheeks flush. 'I wanted to introduce you properly. I actually called you the other day to invite you up to meet Ronda.'

'I really like her,' she says warmly through the tears. He nods and smiles appreciatively. 'I stayed at hers and she lent me this top.' Kate pulls at the fabric to show him.

'I'm glad,' he says. 'It looks lovely on you.' And then he squeezes her hand.

20

Jonny limps out of the main entrance using crutches. Ronda mimics him hobbling, which prompts them to throw their heads back in laughter. Jonny stops and holds his side, it tickles him so much. His pale, white face becomes red and healthy as he wipes away the tears. Kate doesn't think she's ever seen him laugh so hard. She wanders behind them, watching them bumble along the street together. The way they are with each other makes her smile: the side glances, the private jokes, the way Ronda checks her hair in the reflection of every shop window they pass.

'I can stay for a few nights. The doctor said we need to keep an eye on you after that fall,' Kate suggests as they drink coffee outside a café on the seafront. Jonny refused to go straight home to bed; he said he was sick of lying down and needed some fresh air. Seagulls call down to them and cool, salty wind brushes past as they sip on their drinks.

'No, it's your exams. You need to get back to London.' He pours a third sachet of sugar into his mug and stirs. 'You can't miss school just cos I fell off a bloody ladder.'

'You didn't just fall off a ladder!' She pushes back her hair, which keeps flying in her face. She does need to get back to work, and she's got that last study period with Lily tomorrow.

'I'll be around, love, don't worry.' Ronda says quietly.

Kate smiles, relieved. 'Can I see the house before I go?'

Jonny looks pleased. 'Sure. We'll head over after this.'

Jonny's beloved car is back at the house, so they climb onto a bus. She watches as they pass the jumbled mix of boarded-up shops and pretty independent frontages. A lot has changed since she lived here; gentrification has arrived in Margate. She looks up at the striking glass Turner Gallery which sits on one side of the promenade. She instinctively puts her hand on her stomach as she is reminded of her long walks down the stretch, waddling under the weight of her bump. Her changing body, so alien, and her sober, untreated mind a hive of activity. She wouldn't let herself get attached to the tiny growing person inside her; every time she felt a kick, she closed her eyes and wished it would go away. How she yearns to go back and change what happened next. Whenever she thinks like that, she tells herself she wasn't meant to keep her. That she wouldn't have been able to look after her. Something awful would've happened when she was drunk. Maybe she'd have forgotten she was in the bath, or maybe she'd have fallen down the stairs holding her. And then what would have become of Kate? She wouldn't have recovered from that. She would never have rebuilt her life, and the child would never have grown up.

'It's going to be a different town in ten years,' says Jonny as they pass a trendy coffee shop. Kate nods, staring out at the regenerating town; it looks like her, beaten and dragged into the present and then dressed up to hide the scars.

They get off the bus and walk up to a line of stucco terraces which tower on the opposite side of the road to the sea. It is obvious they were once grand, but they now hunch in various states of disrepair. Some of the windows are broken, and the off-white paint is now more of a dirty, cracked cream. Out front, two large skips are wobbling under the weight of plasterboard and wooden slats. As she gets closer, Kate can see the pattern of old carpet and wallpaper poking out of the top.

'It used to be fifteen bedsits!' Her dad comes up behind her and puts the key in the lock, trying unsuccessfully to open the door. When he jiggles it about, a loud clack releases the latch. 'And before that it was a B & B called the Queen of Margate.'

Inside, it looks exactly as she was expecting: floral carpet in varying tones of brown and yellow, muddied and worn by forty years of footprints. Peeling beige paint and burnt, skewed lampshades hanging from the ceiling. On one side of the corridor are a row of numbered doors. On the other, where work has started, the walls have been knocked through and the room spans from the front window all the way to the back of the house. It has produced a grand room with a large sash window that presents the sea as if it were an oil painting. She stays there a moment and watches the dirty waves crash and packs of seagulls dive into the water in search of food.

A cackle of laughter makes her turn around. Ronda and Jonny are standing by the overturned ladder talking to each other. They look like a unit. Before, when she used to go from one toxic relationship to another, she assumed it was because she had just never seen a healthy one in action. Then she met Ben, and something pinged in her mind. *Oh, this is what love is, I'd mistaken it for something else all along!* Love is funny and calm and exciting and easy and enthralling. It isn't scary and full of anxiety and problems to overcome.

They wave her off at the station. Ronda's handbag wobbles on her elbow and Jonny balances on his crutches. Do people change? Or is it just how she sees them that does? Her dad hasn't, he's always been a steady, constant presence in her life. But she has blamed him for so much and turned him in her head into something he isn't. Did she push all the blame over to him to make what she became easier to swallow? She thinks of Susanna and how wrong she got her. And her own mother, and the role she pinned on her.

It is amazing how the mind works, how it distorts the view, enabling her to live in a fantasy world she created. She doesn't have to live like that any more. She isn't delusional, she hopes. She lives in reality now. That's what the Twelve Steps have done for her, over time they have broken down the fake world she thought she resided in – all the anger and resentments that kept her lonely and angry, they're barely there any more. Especially now she's finally spoken to Jonny, she can see everything clearly now.

She thinks about Becky, the last unresolved thing. Once she's fixed that, she can walk into her future as Mrs Hamilton, with the clean slate she's been craving all these years. Kate Sullivan, the drunk girl at school, the girl with so much promise who drank it all away . . . she just won't exist any more.

Jonny and Ronda's faces pull out of view and she settles back into her seat feeling a million miles away from how she felt on her arrival. When she drank, she just felt like life was one long, dark tunnel of misery. Going from one disaster to the next, without ever coming up for air. She never gave herself a chance to recover from a bleak spell as she'd nosedive into the next, trying to erase it from her memory. Since she's been in recovery, she knows if she rides it out and sits in the fear, she'll come out the other end of the tunnel, and things will be OK again.

She texts Becky, saying she is on her way back and is looking forward to picking up where they left off. Putting in her earphones, she watches the bright-blue sky touch the green landscape as they roll through the countryside. She thinks about the time she was on the train back from Margate, full term, waiting to have her baby. How the last six months with her grandmother had been confrontational, and challenging. She was living without alcohol or drugs for the first time in years. Her head was alive with anger, resentment and pain. Back then she had no idea that, for people like her, just removing the alcohol didn't make them better. She still needed the tools to live. She feels sad for that teenager sitting on the train all those years ago, waiting for a baby she knew she wasn't going to keep.

When the rocking motion comes to a stop, she gets up and steps into the busy London terminal. The train seemed so provincial when it pulled up in Margate. It now relaxes into its bay in St Pancras, heat rising off the wheels like a worn-out fighting bull. Kate slips her ticket into the barrier and joins the rush hour crowds hurrying in various directions. The automated tannoy barely has time to gasp for breath in-between announcements.

The image of her baby haunts her as she wanders into the crowd. Its tiny creased lips in a constant pout, its miniscule fingernails, and dark mop of hair. She was numb when she handed the bundle over. Then, she got very drunk. And she didn't stop drinking until the girl she lived with in Finsbury Park, Colette, took her to that first meeting.

Kate decides to play some happy music to distract herself. She sits on the bus and looks out of the window, humming silently to a song. It makes the corners of her mouth turn up, her foot start to tap. She thinks of Ben. How in all the little moments, when she's minding her own business, his face will pop into her mind. And she remembers she is loved, loved in a way she never thought she was capable of deserving. Maybe the path she took has brought her here for a reason. So she could meet a partner and fall in love before starting a family. She'll actually know who the father is this time. Ben will be such a great dad.

For the first time, she wishes they were having a proper wedding, with a first dance and speeches. She can't even remember why they aren't any more. It suddenly feels sad and a little sordid that they are just popping down to the town hall. Like a dirty secret that doesn't deserve to be celebrated.

Kate walks up the steps to the house. It feels as if she's been away for weeks. When Ben's back from Scotland she's going to book in a weekend for them to go and visit Jonny. If she just allows things to naturally happen, rather than expect them to gel from the off, they'll form their own relationship. They might actually get on; just because they are different doesn't mean they won't. No wonder it's all been so strained, she's been standing in the corner with a tight jaw, trying to conduct the conversation. And Ben would love Ronda, she can imagine them giggling together in a corner. She smiles thinking of it.

Kate is deep in thought when she opens the flat door. Seeing the outline of a man in the kitchen she gasps, too shocked even to scream. He swings around and smiles.

'Shit! I thought you were in Scotland.' She puts a hand on her chest, her heart is pounding.

Ben lumbers towards her and wraps his arms around her. She is sure she can smell Becky's perfume. Holding her shoulders, he pushes her away and looks at her with a tired smile.

'I thought I'd surprise you, I wanted to be here when you got back. Is your dad OK?'

'The doctors couldn't believe how quickly he recovered, said

249

he is made of steel,' she says proudly. 'It was an interesting trip, we talked about my mum . . . about stuff I never knew before. And he's got a girlfriend! He seems happier than I've ever seen him.'

'That's great, Kate, you must be relieved. I know you worry about him.'

'We need to go down there and visit him, we've left it too long,' she says.

Ben nods. 'Sounds great.' He pauses. 'I'd really like to get to know him better. He's such a good guy, Kate, you're lucky.'

'Really? I didn't know you thought of him like that.'

'What do you mean? He's got more loyalty and honour in his little finger than my dad has in his whole body,' he says, and then he pauses in thought. He breaks away from her and walks to the kitchen.

Talk of his dad always puts Ben in a bad mood. She changes the subject. 'Have you seen Becky? Has she gone out?' Kate asks, looking around. 'When did you get back?'

He removes the water filter jug from the fridge and starts to pour. His movements are thoughtful and slow. Holding the glass up to the light he frowns, and then pours the water down the sink, cleaning it under hot soapy water before pouring another glass. 'She's gone home.' He coughs.

'Oh.' Kate is disappointed. 'Really? I asked her to stay. Did you see her?'

'Only briefly. I helped her pack the car,' he says, sipping his drink and swallowing loudly.

'So, she just left? And went to her mother's?'

'Yeah,' he shrugs.

'Was she OK?'

'I don't know, I think so.' He shrugs again.

Kate is annoyed, sometimes men are just so useless at gaining subtleties. 'Maybe I should call her.'

Ben's face crunches in the middle. 'Why? I thought you wanted her to go? I thought you wanted it to be just us again.'

'Well I did, but . . . I thought she'd go to Alexa's . . . I'm worried about her . . . I just want to talk to her about something.' She looks at the front door. 'I could cycle over there, it wouldn't take long.' She looks over at her coat and helmet resting on the hooks by the door.

'Can't you just leave it?' Ben says, and there is rough quality to his voice that makes her look over at him in surprise.

'Why?' she asks indignantly.

'Because all you've done since we bumped into her at the restaurant is obsess over her and her feelings, and I'm getting pretty sick of it, to be honest.' He puts the glass down with a bang, and it echoes around the room.

Kate's lips part, she's never seen him like this. 'I . . . shit, Ben . . .' She massages her forehead and stops. She's taken him for granted, just marched ahead with what she's wanted this whole time, without really stopping to think about him, about them. 'I'm sorry.'

He looks up at the ceiling and shakes his head. 'Fuck, no . . . I'm sorry.' He comes over to where she is standing and holds her again. 'I'm just tired, and I've been worried about you and your dad. You've had a stressful few days, I haven't seen you all week,' he tells her. 'Why don't you go and see her after school tomorrow, once you've recovered and rested a bit? I'm just worried you're getting yourself into a state, like . . . like when we met.'

She feels as if she's been knocked, as though he's picked her up like one of those toys in an arcade game and put her back where she should be. 'But that's exactly why I have to do this. I feel like something is festering. I drank the other week. On the train to see my dad I was obsessing about drinking. I feel uneasy about all this stuff with Becky, I need to fix it so I can move on.'

'You're your own worst enemy, Kate. You get so emotionally involved in everyone else. How about you just stop, and just focus on us for a little bit, yeah?'

She looks up at him. His eyes soften at the edges, and he gives one of those half-smiles that gets her right in the stomach. He is right, of course. She probably shouldn't go charging round there.

'Yes, OK, I'll talk to her tomorrow,' she says, agreeing.

He claps his hands together. 'Great, now what would madam like for dinner? I'll make you anything you want.' He opens the fridge. 'As long as it involves broccoli and salmon.'

'Sounds lovely,' Kate says distantly. 'I'm going to go and get changed.'

She trudges up the stairs. Something comes with her, it's the thing that's been following her around since she saw Becky again. That lingering feeling that just won't go away.

She takes off the top that Ronda gave her and throws it into the wicker wash basket. Clare said that the reason for Step Nine is that it clears out your closet so nothing can come back and bite you. You've kept your side of the street clean; you've resolved any problems with the people around you. The closure you get allows you to start again, with a clean slate. She thinks about how naive she was, when she sat in front of Becky and did her Step Nine. Apologizing for petty, stupid, teenage things, when actually there was something far more significant that she apparently needed to make amends for. Becky must have sat there raging.

Kate opens the door to the spare room and flicks on the light, staring at the emptiness of it. The bed is made, and there is no longer a neat row of shoes by the door. Just before she plunges the room into darkness again, she notices a photograph standing against one of the bedside lights. She walks inside and picks it up. It is the photograph of the girls on prom night. It must have fallen onto the floor when she packed the basket away. She looks at their wide eyes and pouting lips. She looks at Becky – she has never noticed the way she's looking over at Kate with respect and a tiny bit of fear. She puts the photograph back and walks out of the room.

'How long are you going to be?' Ben calls from downstairs. 'Want me to choose a movie?'

'Yeah, sure!' she replies, not really caring. 'I'm coming now.'

Kate pauses at the banister. Smells of dinner curl up the stairs. She just hopes she can make everything right with

Becky. The thought of spending the rest of her life knowing someone is in pain because of her is terrifying. She goes into their room and sits on the bed, thinking about Becky and the strange way she behaved while staying with them. If there are unresolved issues between them, why did Becky want to be so close? She shivers. Even though she's gone, Kate can't shake the feeling that this isn't over.

21

Kate has never before noticed how loudly the clock ticks in her classroom. She listens to the reverberating tick-tick-tick as her eyes scan over Lily's detached and anxious face. The young girl has the tangy, rotten smell of yesterday's booze about her. Her eye contours are dark and veiny and shine with sweat. Her beautiful long hair is glazed with grease. Kate wants to cup her hand under Lily's chin, she wants to gently move the hair away from her face, she wants to hold her and rock her like a baby and tell her everything is going to be OK. But she can't. Instead she points her pen at a row of text.

'This is an example of last year's exam question: *How does Carol Ann Duffy present emotions of love and jealousy?* Let's think of some areas of discussion for an essay.'

Lily flinches, her fingers are flicking at the corners of the A4 sheet of paper. 'I dunno, Miss.'

Kate sits back in her chair, frustrated. 'Come on, Lily, you can answer this, we've talked about it in class a few times and you've always had loads to say.'

The girl stays silent. 'I've got to go,' she mumbles. Kate

looks at the clock. Lily was fifteen minutes late and she's been sitting there monosyllabically for not even half the session.

Kate slaps the textbook on the desk, annoyed. 'Lily, do you know how worried your mother is about you?'

Lily looks up fiercely. 'Did you report my eye? Did you tell my mum?' she says, mouth wobbling with a heady mix of anger and distress.

Kate pauses, she takes a deep breath. 'Lily, it wasn't me, it was another teacher. And anyway, I shouldn't have taken your word it was an accident.'

'You said if I came in, you wouldn't. You lied.' Her glassy red eyes are brimming with tears.

'Lily, I didn't mean for it to sound like an ultimatum . . .' she says, not really knowing if that's true.

'My mum went to the police, they are interviewing Callum,' she shouts. 'I hate her . . . I hate her,' she screams, standing, her hands balled up tightly by her waist.

'Lily, calm down.' Kate tries to put her hand on her arm, but it's flapped away. 'You don't mean that, she loves you. She just wants the best for you.'

'She doesn't, and I don't care about any of this. I'm not coming to the exam, Miss, I've come to tell you. And I wanted you to know it's your fault for telling that stupid bitch on me.' She rushes to the door.

Kate feels as if her hands are tied behind her back, she wants to express herself, but she needs to stay within the boundaries.

'Lily!' Kate shouts, and the girl turns with hatred in her eyes.

'Fine, hate me, hate your mum. That's fine. But please, please come to the exam. Because you know if you don't, it will all be for nothing. All the coursework and that first paper . . .'

Lily gives her one more scornful look. 'I just don't care, Miss.' And with that she turns her back and runs away.

Kate coughs out a breath as if she's been punched. She holds out her hands to see them shaking. Fuck, she's totally fucked this up. The passionate outburst has shocked Kate to the core. She is trying to remember the conversation they had outside the shop – had she really said she wouldn't tell anyone about her eye if Lily came for extra tuition? It is all so muddled. She hadn't meant it like that, surely. Has her need to control everything seeped through into this? Her lips start to move, and she lets her head fall into her hands. Please let go, please help me let go of this, she whispers aloud.

After six years has she really changed that much? Have some of her old behaviours started creeping back in, so surreptitiously she hadn't even noticed? She thinks about the cocktail in the club and the terrible thoughts she was having on the train. The worry is so eclipsing she can't work out if this is something that she's doing to herself. They do say that nostalgia for past habits can be easier to live with than the unknown. Does being happy scare her so much that she is sabotaging herself? Did she take things with Lily too far, has she risked her career? And Ben, is she pushing him away, creating drama just so she can distract herself from the fear that things may not work out anyway?

*

257

At the end of the day she shuts down her computer and locks the door to her classroom. Kate walks down the empty corridor feeling numb. If Lily isn't going to come tomorrow, what is the point? She contemplates not turning up either. *Shut up*, she tells her head.

Kate thinks about what Ben said about their relationship being neglected. He's right. She's barely thought about the wedding really, only in terms of herself, she hasn't contemplated how he's feeling. It's only a week away and, with Becky around, they've barely discussed it.

Kate puts her hands around the bars of her bike and lifts the wheel out of its station, walking to the road. She lets the frame rest on her hip as she attaches her helmet fastening. She's not going home; she's going to find Becky and put all this behind her so she can give Ben and their future the attention they deserve.

'Kate!' Her name is called and she turns.

Her mouth hangs open when she sees who has shouted.

'Alexa!' she exclaims. 'Alexa . . . what are you doing here?' Alexa climbs out of her giant 4 x 4. Kate peers into the blacked-out windows to see if Becky is inside.

Alexa shuts the door with a swift swing of the arm. She looks oddly pale compared to everything else, which is illuminated by hazy evening light. Her black hair is tied into a bun and she is wearing large tasselled earrings which shake with her every movement. Her bump sticks out, defying gravity. It looks as if the skin-tight black dress she is wearing is grasping onto it, supporting the weight.

'Sorry, I didn't have your address or number, but I knew this was your school,' she says as she approaches. 'Do you have a moment?' She looks strained, but relieved to have caught her.

'Yes, of course. Is Becky OK?'

'What happened when she was with you?'

'What do you mean? We decided it wasn't the best time to have a visitor, I hope you understand.'

'She went back to Mummy's and had a massive row with her, said some really awful things, and then she left and no one's been able to get hold of her. Mummy was too upset to get any details and she isn't answering the phone. Do you know where she's gone?'

'What? No . . . I've been in Margate,' Kate stumbles.

'I just can't get hold of her, I'm worried. What if she's done something stupid?' Her voice rises as she speaks, and she puts her hands on her stomach for comfort. Kate sees another teacher leaving the school give the pair an odd look.

'Why don't we sit over there.' She points to a bench. Alexa nods and takes a deep breath. Kate helps her down onto the seat. 'I'm sure it's nothing to worry about. She's probably with another friend or something,' she says, trying to calm Alexa who seems to be overly worried.

'She said you'd look after her, that you knew all about it,' Alexa barks anxiously, rubbing her stomach to keep the agitation at bay.

'What do you mean?' Kate is confused. 'That I'd look after her?' Becky certainly doesn't seem like she needs looking after, she's so sophisticated and self-assured.

'You got yourself clean, I thought maybe some of that would rub off on her.'

'Clean?' Kate says, alarmed.

Alexa looks over at her. 'Didn't she tell you?'

Kate shakes her head slowly. 'Tell me what?'

Alexa is stunned. 'She said you knew everything, she said she felt safe with you.'

'What do you mean, Alexa?' Kate asks.

'She picked up a really bad addiction to prescription pills in the States. She promised she hadn't touched them since she'd got back.' Kate thinks back to the pills Becky was holding by the sink and her erratic behaviour.

'She didn't tell me any of this,' Kate whispers. She thinks about sitting in the AA meeting with Becky, how she'd hung on every word.

Alexa takes a deep breath and looks up at the sky in frustration. 'Oh God, I've made a mess of this,' she whispers. She turns to Kate. 'Will you go and see Mummy, try and find out what she said to Becky? She's refusing to tell me anything.' She lifts a shaking hand to her face. 'Maybe she'll listen to you.' Her voice wobbles. 'She always loved you, Kate.'

Kate stares across the street. It is the last thing she feels like doing. 'She didn't love me,' Kate mumbles.

'Please.' Alexa puts her hands over Kate's. 'I've been so busy with the boys, I thought maybe Becky would be able to help with Mummy. I forgot how difficult they were with each other. And that house! It's such a mess, the housekeeper is useless, she's almost eighty but Mummy refuses to replace her. Daddy

260

washed his hands of her long ago.' Kate watches her pale, white skin redden and become blotchy, holding in the tears. Kate wonders how much Alexa has been keeping inside and for how long. 'Please can you talk to Mummy? You know about this stuff.' Her eyes plead with her. 'Becky . . . she needs you.'

'Oh Alexa . . . I had no idea . . .' she whispers. She can't believe she missed the signs; she was so caught up in herself and her paranoia that Becky was trying to take Ben away. Kate licks her lips, suddenly afraid. 'I was planning to find her tonight, things were left . . . unfinished.'

'What do you mean?' Alexa asks, straightening her back.

'I just wanted to make sure she was OK; I didn't want her to leave with any bad feeling.'

'Bad feeling?' Alexa questions.

'It's probably nothing. Ben asked her to leave while I was away, and I was worried she was upset.' She should have taken better care of Becky, she thinks. 'I'll come and see Susanna. Anything I can do to help.'

Relief rides across Alexa's face. 'Do you want me to drive you?'

'It's fine, I'll cycle over.'

They exchange numbers and Kate watches the large, shiny vehicle drive off. The rustling sound of leaves compels her to lift her chin to the trees. Clouds are moving at a pace she's not seen for weeks. The still saturation the heat had layered upon everything has gone. Debris rolls down pavements, like tumbleweed in a sandstorm. She had thought she was going mad, but there really was something going on with Becky.

She's had enough counselling and group therapy over the last six years to know how long things can affect you, they don't just disappear if you ignore them. If something happened to Becky that night all those years ago, she could be self-medicating, using the pills to dull the pain. Addiction is addiction, no matter the poison you choose. Kate squeezes her eyes shut, wishing Becky's cries would stop echoing in her head.

She locks her bike outside the house in Belsize Park. The sun is hidden behind buxom grey clouds, the air feels heavy, as if it's about to drop. She walks towards the front steps and looks up, squinting. Curtains are drawn at every window. She rings on the bell and waits – nothing. She rings again and bends down, peeking into the letter box. She starts to back off down the steps, looking up one last time. Then she sees Susanna peering out of a curtain, their eyes meet, and Susanna nods. A few minutes later the front door is opened a crack.

'Yes?' she says as if Kate were a stranger.

'Susanna, Alexa asked me to come. Can we speak? We're worried about Becky. And you.'

'You've got nothing to worry about, young lady!'

Kate walks forward pushing the door slightly. 'Can I come in?'

Susanna doesn't put up much of a fight. 'I wasn't expecting visitors. And I excused Maria for the day.'

Kate follows her inside, into the dimly lit hallway. Susanna is wearing a dressing gown; there is a stain on it. It could be wine, or urine. A number of smells attack Kate as they continue through the house. She is unsure if they are coming from the furniture or from Susanna herself. She notices a few helpings of dog excrement littered around and she begins to breathe through her mouth.

'Would you like a drink?' asks Susanna.

'No, no. I'm fine.'

'Shall we go in the cosy room?' Susanna asks grandly.

Kate follows her into the living room and watches Susanna as she wobbles back on a lounge chair. Mess is scattered around her: ashtrays, newspapers, overturned glasses. 'What can I help you with?' she says, lighting a cigarette. Kate can tell she is trying to act sober. The attempt would be funny if it weren't so sad.

'Becky, she was staying with me, and we don't know where she is.' Susanna is turning her hands over and inspecting them, as if she isn't interested. 'Did you have a fight? Do you know where she went, Susanna?'

Susanna shifts in her seat. 'I've spent my life being disappointed by her. I'm used to it,' she says simply.

Kate grits her teeth. 'And how has she disappointed you? Because she isn't a model like Alexa?'

Susanna lets out a little punctuated laugh. 'Ha! I never wanted to have another. Mr Cross lied, you know, about having his tubes tied. And hey presto! I should have given her away.' She sniffs. 'You know my body was never the same after that, my career was ruined.'

'Susanna, I don't think you mean that . . .' Kate starts.

Susanna looks at her with cold eyes. 'You wouldn't

understand, dear . . . being a mother is one of the hardest jobs in the world.'

The comment burns, and Kate wants to dig her nails into this twisted, nasty, bitter woman. A woman she could have easily become if she had continued drinking. Festering with resentments, piss-stained and alone. All the anger she has towards herself, towards her illness, rises to the surface.

'I may not know much about being a mother, but I know a lot about giving away a daughter. And it's one of the worst things I ever did, and I regret it every day,' she shouts.

Susanna's mouth hangs open, taken aback.

'But at least I wasn't a mother like you. At least my child has never seen me like your daughters have seen you,' Kate spits. She stands, raising a shaking finger, pointing at the ghastly woman in front of her. 'You can get better, you know, you don't always have to be like this. You can be loved; you can love again.' She gathers her bag and helmet off the floor and begins to walk away.

Susanna calls after her, 'Thanks for dropping by. And by the way . . .' Kate turns to listen. 'I'd be careful with your fiancé around that daughter of mine. You know she has his passport? She's a nasty, thieving cow, that one. I was looking through her bag for pills when I found it.'

'What?' She staggers.

There is a look of glee on Susanna's face that Kate wishes she could knock out of her.

Susanna takes a sip of her drink, satisfied. Kate shakes her head at the woman and continues her mission to leave. She runs for the door. Kate needs to get away from there; Susanna is an apparition of what her future could be, and she has the urge to get away before anything sticks. She can still hear Susanna laughing as she bangs the front door shut and runs down the steps.

Kate is in a daze when she walks through the door of the apartment. 'You're back,' Ben says as he walks over to kiss her cheek. 'How was it? Look, I collected my suit!' He picks up a suit bag he'd thrown on the back of the sofa. He notices her demeanour. 'Hey . . . are you OK?'

'Alexa came to school. Becky isn't at Susanna's,' she says softly. 'I went to the house to see if I could find out where she went.'

'What?' Ben is confused.

'Alexa let her stay here because apparently I'm a good halfway house for the mentally unstable.' She feels like crying. 'But the fact is, I had no idea. I have no idea who she is at all.'

Ben walks over to her. 'Hey . . . hey . . . don't cry.'

'Why did she come here?' Kate asks, even though she feels as if she knows the answer. She starts wringing her hands. 'I knew it, I knew she came back to get back at me, she wants to stop me from getting my happy ending,' she whispers frantically.

'Happy ending?' Ben laughs. 'Kate, you've had a shock.'

'The whole thing, it doesn't feel right,' she says, rubbing her chest trying to soothe the anxiety. 'Did something happen between you two? Tell me.' She looks over and studies his reaction.

He walks across and puts his hand on her shoulder. 'Kate, you're tired.'

She moves away. 'What happened between you two, on the landing, that night after the club?' she asks again.

'Kate, what can I do to make you believe nothing happened?' He puts his arms in the air. 'This is crazy!'

She turns. 'Why does she have your passport?'

'What?' he asks, confused.

'Susanna said she found your passport in Becky's bag.'

'What?' Ben laughs in shock. 'Are you serious?'

'Why has she got your passport, Ben?'

'I have no idea!' he says, his voice thick with exasperation.

She marches towards the stairs. She needs to get the notion of them flying back to New York together out of her head.

He follows behind her. 'This is insane.'

They make it to their room and Kate walks over to the drawer where he keeps his passport, the same drawer Kate caught Becky looking through. She yanks it open, positive it will be missing. The contents shake and she peers down.

There in the middle of the bric-a-brac lies his blue passport. 'Oh,' she says out loud as she holds it up. She looks over at Ben; he isn't smug, he just looks sad.

'Susanna said she saw it in her bag,' Kate whispers.

Ben nods slowly. 'Kate . . .' He rubs the back of his head. 'Do you think you should go to some more meetings? Maybe look into therapy to go alongside it?'

She looks down at the book between her hands. Is she going

crazy? 'I shouldn't have listened to her, she's mad.' She walks towards him, but he backs away a step. 'Ben, I'm so sorry.'

Her phone beeps, she looks down. It is Miriam, the woman who is making her wedding dress. She has used some of the lace from her mother's veil, it was the one special touch she wanted on the bare-minimum wedding day. *It's ready! let me know when you want to pick it up x*

'Kate, do you really think I would ever cheat on you? Let alone with a friend of yours who is staying in the next room?'

She shakes her head. 'No, I'm so sorry . . . I've just been under a lot of stress.' She blinks a tear away. She's losing him, she can feel it.

She pauses and looks at the text again, her dress. She's getting married, she never thought it would actually happen. She never thought she was capable of a healthy relationship. She feels insane, is she is self-sabotaging? What if this is her illness trying to get her alone and vulnerable by pushing Ben away?

'How was Becky when she left?' Kate asks.

Ben sits down on the bed and rubs his face, thinking. 'Um . . . sad. Thoughtful? She said she was really thankful that we had her to stay.' He thinks. 'Actually, she did say she wanted to see you and clear things up . . . she said maybe after the wedding, when we have a bit more time.'

She nods, maybe Becky had wanted to ruin their relationship, to get back at Kate. Maybe she realized Ben was never going to be the bad guy and left, defeated. But here Kate is, ruining their relationship anyway, allowing Becky's plan to unfold even though she isn't even here any more. She wipes her brow as the thoughts tumble.

'You can't really think she came back to get something over on you for something that happened when you were teenagers?' He looks concerned. 'Please, please, can we just refocus a bit? This isn't our problem. Get through the last exam, I know how stressful you find them. Then how about we get hitched, yeah? We can worry about Becky afterwards.' He takes her hand and puts it inside his and squeezes. Her Ben, her lovely, kind, wonderful Ben.

'I'll go to more meetings, and I'll look into therapy.' Kate says. 'I obviously need more help.' She leans her head on his shoulder and closes her eyes.

22

Kate carefully places a name card on the corner of each desk in the hall. When she comes to Lily's she puts it down sadly, her finger tracing the edge of the paper. Mrs Wells spoke to Mrs Johnson the evening before; she said she'd do her best to get her to the exam, but Lily hadn't been home and Kate wasn't holding out much hope. The whole morning has been licked with grey paint – every conversation, every step she has taken feels as if it has painfully dragged out, like it is playing at half speed.

Nothing feels right. Lily, Becky and her relationship with Ben. It is all falling to pieces. Pain is inevitable but suffering is optional, is what Clare would say. Clare. She'll call her straight after this exam! The thought almost makes her smile. She's not been working her programme at all and has been wrestling with all of this stuff on her own. Hoarding it to herself, letting it pile up precariously. If she went through it with someone, bit by bit, and organized it into orderly piles, it would all make sense, she is sure of it.

The sound of the main doors opening brings her back

into the room. The students troop in. They chatter nervously like twittering doves and the sound echoes beneath the high ceiling. She hopes one of them is Lily. Kate pictures the girl ten years in the future, in an office, laughing in her chair at something a colleague has said. She answers the phone confidently and types away at her computer, happy and fulfilled. Then Kate imagines Lily at home, surrounded by empty bottles and crowded ashtrays. The TV on and a cigarette hanging from her lips. Her sparkling eyes dulled and vacant. She looks down at Lily's name card on the desk. *Please come*, she thinks.

Scared, she watches the stragglers join the rest of the year. There are about a hundred sitting the exam – they look like rabbits in headlights. It's funny what a leveller an exam hall is: all the popular kids, all the nerds, the ones that need to work that little bit harder, they all have the same wide-eyed expression on their face.

She folds her arms and watches as Mr Skinner marks each pupil in at the door. Instinctively she holds onto her pendant and drags it up and down the chain. If she comes, she'll be late – Lily is always late. Kate looks out of the window; a throng of birds flies across and then back the other way, as if they can't make up their mind which way to go.

The table she is standing next to shakes, and she looks down. Lily has taken her seat, and she puts a cracked biro on the desk, next to the exam paper.

'You came,' says Kate, mystified.

Lily stares ahead. 'He was cheating on me the whole time, Miss. He never really loved me.' She sniffs and sits up in her

270

chair. 'He always said there was no point me doing my exams, but then I remembered what you said, that I should be in the top set. And the poem, Miss, I didn't want to end up dead like her.'

Mr Skinner comes running over, an annoyed look on his face. 'Everything all right, Lily?'

Kate nods quickly. 'Yes, her pen's just broken.' She puts a fresh one down for her. 'All sorted.' She blasts him a smile, and he walks away.

'I'm so happy you are here. Just try and focus, worry about all that later,' she whispers to her.

As Kate walks away, a smile eases onto her tired, cracked lips. She can't believe Lily came, she hadn't even allowed herself to hope. She stands next to Gus, and he nudges her, as if to say, *See!* She feels as if she could combust with pride and joy. She notices a face looking through the glass door; it's Malcolm. His eyes track the full desks and he gives them both a satisfied nod before walking away. Kate feels lighter than she has for weeks.

The exam is an hour and forty-five minutes long. She spends the time walking from top to bottom of the room, in and out, as if she is on a grid. She tries not to think about Becky, about where she is. She can't get her friend's face out of her mind, the way it looked the other night when Becky was trying not to cry. She hadn't looked angry or bitter, the way Kate expected. Maybe she's back in New York. Maybe they'll never have that conversation, maybe she'll never hear from Becky again. Maybe nothing will happen at all. The thought stumps

271

her; her mind has been so invested in the situation, it just hasn't occurred to her. Her shoulders relax. She has spent this long living in denial about that night, maybe that will just continue.

Kate looks over at Lily who is deeply in the zone. Her pen is speeding across the page, her mouth is moving as she writes, occasional flicks of irritation as if her hand is too slow for the words that are pouring out. Kate starts to wonder if she'll get the top grade.

Just before the end of the exam, Kate notices a commotion outside the door. Her brow furrows, irritated that something might distract her students. She wanders closer to see what's going on. She is surprised to see Mrs Johnson standing there; her arms are crossed and she looks angry. Malcolm and Maureen are listening to her with intense concern. Malcolm tries to get her to walk down the corridor towards his office. Mrs Johnson throws her arms in the air in frustration.

Kate wonders what's going on. She looks over at the students and at Lily, they all have their heads down, no one has noticed. She checks the clock; there are five minutes until the end of the allocated time. She looks back over; Mrs Johnson has gone. Malcolm is standing there, a dark look upon his face.

The bell goes. 'Pens down! No talking!' shouts Mr Skinner. 'Write your names on the first page.'

Maureen's head pokes in at the door. 'Mr Skinner,' she calls. He walks over, annoyed to be interrupted at such an important moment.

Everything slows down then. Kate can't remember the exact

272

moment she realizes; it just occurs to her. She looks at Lily running her eyes over her sheet one last time with a satisfied smile on her face. Kate then looks over at Malcolm, who stares back at her without a trace of warmth. Her heart sinks.

'Miss Sullivan, Maureen needs you,' Mr Skinner walks over to her and whispers.

Kate freezes to the spot. Maureen comes over. She takes her by the arm and pulls her towards the door.

She puts her hands either side of the basin. Her fingers hang over the edge; they look like she is in rigor mortis, they are so stiff and white. Her head is hung, her eyes are closed in pain. Her mind is rushing with a thousand arrows of hurt, almost too thick to make sense of anything at all. She wants to run for cover, she doesn't want to be here any more. If only it were possible to remove her mind from her body just for this next bit, so she could go through the motions without feeling anything at all. She thinks of a sip, just one sip, that could take this feeling away. She groans and turns the tap on; cupping some cold water in her hands she splashes it across her face in an attempt to bring her back to reality. She is reminded of a breathing technique she learnt and she tries it as the excess water drips down into the ceramic washbowl, making a tapping noise. One sip, one sip, just one sip.

'Miss Sullivan, we are waiting for you,' Maureen shouts into the toilets.

'I'm coming,' Kate replies.

She tears off some paper from the dispenser and carefully

wipes the dripping mascara from her face. Maybe she is just a bad person. Even when she tries to make things right, she gets it completely wrong. She leaves the toilet and walks with Maureen along the corridor.

Inside the office Malcolm sits behind his desk. He looks downbeat and stressed. It is rare for him to look like that, even though he should, with the amount he has on his shoulders. 'Sit down,' he says, scratching the back of his head. The hair looks dishevelled, as though he's been rummaging around in it all morning, trying to find the thing that will make sense of what's going on.

'Miss Sullivan, did you tell Lily Johnson that you'd keep an injury a secret if she came to your classes?'

'No . . . I . . . well . . . I bumped into her on the street. She said it was an accident . . .' her mouth opens and closes trying to find the words, '. . . and we arranged for some extra tuition sessions . . . I didn't mean for it to seem like . . .' Her voice is weak, it trails off as she speaks.

'Her mother came into the school, she read Lily's diary.' He holds up a photocopied piece of paper. 'This is quite incriminating, I'm afraid.'

'I . . . I didn't mean . . .' Did she mean to do it? Is she that much of a perfectionist, is she that competitive, that she put a student in danger? 'I'm so sorry,' she whispers. 'It all just got out of hand. I just wanted her to finish . . .'

Malcolm leans forward. 'Kate, you are one of my most promising teachers. I have no doubt that your intentions were in the right place. But we have a duty of care to these kids. Did

274

you know who her boyfriend is? Callum Tate, a notorious drug dealer, he's been farming kids out to county lines. Really scary stuff. Lily could have got caught up in all that.'

'Oh God, I had no idea . . . I . . .'

Malcolm holds up his hand. 'Just take the rest of the day and let's talk in the morning. I may have to take this up the chain. Let me think on it. OK?'

Kate nods, unable to speak. She walks out of the room, her arms slack against her body, devoid of anything at all. She feels like an empty vessel floating on a silent sea.

23

Everything looks exactly the same but is completely different. She is different. After retrieving her bag from her classroom, she changes methodically, on autopilot. Looking up at herself in the mirror Kate slowly unbuttons her work shirt and slips off the sleeves. She unzips the fly of her black tailored trousers and steps out of them. She takes out the pins in her carefully turned bun and shakes out her hair. She puts on her damp cycling clothes. She feels physically uncomfortable, itchy and wet. She doesn't mind, the tangible feeling distracts her from the mental agitation.

The bell rings as she walks down the main corridor. Doors fling open, kids shout and whoop and jump in the air. The sounds reverberate, jolting her. She is tender and rocky, as if she could accidently knock into everyone she passes. She wants to cover her ears, kneel on the floor and scream.

She makes it to the exit. Lily is standing inside reception chatting to Maureen; she is leaning against the door frame, chewing gum and grinning. She notices Kate walking past.

Smiling, she rocks herself off the door frame to speak to her, but Kate bows her head and keeps on going.

'Miss!' she hears Lily call, but she hurries out of the door and onto the street.

Will she get sacked? Maybe that will be for the best. She shouldn't have thought she could do this, live a normal life, have a successful career. *Stupid Kate, stupid*. Shhh, she says out loud. A man walks past and gives her an odd look.

Her phone buzzes in her pocket as she gets out her bike. It's Ben. She doesn't want to hear his cheery voice congratulating her on finishing the exams. She almost cancels the call.

'Hi.' Her voice sounds weird, she thinks.

'Hey!' Ben says. 'How did it go? Congratulations, they're over!'

'Yes.'

'Well. How did it go?' he asks again.

'Ben, I . . . I've been asked to leave for the day.'

'What?' he says, confused.

'I've done something incredibly stupid.'

'What? Kate, you sound weird.' He is concerned.

She doesn't respond at first. 'I'll call you later.'

'Are you coming home? I'm here, I'll wait for you. Kate?' he says, panicked.

She hangs up and stuffs the handset in her backpack. She isn't going home. She's let the voice override everything else, it is guiding her, and she has lost her ability to reason with it. It won't take her long to get there. She cycles away from the high-pitched screams of the kids in the playground.

Kate can't get the image of the baby bundled in the pink blanket out of her head, the feel of her soft, thin skin on Kate's lips as she kissed her goodbye. And the way she had cried for Kate, fingers opening and closing, grasping for her mother, for her touch, her smell. Kate rides faster and faster, trying to wipe the image from her mind.

She always tells herself if she hadn't given the baby away, the little girl's life would have been ruined by her inability to look after a child. But she should never have let her go, she knows from personal experience what it's like to lose a mother. What other lies does she believe, just so she can function, she wonders. Kate has been so proud of her sobriety the last six years, but has she really been living in reality all of this time? Or has she just been picking and choosing what to scrutinize? She's only just resolved her relationship with Jonny, and she never told Clare about the baby, the shame too big to name. It is the most monumental thing about her, and Clare doesn't have a clue. All that work they did together, and Kate only let her in on the stuff that she wanted to deal with. None of the hard stuff. Not the stuff that really needed exploring.

Kate pushes harder on the pedals. She is going to the only place she can think of. A chorus of tragedy is pulling her there. She must find out, she must remember. It is the place where this whole sorry mess begins and ends.

Her bike swings from side to side as she cycles quickly through Kings Cross. Behind her are the brand-new sky-scrapers of the city. She weaves through four lanes of traffic; it is filthy and polluted. She heaves in each dense breath, barely filtering any oxygen through. She looks up at the heavy sky, wondering what it is waiting for – the curling grey clouds look ready to burst. Her chest feels tighter and tighter as she makes her way across town. Just before Regent's Park she turns down the long road that will take her to Camden Town. It has mainly weekday homes of the wealthy, and an army barracks sits on the end of the street. This side of London feels so established compared to parts of the East End which are either ramshackle or sparkly and new.

She gets off her bike. She looks up at the vulture on the swinging board – it is as if he knew she'd be back. The bird gives her a sad sort of smile, as if he was hoping his suspicion was mistaken. The welcome she would have received ten years ago plays in her head: the clink of her favourite drink being put on the bar, someone pulling over a stool for her, beckoning her over with a wicked smile.

She stands in the empty pub. It is four in the afternoon, not quite lunchtime and not quite evening either. It is open and clean. The old nooks and crannies with people huddled talking are gone. She walks to the bar and sits at the counter, stroking the smooth varnish that has trapped the worn chips and cracks of its previous incarnation.

'What can I get you?' It is the same barman from the other week. She blinks.

'Can I just get a soda water please?' she asks.

The barman nods and loads ice into a tall glass, whistling along to a song. 'Lime?' He holds up the sliced piece of fruit between some pincers.

She nods. 'Sure.'

Behind him is an open door that takes you through to a corridor where you can either go up or down. To the flat or the cellar. A filled glass is placed in front of her and she goes to retrieve her wallet.

'Don't worry about it,' he says shaking his hand at her. 'It's just from the pump.'

'Are you sure?' she asks and he nods before setting back off to work, whistling. He looks like one of those people who Kate wishes she could be. Just naturally content. Not fazed by ambition or worried about the future. Just able to enjoy the simplicity of removing glasses from the washer and neatly arranging them in a queue under the giant mirror that spans the bar. When Kate worked here, her mind was a constant hive of worry, of what she did the night before, of where her life was going, of what a terrible person she was for a multitude of reasons. She would bang glasses down with a huff. She'd hate the day shift, and would will the clock to move faster, so that the evening crowd would come in and buy her drinks. That's when her mind would quieten, and she would be able to enjoy being herself again. For a moment.

Kate hops off the stool and moves over to a small table by the front door. 'Thanks.'

She sits there for a while, listening to the innocuous sounds of an empty pub, the kitchen washing up, places being set for dinner, barrels loading down the shaft at the front. She takes a deep sip of her drink. She is thirsty from her cycle, the ice clinks and her teeth smart from the cold liquid.

Kate thinks about the aftermath of her mother dying, the confusion and the sadness in everyone's eyes that they tried to mask from the little girl yanking the hem of their clothes, asking where her mummy had gone. They were all crying and smiling. Lots of, but your mummy is in heaven with Grandma and Grandpa. Lots of, your mummy loved you very much, it's Christmas Day and your mummy would want me to give you the biggest cuddle. Lots of smiles that glistened with tears. Pretending everything was OK. It was confusing. She takes another sip of water.

There is a bang, and the door to the pub clatters on its hinges. She jumps. 'Sorry,' says the man who just walked in.

Kate shakes her head, as if to say not to worry. She watches him go over to the bar and chat freely with the guy serving. He must be a regular. She looks over at the door behind the bar, then up at the clock; she's been sitting there for over an hour.

The door bangs again, and three guys wearing suits enter, easing off their ties. A good sign, early evening traffic has started. The regular leaves his pint on the bar and walks towards the men's toilet. The barman welcomes the relieved and excitable men who have just walked in. Kate picks her moment and slides out of her chair. She walks towards the ladies, but just as she goes past the end of the bar, while the server is bent double removing pint glasses from the shelf below, she ducks through the door at the end of the bar that takes her behind the scenes.

The noise from the pub becomes muffled as she holds onto the banister at the bottom of the stairs. She turns her head upwards, listening to hear if anyone is up there. There are no footsteps. There used to be a spare key behind the coat rack, and she finds it still there.

She uses the sounds of laughter from the pub to mask her ascent up the creaky wooden stairs. She tries the key, but finds it's already open. When she shuts the door behind her the noises from below stop immediately. It is eerily quiet behind the heavy old door, as if the pub below doesn't even exist.

She looks up, half expecting to see Chris's belongings clogging up the hallway. They always joked that it was one broken television and three overspilling ashtrays away from looking like a squat. But now the flat is empty, there isn't a stick of furniture inside.

Touching the magnolia walls, she looks up at the bulbs which hang anonymously from basic plastic light fittings. The living room is full of cardboard boxes with line drawings of glasses on the side. Back then, there would have been someone sleeping under a pile of coats on the sofa and a constant low babble coming from the TV.

She turns out of the living room and moves into the bedroom. It is just a square vanilla box now with a window that backs onto the mews outside. Out of nowhere, Kate is reminded of the cries, of Becky's shouts for help in her sleep. And then suddenly snippets come to her, of Becky, here, in this room: *Please, Kate, I feel weird, I don't like this . . . we should go . . .* The image in her mind of Becky's anxious face takes her breath away. *It's my fault*, she thinks miserably. She thinks about how Becky has never had a boyfriend. She thinks of how Becky

282

reacted when Kate tried to set up a dating profile, and her traumatized cries in the dead of night. Whatever happened that night must have scarred her for life. The cries echo in her mind, transporting her back. Standing there now, piecing it all together, the reason is obvious. Becky must have been assaulted that night. That is why she left and never spoke to her again, she blamed Kate and her drinking for what happened to her.

She walks over to the window and peers down, wondering whether anyone could have heard Becky screaming. There is an old corrugated-iron gate with a large padlock and she remembers the car lot down the back street. Looking around again, she wishes that there was still something that connected the room to the past; instead she could be anywhere. She sits on the floor, her back against the wall and her knees up. She clicks her tongue in her mouth and thinks.

The day after, Kate hadn't thought much about what happened, she couldn't really remember anything. She'd put it down to another embarrassing night to screw up and chuck in the bin of shame and try to forget. She'd fooled around with one of the guys they were partying with. The thought makes her feel a bit sick. One-night stands are just not in her personality, now she knows who she is. But back then it was just another way of self-destructing, of feeling something, anything. She shouldn't have put herself in that situation, but she had lost all self-respect. It makes her feel sad that she treated herself like that, and let other people think it was OK to take advantage of her, even though they must have noticed she wasn't well.

Becky on the other hand would never have done some-thing like that. She was still a virgin when they lost contact. She thinks of Becky's face the next morning. She tries to remember if there had been any indication from Becky about whether she'd been hurt. *God, I was out of it last night, I can't remember anything.* That's what Kate would have said, that was her standard morning-after utterance. She would have gone downstairs straight to the beer pump and helped herself to another pint to stop herself shaking. But was that true that morning? Or was she thinking of another day? Hard to say, it's all so scrambled up into one awful episode.

Kate shifts uncomfortably. She looks down at her wrists and holds them out. She takes one of her hands and folds it around the flesh of the other wrist, trying to mimic the pressure she remembers. She can taste some sort of memory in her mouth but can't quite catch it. Like a dream that's dissolving as you retell it the next day.

She must find out what happened that night and what part she played in it, no matter how difficult it is to hear. Anything is better than this limbo; the uncertainty is making her go insane, like Chinese water torture, drip by drip.

She stands up and walks out of the room, and goes back down the stairs. Just as she walks back out to the pub the barman walks through.

'You're not meant to be back here,' he says, grabbing a few bags of peanuts off the back of the door.

She shrugs. 'Sorry, I got lost.'

'No worries.' He smiles.

Kate tries calling Becky when she leaves the pub. She expects it to go straight to voicemail just as it has every other time she's called, but is still disappointed when she hears the familiar cheery message. She hangs up. She looks up at the dimming sky, frustrated, wishing it would rain down on her, wishing for thunder and lightning. *Where are you, Becky? Come back . . . I don't care if you tried to get between Ben and me, just tell me what happened. Tell me what I did so I can make it right again.*

She bends down and unlocks her bike and then looks back up at the old building. The vulture sign swings, its hinges whining as it rocks in the wind. There are only two things she is sure of: she doesn't want to ever come back here, and she never wants to be that person again.

24

Ben is home when she walks through the door. He looks up at her angrily and strides towards her, holding his phone. 'I've been worried about you,' he says, holding up the handset. 'Why didn't you answer?'

'Sorry.'

'Are you OK?' He notices her demeanour and the anger dissipates. 'Where have you been?'

He lumbers over, his big hands around her shoulders. He guides her to the sofa and gently tells her to sit down. She does what she is told. He sits on the coffee table in front of her. It feels nice, him stroking her face, it reminds her of that first week they met. Ben changed his flight so he could stay with her. He tended to her like a malnourished chick whose mother had flown away and never returned. He cooked for her, he made her hot drinks, she talked, and he listened. He nodded and spoke back, he made bad jokes and she laughed. He kissed her and she slowly felt OK again.

But she never really dealt with why she was standing on the bridge that day, contemplating throwing herself from it.

'What happened at school, Kate?' He moves a strand of hair from her face.

'I've been really stupid, Ben,' she says, massaging the side of her head with her fingers.

'It's OK, tell me.'

'That girl, Lily. I put her in danger to get what I wanted.' She looks up and over at the window, the street lights have just turned on. 'I suppose I was trying to protect myself,' she whispers.

'What do you mean, Kate?' he asks tenderly.

She can see it clearly now, all the stuff she's hasn't dealt with. She's been distracting herself by trying to make everything OK with Lily because, ultimately, all she could see was herself at that age, careering into disaster. And she wanted to stop it. She wanted to stop herself.

'There is something I haven't told you, about me. About my past,' she says, unable to look at him.

He doesn't stop stroking her. It feels nice, it lulls her into a safe space.

'You could tell me anything and I wouldn't care,' he says.

She takes a deep breath. She never thought she would need to tell him. 'When I was nineteen, I had a baby. I gave her away.' His thumb stops stroking her very suddenly.

'What?'

'I wasn't well at the time. I was going to have an abortion, but when I got to the clinic, I couldn't go through with it. I thought if I just got out of London, I could get my head straight. I went to stay with my grandmother in Margate. But nothing changed, I was still stuck in my head. All I wanted to do was get it out of me, hand over the responsibility so I could start drinking again.'

'You gave your baby away?' he says, almost whispering. 'Who was the father?'

She stays silent.

'Who was the father?' he asks again.

'I . . . I don't know.'

He looks at her, differently, a way she's been looked at before, but never by him.

'What do you mean?' he asks.

'It was when I was partying a lot, I must have . . . I must have taken a situation too far and not realized. I didn't even know I was pregnant until I was three months along.'

He nods slowly, taking it in. 'Hey. Come here.' He folds her in an embrace. 'I just can't believe you never told me.'

'I'm sorry,' she whispers.

'You've nothing to be sorry for.' His eyes blink quickly, as if in shock. Her heart groans; was she right to be so open about this?

'I don't ever want to go back to school,' she says. 'I want to quit.'

'But you love your job, that school . . .'

'I think you should take that job in Philadelphia. We should start again there. We could start a family. I'm ready. I want to have a baby, Ben, I want to give birth and hold it in my arms and never let go,' she rushes.

'Let's just take a moment,' he says. 'You've had a rough day.'

Her phone rings. Alexa's name straddles the screen.

Ben picks it up. 'Want me to answer?'

Kate nods, chewing her lip.

He walks towards the kitchen as he answers. 'Alexa, it's Ben, Kate's partner . . . Right. That's great news. Definitely. I'll tell her.' He looks over at Kate. 'Thanks for letting us know. Take care.' He lowers the device from his ear.

'Good news.' He walks back towards her. 'Becky called Alexa. She's staying at a hotel. She's thinking of going back to New York.'

Kate nods thoughtfully. Would that be a good thing? She is so close to finding out what happened that night. If Becky moves away again, it could be kicked into the distance, never to surface again.

'Now, can we please stop talking about her? Can we move on from this?'

Move on from this. She mulls over the sentence. That's the whole point, isn't it: can you just move on? Just draw a line in the sand, and no matter how atrocious the past might be, just make the decision to forget?

Kate nods, but keeps her lips tight.

'Look, forget about work. It's almost the end of the year, maybe Malcolm will think it best you take some personal time.' He strokes her face. 'And we're getting married this weekend,' he says tenderly. 'Remember?'

'Do you think I'm a bad person, Ben?'

'Kate . . . what?' His eyes look at her sadly. 'No. You are the best person in the whole world and I'm so lucky to be

289

marrying you.' A tear leaves her eye. He strokes it away. 'I don't deserve you.'

'Yes, you do.'

When they go to bed that evening, she kisses Ben and brings his hand to her breast.

'No,' he says, moving it away. 'I'm not in the mood.' She nods and gives him a kiss on the mouth. She opens her eyes as their faces meet; his brow is furrowed and his lips are taut and hard. She moves away, trying not to look confused. Before he turns off the light, he turns back towards her, propping his head up on his hand.

'Let's do it,' Ben whispers.

'Do what?'

'Let's move away, let's start again. I'm over all this commuting, and it's not good for you, me being away all the time.'

Philadelphia, with its towering skyscrapers and boat-size cars, and absolutely nothing that connects her to anything. No old haunts, or people she messed about with back in the day. They could run away from it all, get a fresh start where their slate is completely clean, not one speck of dirt or an inch of a scratch anywhere.

'OK,' she whispers.

'What about Jonny?' Ben asks.

She thinks about Jonny, his face full of laughter as he hobbled down the road with Ronda. They will be happy in their huge house on the seafront. They could come and visit them in America. Jonny would love it.

'He'll be OK.' She smiles at the thought of them. She no longer feels any guilt or resentment there. The relief is immense. 'Do you mind if they come to the wedding after all?' She looks up at him.

'Of course not, darling, whatever you want.'

Ben is right. Malcolm asks her the next morning to stay away until next year, to think about what she's done. The suspension will also pacify the Senior Leadership Team and Mrs Johnson, he says. Next year he wants her to start afresh, with renewed passion and drive. Lily will be moving to college, so Mrs Johnson won't have to fret about the situation. Kate feels a pang of sadness when he compliments her abilities, but it isn't enough to make her reconsider their plan to move away.

On the Wednesday she goes to collect her dress. Miriam cries with delight as Kate twirls for her in front of the mirror.

'You look so beautiful, Kate. I was terrified when I first took the scissors to it.'

Kate admires her reflection. When she first had the idea of using her mother's veil, she had brushed it away, thinking it was cursed. But she couldn't stop thinking about it, about how her mother must have felt when she walked down the aisle looking at Jonny. In the end, she decided to do it; there was something magical about having the same fabric wrapped around her that was around her mother, tying them together on the most important day of her life.

'Thank you, it's exactly what I wanted.' She kisses Miriam on the cheek as she says goodbye.

'Have the most wonderful day!' Miriam waves her off. 'Send me pictures!' She claps her hands together in excitement.

On her way home, Kate stops at the local florist and chooses her bouquet for Saturday. She picks sweet peas and daisies dripping with wispy thlaspis. She holds the sample stems in her hand and pretends to walk down an aisle. She laughs with the florist, who excitedly writes down her order for button-holes and a corsage for Ronda.

By the time she arrives home the stems are floppy between her fingers. She looks up at the sky. It feels ominous somehow that the heatwave should break the weekend they are to marry. She unlocks the door and makes her way inside. The living room is sad and gloomy in this light. Clicking on the light, she goes into the kitchen where she pulls down a small vase and fills it with water. She threads the stems and places it in the middle of the counter. Sitting on one of the kitchen stools, she rests her chin in her hand; with the other she gently touches the petals and smiles.

She hears a bang upstairs.

'Ben?'

Her feet are silent on the carpet as she walks. The door to their room is open. She watches Ben as he holds up a T-shirt and folds it expertly onto a pile.

'Hi,' she says. 'What are you doing?'

He turns. 'Kate,' he says, sadly. 'I thought you were out.'

She looks at his neat pile of folded clothes and the empty bag next to it. 'Are you packing already?' He is staying in a hotel on Friday night ahead of the big day. They will next see each other at the end of the aisle.

He pauses, shaking his head. 'I'm sorry.'

She walks in further. 'What for?'

'I have to go back up to Scotland. Just for a night. They messed up a massive parts order. I should have been there to check it.' He scratches his head, stressed. She goes over to him and touches the side of his face. He flinches.

'Right, OK.' She nods practically. 'Well, never mind. You'll just be gone one extra night. It will fly by.'

He nods. 'Yeah.' He is looking down at his half-packed bag. His eyes refuse to connect with hers.

She hits his arm. 'It's one night!' She tries to lighten the mood.

He attempts a smile. 'I don't want to go.' His voice cracks, he scratches the hair on his face. 'I want to stay here.' His eyes look tearful. Ben never gets upset.

She throws her arms around his neck. 'Next time you see me, we'll be saying *I do*,' she whispers excitedly. She feels his body stiffen; his limp arms finally give in and return the embrace.

Once he is packed, they stand at the front door. 'I'll get Jonny to drop your suit at the hotel with your buttonhole.'

He nods. 'Great.'

'I can't wait to marry you, it's the one thing that's kept me sane these last few weeks,' she laughs.

Then, he looks at her with such tenderness she thinks he is going to cry. 'I love you. I always have,' he says, an utterly serious look upon his face.

'I love you too.' She mimics his gravity.

She leans forward and kisses him. For a moment she thinks he isn't going to kiss her back. Then he does. Her whole body shudders with relief.

'See you at *I do*,' she says.

He nods, looking at her intensely. Like that first time she saw him, on the bridge. This time the look scares her. They move apart and he turns. She shuts the door, rests her head on the panel, listening to him retreat down the stairs. Then he is gone.

25

It is raining as Ben leaves. Kate sits in the armchair by the window and listens to the patter of raindrops on the sill. There is something oddly settling about it, even though she feels utterly peculiar. She is trying to imagine Saturday, but can't. Ben's face just won't come into view. She can't picture meeting him at the end of the aisle, and she can't conjure the feeling she'll have when she says *I do*. She makes herself dinner and sits on the counter raising a fork to her mouth in silence. It occurs to her that without the pressures of school and the constant piles of marking to be done, with Ben away, there is little else going on in her life. She is isolated and alone.

When she finishes eating, she picks up a book which is resting on the coffee table and takes the blanket off the back of the armchair, wrapping it around herself. The cool room is a relief after the last few weeks of muggy air. She gives up reading after a few minutes, and stares out of the window, the slanted sheet rain mesmerizing. And then, out of nowhere, an image of her mother springs to mind. She isn't sure if it is from a photograph or a memory, and she starts to cry. Her shoulders shake and her head bobs as she tries to compose herself, and then she stops, and gives herself permission to release the emotion. She doesn't know for how long she sits by the window, with the rain rattling down, crying. It is as if all this time she never mourned her mother, because there was so much anger there. She blamed her for everything, for leaving her with such an awful legacy, for not being strong enough to get well. But none of that was true, she didn't choose to leave Kate behind. Kate wipes her face with the flat of her hand and sniffs.

'I'm sorry,' she says out loud. 'I'm so, so sorry.'

She tightens the blanket around herself as if she is being hugged, and lets out the loudest sigh she's ever mustered. Letting go.

While Kate was completing her steps, Clare had suggested she call upon her mother for strength in times of distress. She said she'd surely be looking down on her, making sure she was OK. Kate had rejected the idea indignantly. That woman wouldn't know how to steer her; she didn't even know how to deal with her own issues. Taken aback, Clare had nodded and said she understood. But now, sitting here, Kate can't help but think that she has been there this whole time, gently guiding her, so softly she hasn't even noticed. The thought makes her whole body tingle.

After a while, basking in that thought, Kate sits up and picks up her phone. She wonders who she can call. The sad thing is that no one really springs to mind, apart from her sponsor, and it's Clare's job to speak to her. She looks through her call history and sees Alexa's number. She pulls off a long single hair from the chest of her sweater; it is brown and curly. Becky.

She holds the phone to her ear and listens to the ringing.

'Kate.' Alexa's voice is breathless.

'Alexa, I . . . I'm sorry to call so late,' she says. It is almost ten in the evening.

'That's OK,' Alexa says. 'Have you spoken to her?'

'No, I'm not sure if she wants to hear from me.' Kate is suddenly worried she's overstepped the mark.

Alexa sighs. 'I'm sure she does, Kate, she cares about you so much.'

Kate isn't sure that's true. 'I'm really sorry I didn't help much with your mum.'

Alexa sighs, 'Oh, don't worry. It's not your fault. And anyway, I think whatever you said did something. We've managed to persuade her into talking to someone professionally, so fingers crossed.'

Kate smiles. 'That's brilliant,' she says. 'Alexa . . . did Becky ever say anything to you about something happening to her when we were younger?'

'What do you mean?'

Kate swallows and plays with the edge of the blanket, unsure where she is going with this. 'I just wish that I had been a better friend.'

'Oh Kate,' Alexa says, 'you were a brilliant friend to Becky. Even when you were both ghastly teenagers. She adored you.'

'I wasn't. I was terrible to her.'

'Kate, we were all horrible when we were teenagers. You know I was always awfully jealous of your friendship. I always remember getting home from a red-eye flight and finding you both curled up on the sofa together, your arms wrapped around one another. I couldn't work out whose were whose. I've certainly never had a friend like that.'

Tears spring to Kate's eyes. Apart from Ben, there isn't anyone she has ever been that close to. 'Will you tell her I've been trying to get hold of her, next time you speak?'

'Of course.' A pause. 'Unless I'm in labour!'

They say goodbye and Kate stares at her phone. She writes a message. *I understand you may not want to talk to me, but I wish you hadn't gone. There is so much more to say. If there is something I've done, please can we talk about it. I'm sorry x*

She sends the message to Becky. She imagines her friend receiving it and throwing the handset across a room. She imagines Becky shouting angrily at her audacity. What does one do with ten years of unresolved bitterness? How does that sort of pain accumulate?

Kate lies in bed. Her whole body is riddled with disquiet, her mind babbles uselessly, lifting up rocks, studying the ground underneath and dropping the heavy items back down with a thud, finding nothing. She tries to count her breaths to sleep, she tries drawing the alphabet with her finger on the mattress to slowly wind herself down into oblivion. Her mind takes her to Ben's stash of wine in the cupboard in the kitchen. Her head begins to throb. She turns over and pulls out a packet of paracetamol from her bedside drawer, taking two.

Finally, she succumbs and flips up the duvet, deciding to get a glass of milk from downstairs. She lifts herself up and checks her phone for the time. There is, in fact, a message. From Becky. It wakes her immediately and she opens it with shaking fingers.

I'm sorry. You will understand x

Kate hurries the phone to her ear and tries to call her back. But it goes straight to voicemail. She lies back down, her breath scant and her mind full. Her eyes focus steadily on the strange patches of light the moon has brought in through the window. Her lids twitch, opening and closing as her pupils dart around. Finally, exhaustion claims her and she falls asleep.

In her dreams she hears noises from the guest room. It is harder to hear than the first night, quieter, less dramatic. She holds her breath so she can hear the soft cries of a girl in distress. Kate gets out of bed and leaves the room. Out on the corridor she puts her ear to the door. 'Stop! Please!' she hears. She is about to burst in when she wakes with a jolt.

She can barely blink, terror has filled her so completely. She knows that she's heard those cries before, in her previous life. That night in the pub something awful did happen. That is the reason Becky came back, she is sure of it.

Somehow, when the birds start to tweet, through pure exhaustion she shuts down and falls asleep.

On Friday afternoon Jonny and Ronda arrive, and she is so relieved to have some human contact she almost cries. Jonny makes his famous spaghetti Bolognese and Kate tries to stay in the room with them, ignoring the torturous voice in her head. She hasn't been able to speak to Ben since he left, he's been too busy, passing her off with rushed and undetailed messages with promises to call her later.

Another sleepless night. She keeps telling herself it is normal before your wedding. But she had expected the anxiety to be tinged with excitement, rather than fear. She can't stop looking at Becky's message and trying to decipher what on earth she means.

She takes out the milk from the fridge and pours a glass. She glugs it down, the cold, thick liquid helping to dampen the fizzing unease. She hears footsteps and turns around. Ronda is wearing a multicoloured silk dressing gown. Her hair, usually expertly pinned up, is long and wild around her face.

'I couldn't sleep,' says Kate.

Ronda smiles ever so slightly. 'That's normal, love.'

Kate offers her a glass and she nods. 'Is it? I feel awful.'

'I don't think anyone sleeps the night before their wedding.' Ronda looks older without any make-up on, but in a nice way. Kate has the urge to hug her then, to lay her head on Ronda's chest and close her eyes, she is sure she would be able to sleep then.

'What's Ben like?' Ronda asks. 'I haven't been able to get a good description off Jonny.' She laughs lovingly at his inability to define other people.

'Ben's wonderful.' Kate says immediately. She stops and thinks how best to describe him. 'Well, Ben is . . . he's passionate, he's caring and kind, and he looks after me,' Kate says, thinking of how insular their relationship is, how without him, she really is alone.

Ronda nods. 'And what are the in-laws like? They didn't fancy flying over for tomorrow?'

'That was sort of our decision. Ben and his dad don't get on that well. They are so different, and I think a lot of pressure was put on him from a young age. He was the captain of the lacrosse team, the homecoming king . . . all that stuff. He doesn't really talk about it, but I think he had a quarter-life crisis in his early twenties, a breakdown. He always says he never wants to be anything like his dad.'

Ronda nods along in thought. Kate has never told anyone this. 'We just wanted to have the day be about us, rather than other people and drama,' she explains. 'I mean, we were planning on just dragging some witnesses off the street!'

'Well, your dad is very happy he gets to be there tomorrow,' says Ronda.

Kate nods. 'I had better go to bed. Big day.'

'You'll be grand, girl. He is a very lucky man.'

Kate stops. 'You know, I was really horrible to Jonny growing up.'

Ronda nods, and squeezes her arm. 'Katie, your daddy loves you more than anything in the world.'

Kate gets back into bed. She closes her eyes and, by some sort of miracle, she falls asleep.

The next morning there is a knock at her bedroom door.

'Come in,' she says softly.

It's Jonny, holding a tray. There is coffee and toast and sliced fruit.

'Ronda asked me to bring this to you. I only made the coffee.' He puts the wooden tray down on the end of her bed. 'She's going to do your hair and make-up, if you want her to?'

He stands there awkwardly, his eyes sparkling.

She looks at the empty screen on her phone. Ben hasn't messaged this morning. But it is their wedding day, is it bad luck to text as well? She looks up at Jonny's face. It's full of pride, with no idea how she's torturing herself inside.

'Yes, I'd love that,' she murmurs softly.

He leaves. She takes a piece of toast and bites off a corner. It sits in her mouth like a dead animal. She can't chew and she spits it out into her hand. The coffee tastes like petrol. She forces a deeper sip. Wishing she had a bottle of vodka hidden under her bed, her mind races through excuses to leave the flat, go to the shop and buy one. *Shut up*, she tells the voice.

Showering, she feels every droplet drumming onto her naked body, her senses on high alert. Her eyes linger on the razor. She has an urge to press the blades down on her skin. Another thought taps. She deserves this; even on days which are meant to be full of love, she only feels pain. It's karma, isn't it? She looks up at her reflection in the mirror. The steam obscures her view. She wipes it clean but the mist quickly creeps back over.

When she comes out of the bathroom, wrapping her dressing gown around herself, Ronda is there, holding a make-up bag and a hairdryer. 'You ready? Your dad has set up a mirror downstairs for us.' Kate follows her.

There is something therapeutic about having someone touch your hair, pulling the strands through a brush and waving warm air through it. Just that feeling of tender pressure makes Kate want to cry. Ronda gives her warm smiles and excited taps on her shoulder, an occasional frown the only sign she has noticed something isn't quite right. Kate tries to focus on a good outcome. She pictures Ben putting on his suit right now. He's looking in the mirror, giving his handsome reflection a sideways glance. *Why haven't you called?* she wants to scream.

'And there!' says Ronda with a flourish.

Kate opens her eyes to see her long, tousled hair in a messy side plait. Some of the spring flowers have been used as decoration. Her make-up is simple and elegant, quite different to what Kate was expecting from a red-lips devotee. Ronda hands her the tube of muted gloss she has applied to Kate's lips.

'Here, put this in your bag for later.' She closes Kate's fingers around it.

Kate nods. 'Thank you, I love it.'

She stands and walks closer to the mirror. She looks prettier than she ever has, as she should on her wedding day. She goes upstairs and puts on her dress. For some reason she doesn't feel like she is going to be kissed today. She feels like a little girl going to communion.

She sits on her bed and listens to the quiet. She thinks of the night a few weeks ago when she drank that drink, when

303

she *knowingly* drank that drink. Maybe she broke the spell then. Maybe that's when she let go of her peace of mind. She looks at her phone one more time and picks up the bouquet of flowers.

Her phone vibrates. She looks down and opens the message. It's Ben.

I'm sorry, I can't do this. Becky coming into our lives has changed everything. I wish I could explain. But I can't x

Her eyes open and close in shock.

26

The next moments come in flashes of time that are completely meaningless. She can't speak, can't cry. She lies on the floor and curls herself up, trying to make herself as small as possible, because she doesn't want to exist any more. She balls her fist and hopes that her nails will puncture the palm of her hand. In the distance she hears Jonny shouting for her to come downstairs. It is the faint sound of someone calling from another place, a place where this message doesn't exist, a place where Kate is still getting married today.

Clinging to the banister, she makes it downstairs, where she lays her cheek on her father's jacket, her eyes squeezed shut, too scared to open to this new reality. She wishes the pain was physical so she could bandage it or have surgery to remove it. Taking her head from the comfort of his shoulder, she looks up at the faces that watch her in distress.

'What happened?' Ronda whispers, gripping the back of the chair. Kate can't talk. Her lips feel stapled shut.

She tries to form some semblance of a sentence. 'Her . . .' she tries to explain. 'He's with her.'

Jonny and Ronda look at each other, confused. 'Who, love?'

'Becky.'

'Becky?' says Jonny, surprised.

'I was right all along.' Kate stands like a ghost, all in white, holding her mother's pendant as she rocks back and forth.

Thoughts tumble. Her mind creates scenes of them together. They are laughing at her in her wedding dress, waiting to go to the town hall. They are sitting on the train at this very moment, watching the graffiti slide past as they exit London en route to the airport. They are probably sipping champagne at Terminal 5, tapping their glasses, congratulating each other on their escape from the crazy lady back home. 'What a close shave,' Becky will say, leaning in for a kiss. Ben, her Ben, but not her Ben any more, will nod and smile, under a spell.

Her mind falls on the stash of wine under the sink. She stands, already deciding that she's going to open a bottle and glug, glug, glug until she can't feel anything. She wants the alcohol to rain down on her, on her dress, on her hair, on her every fibre. Because, after all, there is nothing to lose any more. She wobbles as she stands. Jonny tries to steady her, but she pushes him away. Walking forcefully, she yanks open the kitchen cupboard. The bottles clink together and she pulls one out with abandon. The cutlery in the drawer jumps as she pulls it forward, knives and forks banging together as though in a sword fight. Grabbing the corkscrew, she digs the point into the foil around the top of the bottle.

'Kate, don't,' her dad says, coming towards her.

Ronda joins him. 'Why don't we take you to one of your

meetings? Don't let him do this to you, Katie.' She approaches Kate as if she is a chicken Ronda is trying to catch.

'I did this!' Kate screams. 'I did this.' Feeling a sharp prick, she brings her finger to her mouth. Blood collects as she sucks. 'She hates me because of what happened,' she moans. 'She did this to get back at me.'

'What happened?' Jonny looks baffled.

Kate promised Jonny she would never drink again, but he doesn't understand this pain. He would crave oblivion too if he felt this. She drags a glass from the shelf and crashes it down on the surface. She wishes it had broken in her hand, she wants to bleed all over the kitchen floor. The wine makes a satisfying glugging noise as she pours it into the bulb of the glass.

'Just stop for a moment.' Ronda walks towards her.

'Do you want one too?' Kate snaps, removing another glass. 'I'm not really into sharing but please, join me.' Her voice is facetious and angry.

Here she is. *The bitch is back. Fuck everyone, fuck you and you and you and you.* She tried to live a different sort of life, be 'normal', get a career and have a relationship, make a home. It hasn't worked because that isn't who she is. Her destiny isn't to feel fulfilled. Her destiny is to die unhappy. Her mind rushes on, crushing her willpower . . . *You can't fix this, you can't. There just isn't any point in trying any more, it will get you eventually.* She may as well surrender now.

'Don't push us away, Kate,' her father pleads.

There just isn't any point to anything any more. Kate looks

307

him in the eye and raises the glass to her lips, she watches as the liquid starts to fall towards her mouth. She closes her eyes and waits for the luscious wine to touch the tip of her tongue and take away the agony.

And then a voice from within: *Stop!*

A sound so primal, a voice so familiar, one she hasn't heard for the longest time. It read to her five-year-old self as she fell asleep, sang to her after a fall, screamed as she ran towards a busy road.

She moves the glass away from her lips, puts it down. In shock. She looks over at Ronda and Jonny, who stare back at her. The good voice, the one who is always kind and positive. It is *her*, her mother.

Swallowing thickly, she whispers, 'She's been here the whole time.'

'What, love?'

Before she can reply, the doorbell rings. The three of them look at each other.

'Ben,' Kate whispers, the whole of her body screaming it so. He changed his mind. He made a mistake. He realized Becky was just trying to get revenge. This is all a huge mistake.

Kate charges forward. Jonny goes with her, jumping ahead as they arrive. He puts his hand flat on the door to prevent her opening it. 'I don't know what he's playing at, but let me deal with him,' he says gruffly.

Kate rises to her tiptoes and looks over his shoulder as he opens the door. Standing there, make-up free, all in black, with a suitcase by her feet, is Becky.

'What . . .' Kate starts. Her voice wobbles. 'What have you done?'

Becky looks up at her, eyes wide and full of regret.

Kate fights to get to her, but Jonny blocks her easily. Her small frame bangs against his back. 'Where is he?' she screams. 'Round the corner in a car? To whisk you both off to JF-Fucking-K?'

Picking up her bag, Becky walks up a few more steps towards them, searching Kate's face for something. 'Did he . . . did he tell you?'

'What? That you've been fucking behind my back?' She is screeching now. 'You think I deserve this, don't you?'

'No . . . Kate . . .'

Kate can't bear it any more. She retreats upstairs. The other voice starts its work: *You deserve this, for whatever happened to Becky that night. It's your fault. You put her in danger. You let your best friend get hurt.*

She feels a hand on her back. Becky has got past Jonny and followed her inside.

'That's not what happened, Kate.'

Kate hurries away from her, her hands over her ears, not able to hear it. Becky follows her.

'Kate, he was meant to tell you!' she cries. And then, 'Fucking coward,' under her breath.

Jonny leaps up to the top of the stairs. 'I think you should go now.'

Becky just stands there, staring at Kate, her wedding dress. 'You look beautiful,' she whispers sadly. 'Oh God.' She begins to sob. 'I shouldn't have started this.'

'Started what?' Kate screams. She can feel Jonny's hand on her shoulder. 'Did you want something I had for once? Do you really hate me so much you want to see me ruined on my wedding day?'

'I told him if he didn't tell you, then I would.'

'Becky, I think you should go,' says Jonny again, firmly.

'I really think you should let me talk to Kate.' She sniffs away her tears and looks at Jonny with new-found purpose. 'I have to tell her what happened that night.'

He looks between both the girls. 'It's up to Kate.'

Kate shakes her head. 'No.'

'Kate, I did this for you.'

Kate looks at her in shock.

'Let me explain, and then I promise I'll leave you alone.'

Kate looks over at her. 'Are you with him?'

Becky shakes her head. 'No, Kate. That's not what this is.' She looks over to Ronda and Jonny. 'Will you give us some time? There is a lot to say, and it would be good to have some privacy.'

Jonny looks over at his daughter, for permission. Kate nods silently. They begin to leave, and Ronda puts her handbag over her shoulder.

'We'll get some coffee. We'll be just around the corner – call us if you need to.' Ronda pulls Jonny through the door and closes it behind her.

They are alone, silent. Kate's knees feel like jelly. She holds the wall for support, her other hand clasped around her pendant. She looks down at her dress. The front panel with the lace from her mother's veil. She blinks, her eyes rest shut for a moment. She is transported back to the bridge, to the moment she contemplated jumping. Her fingers were freezing from the cold wet metal, the rain like tiny pins darting in her face. She should have jumped.

Becky speaks.

'I've thought about you every day, and about what happened that night.' She looks up at Kate with genuine tenderness. 'When I saw you at the restaurant, I watched you for a while. It was so good to see you well and happy. You looked so carefree. I was relieved. I often wondered what happened to you, whether you found the help you needed . . . but then I saw who you were with. I recognized him, Kate . . . though I couldn't quite place it at first.'

'From New York?' Kate asks meekly.

Becky shakes her head. 'I couldn't believe it could be him. The coincidence was too huge. I was going to leave. I even walked out of the door, onto the pavement. But something pulled me back, and I followed you into the toilet.'

Kate thinks back to their first meeting, at the basin. 'You . . . followed me?'

Becky nods. 'I had to know.' She places a hand on the side of her head and pauses. 'I've not been well, and I thought maybe I'd got it wrong. I couldn't be sure . . . the pills . . .'

'What are you talking about?'

'Then I was going to tell you, the night you apologized. I just couldn't, Kate. You glowed when you talked about him . . . and I wasn't sure . . . then all that stuff with my mum . . . it all spiralled and suddenly I was staying with you. I decided to look for clues.'

'That night you were in our room . . .'

Becky nods. 'I found his old passport. It had a photo of him from college. I have that face etched in my mind, I've never been able to get rid of it.'

'What are you talking about?'

'I couldn't believe what was going on. The thought that you've had sex with him, that you were going to marry him. It made me sick to my stomach . . .'

'What are you talking about, Becky?'

Becky clears her throat. 'I've never been able to get over that night in the pub . . .'

'What are you saying?' The pressure is unbearable.

Becky motions to the couch. 'Sit down. I have to tell you what happened that night.'

'No.' Kate is suddenly terrified of what she's going to hear.

'Sit down.'

Kate does as she's told.

That night – about ten years ago

Becky leans on the bar. Her jaw tightens as she watches Kate, who's had the drink to send her over the edge. Becky knows the signs well – pupils like pinpricks, movements slow and clumsy. She sighs. What did she expect? That Kate would actually stick to her promise and not get too wasted tonight? That she'd help her tidy up, like she said, and refuse a lock-in?

I'm an idiot, she thinks. If the definition of insanity is doing the same thing over and over, and expecting a different result, then maybe Kate isn't the crazy one after all.

Becky misses the real Kate. She sees her less and less these days. Real Kate, the sober one, is kind and generous, conscientious and sweet. She cares passionately about their friendship and hates to mess her around. Real Kate promised that their last night together before Becky went to university would be special. She swore they'd finish their shift in the pub and go out, just the two of them, like old times.

Becky is annoyed with herself for trusting Kate. None of her promises or vows mean shit any more. Infuriated, she clenches her teeth. She already knows what will happen tomorrow. Kate will cry and apologize and expect Becky to shrug her shoulders and forgive her. She's sick of it.

There was a time when Becky was at her happiest gripping her best friend's hand as they twirled on the dance floor, or ran down the streets laughing in the early hours of the morning, or gossiped hungrily as they touched up their make-up in the bathroom during a raucous house party. Nowadays Becky spends more time holding Kate's hair back while she pukes, or stopping her getting into drug dealers' cars, or yanking her back onto the kerb just before a bus crosses her path.

Being friends with Kate Sullivan isn't fun any more. It's exhausting and scary.

Becky takes another sip of her drink and watches Kate show

the remaining table the tattoo on the small of her back. She is swaying and laughing, enjoying their reaction. Kate's lacy knickers are on show. The men nudge each other suggestively. She is too drunk to notice them leering. Becky studies the three guys. They can't be that much older than her. She's not seen them in here before. A song comes on that Kate loves and she whoops, her arms in the air like an excited three-year-old, and she begins to dance, encouraging the boys to join her. The loudest one, with a shaved head, stands up readily and gyrates his hips against hers.

Becky twists the volume down on the stereo. The group moan over at her. She shrugs. Necking the rest of her wine, she walks over.

'I'm sorry, we have to close up now.' She attempts to sound authoritative.

They look at her as if she is pathetic. The boys' lurid smiles falter at the suggestion. 'Come on, we're just getting started!' says the skinhead, taking Kate's hand and pulling her towards him.

'Come on, Becky,' slurs Kate. 'We're having a great time. Let's just hang out here . . .'

'Kate, Chris said no lock-ins while he's away,' Becky reminds her. 'We're going out tonight, remember?'

'Let's do some shots!' Kate jumps in the air, rushing to the bar as if she didn't hear her at all.

Becky breathes out a heavy sigh. She watches the scene unfold and thinks maybe Kate needs to fend for herself for a while. Maybe the shock of having no one there to pick up the pieces will force her to face up to her problem. Becky's tried and failed for years – maybe it's time to admit defeat.

'Great idea!' shouts another of the boys. He's got a posh London accent, his hair quiffed neatly at the front. He wears a salmon-pink shirt with the top button undone and dark stitching of a polo player in the corner of the pocket. Becky wonders again where they've come from. They are not Camden's usual clientele. They belong on the King's Road, or in Knightsbridge. Although there is nothing gentlemanly about these boys. Their sleazy eyes creeping over Kate's body are making her feel a bit sick.

Becky turns to see Kate pouring liquid into shot glasses. 'Tequila!' The tray shakes precariously as she carries it over.

'Yes! Get in,' the posh boy in the pink shirt shouts as he picks one from the tray, extending a little finger.

'OK, well, after these . . .' Becky says feebly, looking around at the mess that needs tending to. She feels outnumbered and weak and wishes she could just leave.

'Here you go.' The skinhead in the polo shirt nudges her.

She takes the shot from him. *Fuck it*, she thinks. One more night in this dirty pub, in this disgusting part of town. Besides, if she's going to have to do all the cleaning, she needs a bit of a pick-me-up. Kate will probably just sit at the bar smoking and talking shit, choosing the music, crying over why someone doesn't love her any more. What's Kate going to do when Becky isn't here? She'll probably get the sack. Serves her right. *Sayonara, sister.* Becky downs the shot.

'More!' shouts Kate, her arms in the air again. She is now

315

on a mission. It is almost futile to attempt to derail her. She'll either get aggressive and tearful, or mute and zombie-like. Drinking with Kate Sullivan is like playing Russian roulette. Becky never knows where she'll end up. A house party, a hospital, a crack den or a canal boat. Becky used to find it exciting – exhilarating, even. And she used to love the way Kate needed her when things went wrong, be that as a shoulder to cry on or someone to rant at. No one has ever really needed her before, no one ever really cared whether she was there. Her mother certainly doesn't. She actively prefers it when Becky isn't around. But Kate cares; even if she'll flit off with some boy for a while, she'll always come running back.

Becky is off to university on Monday, and now, standing there watching her friend, she realizes she just doesn't care any more. Maybe she's outgrown the friendship, maybe she's ready to fly the nest. All she knows is she suddenly can't wait to get away from her best friend.

'No, Kate, we really have to tidy and cash up, remember?' Becky is wiggling her eyebrows, trying to get Kate to remember the conversation they had earlier that night.

'Just one more!' Kate says, giving one of the guys the eye. In Kate's head she must think the look she gave was subtle and sweet. But for Becky, watching from the outside, it looks desperate and clunky. *Oh Kate, you used to be the coolest girl in school, now look at you.*

Becky gets up and goes to the bar where Kate is already pouring yet more shots. She grabs her shoulder. 'Kate, I know you want to stay, but come on, it's our last night together . . . you promised.'

'Don't be silly!' Kate says in a patronizing voice. 'We've got loads of nights we can do that; this is really fun. Come on!'

'Kate, those guys are so drunk and letchy.'

Kate swats her elbow out of Becky's hand, annoyed. 'Oh, come on! Why do you always have to be such a party pooper?'

Becky looks over at the three guys, who are intently chatting, like a pack in a pre-game huddle. 'Please, Kate, I feel weird, I don't like this . . . we should go . . .'

Kate turns to Becky. Her face has gone from carefree to snarling in seconds. 'Go home if you want to.' She spits out the words, stumbling backwards as she talks.

Angry heat rises up through Becky. *Fuck you*, she thinks, *fuck you*.

'You really want to stay?'

Kate nods. 'Yup.' Her glazed eyes scan the room, falling back on the boys who have caught her attention.

'Fine. But just so you know, after tonight, that's it. I never want to see you again.' She looks at Kate to judge her reaction, but it is almost as if she stopped listening to her entirely.

One more night, then that's it, then Kate is on her own, Becky decides as she follows her back to the table, frustrated she can't bring herself to leave Kate here.

'Yes!' The guy with dark floppy hair and glasses pipes up. He's barely said a word before now. 'I love this shit, man.' His American accent slurs as he awkwardly picks up one of the tiny shot glasses. He is definitely the most drunk out of the guys; his eyes can't seem to focus on anything at all.

'He doesn't know how to drink like a Brit,' says the one with the shaved head, ruffling his hair. 'I promised his dad I'd teach him a thing or two while he's in town.'

The American guy laughs along. 'London is wild.'

The skinhead seems intent on taking charge of the situation, telling all the jokes, directing the line of conversation. He sniffs profusely and takes frequent toilet trips. Kate joins him on a few. Becky has never taken drugs. The idea of them scares her. As she sits there she tries to have a good time, she tries to involve herself in the conversation, but it's nearly impossible. They're all high and shouting over each other. Spit flies out from every corner as they all try and get a word in edgeways. Everything is me, me, me – *I feel like this about that, I think this should happen with this* – not really listening to what anyone else is saying. They are all on their high horses riding off into the sunset in different directions. Becky wants to put her fingers in her ears.

When the claustrophobia gets too much, she pulls herself away from the noise of the group. She needs a breather, it's too intense. She wishes she could go home, but she just can't bring herself to leave her friend here, on her own, with these guys. Going to the tap, she pours herself some water and downs it, before cracking open a Coca Cola and pouring it into a tall glass. She walks over to Kate and puts it in front of her. 'It's a vodka Coke,' Becky says, lying. Kate nods, and takes a sip. Maybe that will sober her up a bit.

'Who wants a bit of mud?' the skinhead asks, holding up a tiny clear packet containing off-white granules. 'A bit of MDMA to take the edge off the coke?'

'Me!' shouts Kate excitedly. The packet gets passed round the group. It comes to Becky. Everyone looks at her. Kate rolls her eyes as if she is waiting for Becky to refuse.

She has never taken MDMA before. She should stay lucid in case Kate gets into trouble, but a sudden splurge of rebellion strikes her. She's bored of being the good one, the one who looks after everyone else and excuses their behaviour. She wants to be the naughty one for once. Licking her finger, she copies how everyone dunked theirs into the nest of powder, removing it with a few granules stuck to the end. She puts them on her tongue and swallows. It is the most acrid taste she has ever encountered. She coughs, and quickly takes a sip of drink. The skinhead laughs.

Sitting back, she is shocked at what she's done. She bites her lip, feeling scared. She doesn't want to feel out of control. And then . . . nothing happens, and she's relieved. Just as she gives up on the drugs working, Kate slides into the seat next to her and nestles her face in the dip of her neck. 'Don't you just feel wonderful?'

Becky is about to answer when she feels a wash of pleasure run through her. Any negative thoughts have been removed and she feels light, and swishy. Everything slows down, or speeds up, she can't quite tell which. Kate strokes her arm, which feels orgasmic. She closes her eyes, enjoying the pleasure and the connection to her friend, free from any bad feeling. But then Kate disappears from her side.

Becky's eyes blink open, and she watches Kate join the skinhead on the other side of the table. She giggles in his face and rubs her nose against his, and they kiss. The drugs won't allow Becky to feel disappointed. Someone touches her hand; she looks down and over at the boy with the pink shirt next to her. They smile at each other as if they are both acknowledging the same feelings. They hold their hands up to the light; she can't believe she has never realized how beautiful they are. She feels so safe and cherished, inside this bubble of love.

The next time she opens her eyes they aren't in the pub any more, they're upstairs in Chris's flat, in the bedroom. The remnants of the drugs linger, but she is cold, and grim reality is edging its way back in. She realizes she can't feel her legs; she looks up and sees the room is spinning. *How did I get up here?* she thinks. Starting to feel sick, she attempts to lift herself up, then she realizes something is on top of her. She looks down; pink-shirt boy is asleep on top of her, snoring. She feels below with her hands; she is still wearing all her clothes, so is he. She wonders what time it is, and she wishes she was home in bed, on her own.

Her unruly hair is stuck to the side of her face. She turns the other way. She sees the skinhead kissing Kate, who is motionless on the floor, cushions scattered around her. Their lips disconnect and Kate's head rolls. Her eyes are closed, her lips parted as if she is asleep.

Confused, she watches the skinhead undo Kate's bra. But Kate isn't taking off his clothes. Kate isn't moving at all. In fact, she is completely passed out. Becky tries to shout, a wave of nausea washes over her and she swallows it back down. She blinks; is she going to faint? She takes a deep breath and opens her eyes again. Kate . . . Kate . . . he's doing something to her. She needs to help Kate . . . Becky tries unsuccessfully to push the boy off her. She shouts, 'Stop it . . . please! Stop it,' as she tries to get up to help. The boy with the skinhead looks over at her and grins wildly, as if he knows she doesn't stand a chance in hell of overpowering him. He points over at her. 'Don't fucking move,' he snarls, lifting out a folded blade from his back pocket. Then he brings the knife to Kate's neck and acts out a cutting motion, making it clear what will happen if Becky moves one more inch.

Then she hears soft moaning; it's Kate. The moans aren't pleasurable, but startled, scared, helpless sounds. The blurry outline of the skinhead on top of her. 'No, please don't,' Kate is crying now. 'Help me,' she softly cries, as if she knows there is nothing she can do to stop this happening to her. He slaps the side of her face and Kate must have passed out again, because the room goes eerily quiet.

Becky watches as he climbs off her and lets out a satisfied groan as he touches her leg. Then he leaves the room. Becky's whole body relaxes with relief. She tries to push the boy off her again, and struggles. She looks over at Kate's slack, half-naked body; it is stretched across the floor, her ribs extended like a hanging carcass.

Then her whole body shakes as the door is flung open with a bang. There he stands, the smirking skinhead, his face shimmering with sweat. He walks through, dragging someone else behind him. It's the good-looking American. He is being towed forward by the fabric of his T-shirt.

'Your turn,' says the skinhead. 'Come on,' he says, gesturing to his belt buckle.

The American sways. 'But . . . dude . . . I don't . . .'

'Come on, Ben, she's gagging for it.'

At that moment Kate's head bobs up, she mumbles something softly.

'See?' The skinhead nudges him.

Becky watches, eyes wide, like an animal in the hedgerow at twilight. The American stumbles as he is rushed to undo his belt buckle, and messily lumbers up to Kate's limp body, pushing a knee outwards. Becky musters everything she can and shouts. 'Please! Stop, don't . . .' she sobs.

The skinhead turns and walks over. His hard black boots stop right by her face on the floor. Bending down, he grabs her by the hair. 'Shut the fuck up – or you're next. Got it?' he whispers furiously in her ear. He bangs her head aggressively on the floor and brings his foot back.

'Don't,' she gasps, as the most overpowering pain thwacks into her stomach. The blow has winded her and she coughs. Laughing, he walks away. Closing her eyes, she turns her head the other way. And all she can hear is the sound of the

American's belt buckle clinking against itself in time with the movement. A lone tear scurries down Becky's face as she tries not to listen.

When light streams into the room the next morning, the boys have gone. Becky looks over at her friend who has been haphazardly redressed. Kate sits up, dazed. She looks like a racoon, her eye make-up down her face. There is a red cut on the side of her face and dried blood is smudged down her cheek. Licking her dry lips, she looks around. Becky watches her, waiting for some sort of clue that she knows what happened.

'God, I was out of it last night, I can't remember anything,' Kate says, standing up. She shuffles around looking for her cigarettes. 'Oh God, did I fool around with that skinhead?' she says, laughing, then she grimaces and goes quiet. Confused. She must still be a little bit drunk. This happens to her in the morning. She goes through a period of searching, trying to remember. Usually Becky fills in the blanks.

Becky stays with her for a while, but she can't bring herself to say anything, even though Kate keeps looking at her expectantly. Kate is suddenly very keen to tidy up before the day-shifters arrive. As they work Becky sees her occasionally look out of the window, thinking. Every time Becky builds the confidence to say something, the guilt that she just lay there stops her.

'I've got a family meal, got to go.' Becky says, already at the door.

Kate looks over with surprise. 'Oh, OK . . . Look, I'm sorry last night didn't go the way we said.'

Becky shrugs. 'That's OK.'

'We'll do it the first weekend you get back?'

Becky nods, opening the door wider.

Kate walks over and kisses her cheek, so tenderly Becky feels sick. 'I'm sorry if I was a dick last night. I shouldn't have done those shots.' She laughs, sort of, checking Becky's face for clues. Kate waits again for Becky to tell her what she did, what happened.

'Don't worry about it, you were fine,' Becky mumbles before opening the door and walking through it.

Her walk turns into a jog as she hits the pavement. The jog turns into a light run and then the adrenalin hits, and she sprints as fast as she can, away.

The rest of the day she thinks about whether she should call Kate and tell her. She keeps checking to see whether Kate has rung. She's expecting her to call, crying, saying she's on her way over to the police. But she never does.

And so Becky packs her belongings and makes the lonely drive up to university. She attends freshers' week and meets her new housemates. Far away from Kate. Far away from Camden.

Days turn into weeks, weeks turn into months. She doesn't want to speak to Kate. The guilt of what happened, and what she didn't stop happening, is too much to bear. The years roll by and it stays with her, ruining every good thing she finds, stopping her from ever fully being able to enjoy sex, or

324

friendship or love. And then she sees Kate at the restaurant, and she looks so happy, and Becky feels relief, finally. But then she sees who Kate is with and her blood runs cold. When Kate asks for forgiveness, during her Step Nine, Becky sits there listening, waiting for the right moment to tell her that she too has something to make amends for.

27

'It didn't happen to you. It happened to me . . .' Kate says aloud, trying to make sense of what she's been told.

Becky nods. Her eyes are full of tears. She looks haunted.

Kate thinks. For the first time she doesn't push the memory away. She closes her eyes. It's dark. Someone is kissing her, stroking her hair. It feels nice. She's enjoying the sensation of someone looking after her tenderly. And then nothing. Only noises, a hand tight around her wrist. She can't move, she wants to find Becky and go. A sick feeling of panic, of being held in place and unable to move. 'Becky!' she calls out. There is muffled laughter.

'But Ben would never hurt anyone,' Kate whispers incredulously. Her finger extends to a point. 'You're making this up. This is all part of your plan . . . to get between us . . . because you've always wanted to get back at me . . .'

'No, Kate.' Becky shakes her head in frustration. 'Actually, fuck that, you know what? Some days I wondered whether I should bother. I thought maybe you deserved it for all the shit

I put up with. How you treated me, and how everyone always let you get away with everything . . .'

'OK then, why the hell were you all over him? You acted as though you wanted to fuck him, for God's sake!' Kate laughs angrily.

'No . . . that meeting we went to, when they talked about falling off the wagon and I asked you if you could ever see yourself relapsing. You talked about having Ben. I was scared, Kate. I thought if you knew he did that to you . . . I mean, how could anyone recover from that? An affair, maybe . . . but that . . . this . . . I got this crazy idea that maybe I could get him away from you another way. I thought I could convince you to leave him. By tricking him into an affair. Then I would never have to tell you who he really was, what he really did.' Becky shakes her head, her hand wipes her hair away from her face in agony. 'Which was bonkers, I know . . . but you know what? He didn't want me. He loves you, more than anything. He isn't the monster I was expecting.'

The sick feeling creeping through Kate rushes faster. 'Ben's . . . not . . . a monster,' she says weakly.

Becky continues, ignoring her. 'That night on the landing, he wouldn't kiss me. So I told him I knew what he did, that it was us that night in the pub. He had no idea, Kate, he couldn't even remember where he was when it happened. He was crushed. I gave him an ultimatum: he needed to tell you the truth, or I would.'

Kate coughs, and almost laughs. She stands up and paces.

'Becky, you don't remember it right . . . You've got it wrong!' She is almost relieved. This is all a big mistake.

'Then why isn't he here, Kate?' Becky moves towards her. 'If I'm wrong. Why isn't he here?'

Kate clenches her jaw. This is madness. 'Ben wouldn't hurt anybody.'

'I should have been able to stop them back then and I didn't. I had to stop him this time.'

'No . . . Becky,' Kate moans. 'You've got it all wrong.'

Becky hands her the old passport that she stole. 'Look at the photo, Kate.'

Kate shakes her head fiercely.

'Look at the photo.'

Kate does as she's told. All at once she is transported back there, to that night. Being pulled and pushed and Becky's shouts to stop, and then, with a flash, a face right up close to hers. The heat of breath, floppy hair brushing against her in rhythmical jerks. Ben's kind and thoughtful face is younger, his eyes glazed and vacant, his jaw hairless and smooth.

That sore feeling the morning after, and the remnants of kissing, someone's hand down her knickers. The touches had become less and less tender and more brutal. But she couldn't really remember, she was too out of it. Becky hadn't told her what happened, so it was easier to pretend it wasn't that bad. Hide behind the denial, use it to shield her from the deep shame of not knowing what she had let happen to her. The fact that she couldn't even remember whether she'd had sex or not. In her mind it was her fault. It was her stupid, stupid fault.

Then she looks up at Becky. There is something she doesn't know. The baby in the blanket, and its dark mop of hair. And how Kate has always wondered if that was the night she conceived her child. Her hand clutches her necklace. Ben, he is the father, there is no mistaking the similarity of the baby's face etched in her mind, the same dark-brown hair and turquoise-blue eyes. Kate moans, she chokes a cry and tumbles forward, gripping her stomach. She thinks back to the bridge, and how when she saw Ben, she had felt as if she was coming home. There was something nostalgic about his smell, about his embrace, about his kiss. But it wasn't serendipity, it was something far darker. Becky is telling the truth. It was him.

'I'm sorry, Kate. I'm sorry for letting it happen and then running away,' she cries.

Kate shakes her head and moves towards her. 'No.' She slips her arms around Becky's shoulders and they cry together, their shaking bodies moving in tandem. 'I should never have got us into that situation. Please, it happened because of me.'

'Kate, stop it. No one is to blame but them.'

They cling onto one another, sobbing. Slowly, they calm and part.

A tap on the door. Jonny's face peers round; he surveys the scene.

'Come in, Dad.'

Ronda is behind him, holding a card tray with coffee cups.

'Is . . . is everything OK?'

'I'll go now. I have a flight to catch. I'm glad you are both here. Look after her for me,' Becky says, giving Kate a last glance.

Kate looks at her; they both stare, knowing that whatever has happened between them is over now.

The door closes and Kate caves in to the misery. The sadness of how hopeless she used to be, what she let happen to her, the pain she inflicted because she hated herself. How she would crave attention and love so much that she allowed herself to be used like a piece of meat, thrown from one hungry predator to another. She had no control over her mind, or her body. Her phone beeps. Ben's name is on the screen. Her fingers are wet and slippery from her tears. She can't open it at first.

I know she's told you. I should have, but I'm a coward. That night, it is the worst thing I have ever done in my life. I never thought I was capable of something like that. It's not who I am. I've strived to be a better person every day. I can't believe it was you. You have to believe me; I had no idea. I'm not saying you ever have to see me again. I just hope you can forgive me one day. I am going to make this right, I don't care about the consequences any more. I love you, Kate.

The words pierce her like shards of glass through skin. Ben, her Ben. Her lovely man, her knight in shining armour who was going to save her from herself. He is the very person she should have been running from.

'What can we do, love?' Ronda asks, squeezing her shoulder, giving Jonny a worried look. 'What happened?'

Kate shakes her head. She can't tell them. She can't explain this to them.

Her eyes wander across the living room to the kitchen, and up to the shiny green bottle on the top of the counter.

Ronda notices where her eyes have drifted off to. 'What would you do normally when you've had a shock, love? What do they say in those meetings?'

Her mind is twisting and growing, like thorny brambles on a time-lapse. How has she got herself here? Everything was perfect just a few weeks ago.

Or was it?

Now she knows the truth, she knows it wasn't real.

She is in-between the darkness and the light. There are two paths on offer. Her hands are nestled on her lap inside the fabric of her white dress. The dress she had imagined Ben removing, the dress she had thought of crumpled on the floor as they kissed on their wedding night.

'Clare,' she says breathlessly. 'I should call my sponsor.'

Ronda kisses her forehead. 'We'll give you some privacy, love.'

Jonny squeezes her arm. 'Whatever's going on, we're here for you.' Kate feels cushioned by their love.

The phone rings and Clare picks up. She always picks up.

'How was it?' she squeals. 'Send me a photo, please!' she cries. There is an almighty pause. 'Kate? Kate, is everything . . . ?'

'I'm not married. I'm not getting married. I've been lying to you this whole time. There is so much stuff I haven't told you, about my past. About lots of things, really. I relapsed a few weekends ago . . .'

'Oh Kate . . .' Clare says quietly. 'Tell me everything.'

It all pours out of her. The baby, the way she gave her away so she could drink to oblivion. The truth about her dad, about her mum. The fact she hasn't been going to meetings regularly or working her programme at all. That she's been hiding behind her 'perfect' life, cherry-picking what she wants to see, because she thought that she had the protection of Ben and her future shielding her from her past. And finally, about that night, what happened, and who it was.

'It was all my fault,' Kate whispers. She stands up and walks over to the bottle of wine.

'No, Kate, it was them, they did that to you,' Clare whispers kindly. 'Just because a girl is drunk, doesn't invite a boy to do . . . There is nothing you could possibly have done or said that would justify what happened. They did this, not you.'

'But I didn't care about myself, I let it happen,' she murmurs.

'Kate, you were ill, and you were taken advantage of, you didn't let it happen. It sounds like that boy went out that night to intentionally hurt someone. I'm walking out of the door. We'll go straight to a meeting. We'll start again; you are ready to do this properly now. No stone unturned. Everything is going to be OK.' Kate can hear a door banging, and the background noise changes from quiet and still to frantic and noisy.

She picks up the glass of wine again, turning it, watching the liquid slide against the bowl of the glass. 'Will I have to forgive him? When we do the steps again?'

'Kate, you don't have to think about this stuff at the

332

moment. Just let's focus on today, on getting you to a safe space, OK?'

Kate nods and thinks back to Ben's text: *I never thought I was capable of something like that. It's not who I am.* She understands what it's like to look back at something you've done, and feel like it was another person entirely. If anyone understands that, it's her.

She lifts the glass to her lips. The smell of oblivion teases her.

A door clangs shut. 'I'm in the car, I'll be at yours in five, OK? Kate? Are you listening to me? Kate ... Kate ...' The engine revs. 'Look, there is only one person who needs to come to terms with what happened, one person you need to ask for forgiveness and forgive ... the most important amends, Kate. Yourself, Kate, you have to forgive yourself.'

She stands there holding the wine. Her chin rises, she looks out of the window, trees rustle and birds circle. Kate can hear Jonny and Ronda murmuring to each other at the top of the stairs, wondering if they should come down. She looks at the plughole below and tells herself to pour. Thinking how, at the end of the day, it's just her standing in a room, hoping to make the right decision. On any given day that's all you can wish for. Hope.

'Kate, I've got to put the handset down, I'm a few minutes away. Don't do anything stupid, OK?' Clare hangs up the phone.

She looks at the glass again. All at once, Kate knows. She is only alone if she chooses to be.

*

Kate picks up her phone and looks at the message from Ben. She needs to hear his voice, just one more time. He answers immediately. 'Kate.' He sounds croaky and distant. She can tell he is outside, standing on a busy road.

'I thought I knew you, because you were the one. But it was because we'd met before,' she whispers.

She can hear him sob. He sniffs, and then sobs again. He clears his throat and tries to speak.

'I had a breakdown after that trip to London. I just couldn't cope with what I'd done. I . . . I wanted to go to the police. But I told my dad what happened and he wouldn't let me. I tried to learn to live with it . . . and then that night I met you, on the bridge. I felt like I knew you too, like I was meant to be there to stop you. Protecting you was something I was good at. With you I make sense. I thought I could make up for any past mistakes, if I could just make you better . . . but I had no idea who you really were . . .'

'The baby. It was your baby, Ben.'

He groans.

'Where are you?' she asks.

'I'm standing outside the police station. I'm going to hand myself in.'

A flash of an image: Ben behind bars. It doesn't help, it doesn't make her feel better.

'Don't, please, if you're doing it for me. Please . . .'

'I can't go on knowing what I did, Kate. I need to tell them, I need to take whatever punishment I am owed so I can move

334

on. Close the door on it properly.' He pauses. 'I'm not that person . . .' He begins to sob again.

'I know,' she murmurs. 'I forgive you.' A lone tear rides down her face as her shaking hand hangs up the phone. *I forgive you*, she whispers to the empty room.

Then the doorbell rings. Clare has arrived. Then the sound of footsteps running downstairs, and Jonny and Ronda rush into the room with Clare and she is safe.

EPILOGUE

Exactly a year later

Kate unlocks her bike outside school.

'Bye, Miss!'

She turns and waves at Jake, one of her students who has just completed his last English exam. 'Well done, Jake! Have a great summer,' she calls back.

He puts his arm around his girlfriend and bounds off grinning, the weight of two years' work and stress lifted. Kate frees her wheels and walks leisurely along Mare Street, and over to Broadway Market. It's mid-week, so only a scattering of stalls are set up and a few people mill around. Now the exams are over she can finally take stock of her year. It had begun in a blind panic, as the things that she thought were holding her together fell away in one fell swoop. Her relationship with Ben; their beautiful flat that she couldn't afford on her own. And she finally had to admit to losing the six years of sobriety she had under her belt. There were so many things she had to start again.

Clare had held her hand as her wobbly voice came clean to a room of other addicts about her relapse. And to her surprise, it wasn't awful. They rallied around her, gave her the support she needed in those early days. She handed herself over to it and spoke in every meeting she went to. She reconnected with old friends in recovery and made her programme a priority again.

She gets out her phone to call Clare, as she tries to every day now. She holds the handset out in front of her so the camera gets a good view of her face.

After a few rings Clare comes into view. She has a big grin on her face, and a cheeky-looking toddler on her lap who cheers when he sees Kate.

'Congratulations!' Clare shouts. 'You did it! Did that Jake kid turn up?'

'Yep, full house.'

'Oh Kate, well done. You've worked so hard this year.'

'Thanks, Clare, I couldn't have done any of it without you.'

'You did the work. You came back and started again. Not many people would have been strong enough to face what you had to face and not drink on it.'

Kate looks up at the rich blue sky and blinks. 'I spoke to Becky last night.'

'Oh yeah? How is she?'

'She's great, she's a year sober now too.'

'That's so cool.'

'Yeah, I think I'll go see her over the summer in New York. We both have so much to say. And we'd both like to apologize for things.'

'Did she understand? About Ben?'

'Yeah, I think she understands. I know she wanted me to press charges. But I wouldn't get the closure I need by doing that. He isn't going to hurt anyone else; he isn't a bad person. And he paid for what he did in other ways. And I told her about the other guy, dying so soon afterwards in the drink-driving accident.'

'How did she feel about that?'

'I think she was relieved that he never got the chance to do it to anyone else. I think she carried a lot of guilt around because she didn't report it. But, also, you know. It's never nice hearing that someone died.'

'I'm proud of you, Kate.'

'Thanks, Clare.'

'Are you going to pick up your sobriety chip tonight? Sorry I can't make it.'

'Yes, and a big group of us are going out for dinner to celebrate.'

'You made it, your first year! Have you thought about the other thing?'

'Oh, I knew you'd bring this up!'

'Well, we agreed you wouldn't date for a year, and you've done it. I know life isn't all about finding Mr Right, but you've always said you want to settle down, and have kids. You might need to start putting yourself out there again.'

Kate looks out to the market. A familiar outline wanders across her view pushing a bike, wearing neon-yellow Lycra cycling shorts. She nearly snorts when she realizes who it is. He sees her and waves. She smiles and waves back.

'Clare, I've got to go.'

'OK . . . have a great time tonight!'

'Thanks! I'll pop over on the weekend, I've got a present for that mad toddler of yours.'

They exchange goodbyes just as Gus stops in front of her.

'I swear I didn't follow you,' he says.

She laughs. 'Those shorts are . . .'

'They're pretty much the coolest thing you've ever seen, right?'

She nods and laughs again. 'Most definitely.'

'You want to go for a post-exam victory ride? I swear I won't think it's a date or anything.'

She's been rebuffing his advances all year. Clare had thought it best she didn't have any distractions from finding her feet in sobriety again.

'Yeah, that would be lovely,' she says, standing. He looks surprised and thrilled. Then she adds, 'And . . . we can call it a date, if you want?'

He nods slowly, grinning, as if he can't quite believe his luck. And, both pushing their bikes along the pavement, they look over at one another and smile.

ACKNOWLEDGEMENTS

Firstly, I would like to thank my agent, Teresa Chris. Since that first phone call as I walked over the Millennium Bridge, her passion and ambition for my writing has never wavered, and there is no one I would rather unpick a dubious plot point with. This is happening because of you.

To everyone at Quercus: thank you to the dream team Stefanie Bierwerth and Katherine Burdon, for the time, effort and dedication you've put in to getting this to market. It has completely astounded a novice author like me. Thank you to everyone on the publicity team, especially Joe Christie and Katya Ellis, for all the hard work and passion championing my book. Rachel Neely, thank you for believing in this book enough to want to publish it. It blows my mind every day and I loved working with you.

My sister, Juliet, who is my most avid reader and only ever says the best things. My dear friend and fellow writer, Charlotte Philby, thank you for answering my feverish text messages with equally rambling replies, which somehow always set everything on the right course again. Isolde Walters – thank you for being such a brilliant and helpful reader in the early stages. The teachers and doctors who helped fact-check – Mathilda Sutherland, Chris Fairbairn and Matt Sears, thank you for answering my random questions with such aplomb.

Jane Lythell and Clare Christian who both gave me their time and advice when I first began writing. I would have surely fallen at the first hurdle if it weren't for you both.

My friends: Ben Coleman, Lucy Francis, Sophie Nevin, Candice O'Brien, Erica Sutton-Teague and Bridie Woodward for cheering me on from the sidelines through the wilderness years to these much more grown-up ones.

Linda Stevens, Nick Hofford, Cathy – thank you from the bottom of my heart. Your wit and encouragement will stay with me forever. Karen Smith, I would never have the confidence to follow my dreams if it weren't for your reassuring voice on the end of the phone.

Mum and Dad, you underpin everything, thank you for always being there, through successes and disasters.

My husband, Dan Savidge, for supporting me through this endeavour in every way, from whisking a toddler away at just the right moment, to encouraging me forward when it's been tempting to give up – I would never have finished this without you.

And to J and L, you are my prize.